TANYA

Aut
NECESSARY

Baggage Claim

A NOVEL

Praise for
Necessary Arrangements

"Writing with unflinching honesty, Tanya Michna tackles a heart-breaking situation with grace and empathy. *Necessary Arrangements* is a novel about the power of love in a broken world. Tanya deftly captures the complications of finding joy in the everyday acts of love, life, death, and sisterhood; this is a poignant story that will touch the heart and make one wonder 'What would I do?'"
> —Patti Callahan Henry, author of *The Art of Keeping Secrets*

"A heartfelt and moving story about holding on and letting go, about family ties and the love that binds us, strengthens us, and ultimately allows us to triumph."
> —Lisa Wingate, author of *A Month of Summer*

"The sisters' sensitive dynamic and the portrayal of Asia's manifold struggles ring true. It's hard to imagine readers finishing this with dry eyes."
> —*Publishers Weekly*

"It is the best of dramatic stories that speak to you so deeply, the gift of laughter is required to capture every last nuance of emotion. You'll cheer through the characters' struggles as well as their triumphs. . . . After reading *Necessary Arrangements*, you'll be as certain as I am that this is the timeless, unforgettable story that Tanya Michna was born to write."
> —Anna DeStefano, bestselling author of *Because of a Boy*

continued . . .

Written by today's freshest new talents and selected by New American Library, NAL Accent novels touch on subjects close to a woman's heart, from friendship to family to finding our place in the world. The Conversation Guides included in each book are intended to enrich the individual reading experience, as well as encourage us to explore these topics together—because books, and life, are meant for sharing.

Visit us online at www.penguin.com.

"Michna does a good job of showing the emotional impact of cancer. . . . The novel has its share of sad moments but steers clear of some of the harsher realities, making it a cathartic (but not too painful) read for those who have dealt with illness, and an enlightening one for those who haven't." —LifetimeTV.com

"Family, love, and cancer play pivotal roles in this heartwarming and, at times, heart-wrenching story. The author writes beautifully and handles the subject matter with grace and humor. Having a box of tissues nearby is highly recommended." —*Romantic Times* (4 stars)

"Powerful, yet beautifully told, *Necessary Arrangements* is an eloquent story of family love and devotion, constant courage and unwavering support when cancer claims one of their own. This is book will hold you captive long after you have finished it. Don't pass it up."

—Writers Unlimited

Also by Tanya Michna

Necessary Arrangements

Baggage Claim

TANYA MICHNA

NAL Accent
Published by New American Library, a division of
Penguin Group (USA) Inc., 375 Hudson Street,
New York, New York 10014, USA
Penguin Group (Canada), 90 Eglinton Avenue East, Suite 700, Toronto,
Ontario M4P 2Y3, Canada (a division of Pearson Penguin Canada Inc.)
Penguin Books Ltd., 80 Strand, London WC2R 0RL, England
Penguin Ireland, 25 St. Stephen's Green, Dublin 2,
Ireland (a division of Penguin Books Ltd.)
Penguin Group (Australia), 250 Camberwell Road, Camberwell, Victoria 3124,
Australia (a division of Pearson Australia Group Pty. Ltd.)
Penguin Books India Pvt. Ltd., 11 Community Centre, Panchsheel Park,
New Delhi - 110 017, India
Penguin Group (NZ), 67 Apollo Drive, Rosedale, North Shore 0632,
New Zealand (a division of Pearson New Zealand Ltd.)
Penguin Books (South Africa) (Pty.) Ltd., 24 Sturdee Avenue,
Rosebank, Johannesburg 2196, South Africa

Penguin Books Ltd., Registered Offices:
80 Strand, London WC2R 0RL, England

First published by NAL Accent, an imprint of New American Library,
a division of Penguin Group (USA) Inc.

First Printing, May 2009
10 9 8 7 6 5 4 3 2 1

Cover photographs: Luggage © 2008 Jupiterimages Corporation.net; bedroom by Lisa Romerian/Botonica/
Jupiterimages; flower (detail) by Luca Trovato/Botanica/Jupiterimiages.

ACCENT REGISTERED TRADEMARK—MARCA REGISTRADA

LIBRARY OF CONGRESS CATALOGING-IN-PUBLICATION DATA:
Michna, Tanya.
Baggage claim/Tanya Michna.
p. cm.
ISBN 978-0-451-22498-9
1. Divorced women—Fiction. 2. Female friendship—Fiction. 3. Domestic fiction. I. Title.
PS3613.I3455B34 2009
813'.6—dc22   2008052204

Set in Janson • Designed by Alissa Amell

Printed in the United States of America

Acknowledgments

Thank you, Jane Mims and Rachelle Wadsworth, for answering so many questions and providing invaluable support! The world of higher education is better for having each of you in it, and my life is infinitely richer because of your friendship.

Baggage Claim

One

✦

Bumpy Landings

What am I doing?

As soon as Elisabeth Overton deplaned, the question hit her full force. Last night, Beth had been too busy implementing her spontaneous plan to second-guess herself—she'd hesitated only once, when her Visa was declined, but she'd assumed computer error and used her American Express instead. Today, she'd been too preoccupied with making it through the flight *safely, please God* to think beyond it. Even though Allen had pointed out over the years that, statistically, she was safer in a plane than a car, the skies would never feel friendly to her.

It was completely illogical, she knew. After all, Beth's own mother had been killed in an automobile accident decades ago, while Allen had spent much of their marriage racking up frequent-flyer miles without experiencing so much as a drop in cabin pressure. Still, Beth had been airborne only a handful of times in her life, the first not until her twenties, and she associated planes with her husband being gone, not with exotic travel or romantic getaways.

Until now. What was her impulsive dash from Atlanta to Houston if not a romantic adventure—albeit one that fell in the middle of her husband's business convention? Since neither she nor Allen was given to spontaneous gestures, she couldn't quite imagine his reaction to this surprise. But having braved the journey with a mixture of faith, grim determination, and a miniature bottle of chardonnay, she refused to think negatively. She was here now and planned to seize the day. Just as soon as she made a quick stop in the ladies' room.

Her feet not entirely steady, Beth exited the Jetway into the airport terminal. Glancing around the seating area, she was struck by a memory that was surprisingly vivid, considering it was years removed from this sunny Thursday afternoon.

The freezing night of December twenty-third, back in the age when loved ones were allowed to wait at the gate, excitedly scanning the faces of disembarking passengers. Joy hadn't yet turned four. Earlier that fall, Allen had been hired for his first sales position, parlaying his charm into commission checks. Because of weather delays, Beth had fretted that he might not get home by Christmas, painfully aware that the doll "Santa" was bringing Joy would be no substitute for a missing father. Beth had bundled her daughter into a cherry red secondhand winter coat and braved the freeway drive to Hartsfield International. Allen's flight being cleared for landing was the best gift their family received that year. They'd watched his plane taxi down the runway. Even now, more than twenty years later, Joy's shrill welcome of "Daddy! Daddy!" echoed in Beth's mind. If she closed her eyes, she could see Allen's handsome face, flush from the cold and his latest career triumph. He'd hugged his daughter, then swept Beth into his arms and kissed her breathless.

Time was a study in contradictions. While so many events in Joy's childhood seemed to have taken place just yesterday—*how is it possible* my *baby is expecting a baby?*—that passionate kiss seemed like something from a lifetime ago.

Beth had been thrilled by yesterday's announcement that Joy and Peter, blissful newlyweds, were expecting. But it had been a jolt, too. *I'm going to be a grandmother?* Beth would be forty-five in a few weeks. Some women her age were having babies of their own! Forty-five should be vital and confident. Forty-five was not too late for passion.

Was it? She frowned, her thumb worrying the anniversary band she wore on her left hand.

Because Allen was gone so often, it had been easy to pretend that nothing was missing from their marriage. But ever since Joy had moved out of the house two years ago, during her final semester of college, Beth had tried to dutifully ignore a growing discontent. She was active at church—led a women's weekly prayer group, compiled the monthly newsletter, and participated in peer counseling. She volunteered for an adult literacy program, dabbled happily in her garden, hosted scrapbooking parties, and belonged to a monthly book club. Yet there was an inescapable void in her life.

Her father, the late Reverend Howard, had raised her to be grateful for what she had, to seek out ways to give, not to ask for more, and God knew, Beth had been lucky to have such a long, happy marriage. At least a dozen couples she and Allen knew had divorced over the years, and most of them hadn't had as rocky a start.... Beth reminded herself every day that she'd been blessed, but no matter how hard she tried, her gratitude was fading.

Teetering between guilt that she didn't better appreciate what she had and the anxious hope that perhaps this trip could give her even more to appreciate, she veered left toward the restroom and almost collided with a tall blonde.

"Oh! Sorry," Beth stammered.

The younger woman spared the briefest of nods before resuming her long-legged stride. She didn't look like she'd suffered a clumsy moment in her entire life.

While Beth wouldn't describe herself as a klutz, she was definitely off balance at the moment, her head spinning with long-suppressed thoughts and the unfamiliar booze. She'd never been much of a drinker, and the fortifying wine on the plane had left her dizzy.

Another old memory came into focus, Allen teasing her gently at a Virtu-tronix company dinner, thrown in honor of a new VP. A passing waiter had handed Beth a champagne flute for the toast and Allen had laughed at her ingrained reluctance to drink it. Her father had cautioned his congregation to abstain from alcohol.

Didn't Jesus turn the water into wine? Allen had whispered, gray eyes dancing with merriment. *Sounds like an endorsement to me.*

Beth had always been glad that Joy inherited his expressive silvery eyes, rather than Beth's mundane brown. But when was the last time Beth had seen that gleam in Allen's gaze? Would she see it today, when she surprised him with her presence and the news that they were going to be grandparents? They could celebrate here in Texas, away from the routine familiarity of their Alpharetta home. Their most romantic moments had been on vacations—the sales-incentive package he'd won for two glorious nights in Hilton Head, the cruise he'd taken her on for their fifteenth anniversary, the time he'd said he couldn't take off work to spend Joy's spring break in Beth's hometown but made last-minute changes to his schedule in order to come with them.

Beth was glad she'd ignored any half-formed misgivings about intruding on his convention. Even though Allen was here for work, surely he'd be pleased to see her. If the situation were reversed, *she'd* be touched by his desire to surprise her.

This spur-of-the-moment trip was probably just what they needed.

⟨❦⟩

Dr. Carlotta Frazer *needed* this trip, the detached and impersonal sanctuary it would provide. She was so manic to reach her destination that she'd narrowly sidestepped three separate collisions during her ten minutes in Houston Hobby. Given her extreme sleep deprivation the past week, she was impressed her reflexes were still sharp, but if she kept up this pace, someone was going to get hurt. Plus, her hurry made no logical sense. Even if she made it to baggage claim in record-breaking time, her luggage probably wouldn't be there yet.

Slowing her gait, she struggled to regain her normal composure. Excessive emotion was unlike her. Yesterday was a prime example. She'd made it through the graveside service without once succumbing to emotion.

"I wish you'd reconsider going to the conference," Beverley Murrin had said at the memorial. Had there been disapproval in the dean of faculty's gaze, intermingled with the condolence behind her bifocals? *"No one would think less of you."*

Quite the contrary. People would probably think better of Carly if she'd sobbed through the ceremony, if she'd canceled her conference presentation, if she'd stayed behind to take care of her mother instead of foisting Helene on someone else. Ironically, Dr. Samuel Frazer would have perfectly understood Carly's unsentimental return to work, but she preferred not to dwell on any similarities between her and her late father.

She'd long since learned to ignore comments about how much she was like him. People meant it to be flattering. Samuel Frazer had taught organic chemistry at Emory and was considered a genius.

Carly had eschewed science for liberal arts and was an assistant professor of history at Ramson Neil, a small but prestigious private Georgia college. She'd been there six years last fall, hired on while she was a doctoral candidate still finishing her dissertation, and was mere formalities away from becoming a tenured professor at thirty-two. It would make her the youngest person to ever receive tenure at Ramson Neil. Even though she hadn't known it at the time, she'd been working toward this goal since high school. Instead of worrying about pep rallies or the prom, she'd poured her efforts into advance-placement classes. When she'd graduated—valedictorian, naturally—she already had enough hours to qualify as a second-semester college sophomore, majoring in women's studies. She'd followed her bachelor's degree with an accelerated master's program in comparative history and eventually her PhD. Her dissertation, *Female Perpetuation of Male Dominance in European Politics from the Renaissance to the Enlightenment,* had spawned several articles in well-respected journals. Most recently, she'd sold a book comparing women who'd held positions of power in centuries past, questioning whether any of them were true precursors to feminism or if they had, in fact, behaved more like their male predecessors, furthering the status quo.

She clung to the soothing litany of accomplishments the way an insomniac would turn to a cup of warm milk. *The way an alcoholic runs for whiskey,* her subconscious suggested cynically. Carly ignored the thought; her successes were not a self-destructive addiction. They were . . . proof.

You're brainless, he'd raged, waving a fourth-grade science test in her face as if the C were an inexcusable war crime. *Just like that Dunwoody debutante who gave birth to you!*

Shuddering, Carly jerked to an abrupt halt, barely hearing the complaints of the pedestrians behind her. Even though she'd seen her father's body lowered into the ground with her own eyes, it seemed impossible that the hulking giant was dead. Then again, she *was* on the cusp of major academic achievement; Samuel was perverse enough to die rather than admit he'd been wrong.

Surreal that the man who'd taught her to drive, barking out corrections if her hands so much as strayed from the mandated "ten and two," had been killed behind the wheel of a car. He had turned to say something to his wife and run a red light. The family in the minivan he'd hit had walked away with painful but minor contusions. At the time of the accident, Helene Frazer had been sitting in the back with a mahogany writing table that had only fit in the car by moving the front passenger seat all the way forward. The crash had left Carly's mother with a concussion and serious ligament damage in her right leg. The doctors felt that surgery on the torn MCL wasn't the way to go, but Helene would need significant physical therapy—anywhere from six weeks to three months because of her age and emotional state. Samuel had been killed only because of the way his head had been angled; the impact had snapped his neck.

He's dead. Carly tested the words in her mind, waiting to feel something, anything, even relief.

But she was more emotionally invested in the recommendation report from her tenure review committee than the loss of her father. She'd been given a copy of that report. Without specifying their identities, it stated that two of her peer committee members found her "adequate" for receiving tenure at Ramson Neil. . . . The third had "reservations."

She was far more than adequate. She was Carlotta freaking Frazer, and every piece of criticism her father had hurled at her when she was a defenseless child had been a lie. Once the provost and board of trustees approved her tenure at one of the best private colleges in the southeast, she'd have tangible evidence; Samuel Frazer hadn't been tenured until he was thirty-six. The committee report, however unfairly lukewarm, was a two-to-one recommendation in her favor, and Dean Murrin was fully aware of Carly's track record and publishing history.

The tightness in Carly's chest dissipated. She would attend the International Conference on Feminist Historicism as scheduled, to discuss fourteenth-century writer Christine de Pizan. Then she would go home, get Helene settled into physical therapy, and fall back into work. Teaching this summer, fleshing out and polishing the draft of her book—it had all been painstakingly planned.

At some point, that mocking inner voice added, *you should probably also sleep.*

Despite her earlier effort not to rush, she involuntarily lengthened her stride. As if to escape the waiting nightmares that circled like vultures.

She swiftly navigated two sets of escalators without running anyone down and soon found herself at the baggage carousel. When her navy suitcase was one of the first pieces to tumble down the conveyor belt, Carly could almost believe she'd conjured it through sheer force of will. She grabbed it and hurried outside, her good fortune lasting long enough for her to find a cab without a wait.

Once she was sitting in the taxi, however, her lack of sleep caught up to her. She was lulled by the white noise of the wind (naturally, the air conditioner wasn't working in the ninety-degree May heat). It would be so easy to let her heavy eyes close, but she had no intention of falling asleep in the back of some stranger's cab or arriving at the conference hotel groggy and disoriented. Remembering that she'd promise to phone Helene when she arrived, Carly removed her cell phone from the side pouch on her purse.

She dialed her home number and Daniel Cross answered on the first ring, just as if he still lived there. "Frazer residence."

At her ex-husband's familiar baritone, a pang sliced through Carly, sweet and brutal. "You sound so professional," she said after a split-second hesitation. "You'd make someone a great receptionist."

"Carly. You made it to Houston?"

"Just. The flight was delayed for a bit on the tarmac." She watched the skyline rising ahead like an oasis in a concrete desert. "I thought I should call and make sure Helene didn't worry."

"She's sleeping right now. I can wake her if you want," he offered, although his tone was reluctant.

"No, I'm sure she needs the rest." Carly suspected Helene was faring better under Daniel's solicitous care than she would under her own daughter's. Helene had always adored her former son-in-law, and though she'd never protest outright, too conditioned by her long marriage not to voice a dissenting opinion, her mother's disappointment in the divorce had been transparent.

Carly's in-laws, on the other hand, had probably danced a damn jig when Daniel disentangled himself. Her relationship with them had started off on the wrong foot on the night of the engagement, when she'd walked into a room just in time to hear Mrs. Cross call her a "cold fish." In the divorce, Daniel had given her the house and she'd ridded her-self of the Crosses. An excellent settlement by any attorney's standards.

Feeling childish for her petty thoughts, considering that Daniel had stepped in and made it easy for her to attend this conference, Carly tried to sound grateful. "So everything's going all right there?"

"I think she's still in shock, but we're managing. Some people brought by casseroles, so we don't have to rely on my cooking. If you have time to check back later, she'd love to hear from you, but otherwise, have a good trip."

"The last time you told me to have a good trip, you hired a lawyer while I was gone." *Damn it.* So much for the appropriate gratitude.

"Carly." Daniel spoke in that terrible soft voice, the pitying one. "I—"

"Please, forget I said that." She instinctively shied away from his compassion, just as she'd ducked the conversations he'd tried to initiate after leaving her. "It was bitchy of me. My only excuse is that I'm tired and preoccupied."

"I'll tell Helene you called."

"Thank you. Goodbye, Daniel."

She snapped the phone closed with a click, thinking back to that trip a year and a half ago, when she'd left for a sabbatical in Europe. Daniel had taken her to the airport. It had been a strained time for them—she'd known that, even with her head buried in research—but when he'd wished her a good trip and kissed her, it had been the same kiss. Their Kiss. The one he'd surprised her with halfway through their first date, the one they'd shared after she accepted his proposal. She'd never honestly thought that . . .

The marriage might have failed, but Daniel was the one who'd walked away. Her steadfast, tenderhearted husband, as it turned out, was a quitter. *She* was Dr. Carly Frazer, and she was a winner.

❧

Beth was so excited she was practically bouncing on the balls of her feet as she watched for Allen's blue suitcase to go by on the metal oval.

Joy and Peter, on their way out of town for a long weekend with his folks, had given Beth permission to tell Allen about the baby. When she'd decided to do so in person, she'd gone to his closet and snagged a piece of luggage he'd been given as a corporate thank-you for record-breaking software sales. They'd started their life together with almost no money and a substantial loan from Allen's parents, but he'd been a wonderful provider. Virtu-tronix was the third company to hire him as a salesman and the one he'd worked for the longest. He was promoted last year to senior sales manager and she suspected he'd had a busy week here at the expo, where vendors like his company set up booths and wined and dined would-be clients.

I'm capable of staying out of his way while he works. He had to come back to his hotel room eventually, though. They stood a better chance of recapturing their spark on neutral ground. She always felt more daring in places that didn't remind her of her daily roles—wife, mother, church newsletter editor. When she'd made a point of seducing her husband one night during their Caribbean cruise, he'd expressed as much surprise as appreciation.

Sensuality did not come easily to Beth. During her adolescence, her father had preached against the temptations of the flesh. That hadn't been quite enough to keep her nineteen-year-old self from giving in to Allen's charms once she went away to college, but, as her father had always predicted, there *had* been consequences. A memory tried to surface—Allen's outrage when she'd given him the news she was pregnant—but she pushed it away. Knowing how much he'd grown to love their child, Beth had always felt like it was a betrayal to think about how he'd responded to her announcement. Even if he hadn't planned to get married months before getting his degree, he'd been an exemplary husband and father, mellowing over time. When he was in town, he looked forward to weekly poker games with buddies, kept Beth company outside while she gardened, and glowed with paternal pride whenever Joy walked into the room.

This weekend, Beth wanted to bring their relationship full circle. They hadn't exactly rejoiced that they were having a baby, but now they could share their happiness over their daughter's baby news and be proud of the life they'd created together.

There it is! Murmuring a happy "Excuse me, please," Beth leaned between two men and reached for her suitcase. One of them, returning her smile, grabbed the handle before she could.

"Here you are, miss."

"Thank you." Her grin widened when she thought of the lavender satin lingerie inside and her husband's potential reaction to it.

Outside the airport, a line of yellow-and-orange cabs waited at the curb. She fished a piece of paper from her pocket. Even though she always called Allen on his cell rather than in his hotel rooms, she'd made it a habit when Joy was younger to make sure she knew his precise travel information in case of emergency. Beth read the location to a taxi driver, who nodded several times to indicate his understanding.

Her pulse kicked up a notch. She was really doing this! Smoothing a hand over her skirt, she felt younger and prettier than she had in years. Granted, the skirt had an elastic waist—she wasn't nineteen anymore—but it was a swirl of feminine colors that made her think of Impressionist paintings she'd seen at the High Museum, loving their hazy, soft-edged view of the world.

Wanting to spread her good mood, she tipped the cabbie extravagantly and rolled her suitcase inside, where she made her way toward the check-in line. The portable posts corralling travelers—the retractable belt kind, not velvet ropes—and occasional calls of, "Can I help the next person, please?" made her feel as if she were at the bank. *Yes, I'd like to make a deposit on my future.* She grinned at her own idiocy, but even bad puns were no match for pure optimism.

"Good afternoon." A man in a green blazer greeted her from behind the counter. "And did you have a reservation with us?"

"Not exactly. My husband had the reservation."

"So, I should look for your room under his name?" Confusion evident in his voice and hazel eyes, the young man tilted his head. He reminded her of a lost cocker spaniel Joy had wanted to keep before they'd found its owners.

"My husband checked in earlier this week. I just need a key. I'm here to surprise him. It's Allen Overton," she said. "O-v-e-r-t-o-n."

The man hit some computer keys. "Ah, yes. He arrived a couple of days ago. But there's no second guest listed on his reservation."

"That would be the 'surprise' part of it," she said cheerfully.

The hotel clerk frowned. "Ma'am, I'm afraid I can't issue a room key to someone who shows up unannounced and isn't on the reservation."

"Someone? I'm his wife!" She extracted her driver's license from her wallet. "See, Elisabeth Overton."

He squirmed. "No disrespect, ma'am, but you having the same last name doesn't really prove anything. We value our guests' patronage and their privacy. What if you were some crazy ex who wanted access to his room for some sort of revenge?"

That was the most ridiculous thing she'd ever heard. "Do I *look* crazy to you?"

"Why don't I just dial up to his room and let you talk to him?" He reached for a forest green house phone.

You're ruining the moment, junior. She took the receiver with only a mild glare when he handed it to her. There were several rings, then a mechanical voice informing her that the hotel guest she was calling was not in the room at this time. Now what?

"Do you know where the meeting rooms are for the DDS Expo?" she asked.

"DDS like dentists?"

"No. It's a software convention."

"Well, it isn't held here." He consulted his computer, once again tapped keys, then shook his head with more confidence. "Nope."

She'd hoped it would be an on-site event, but occasionally the participating companies needed more space than the hotel could provide. Other times, the company chose to put their people up somewhere less costly than the expo hotel. This place definitely looked budget-conscious.

"Do you have a supervisor I could speak to?" she asked. She wasn't trying to get the guy in trouble, but surely there was someone who could be reasoned with around here. Even though it was merely afternoon, she'd already had a long day. She didn't want to spend the next few hours loitering in the lobby and second-guessing herself.

"Ah, he took a late lunch, ma'am. But we have a lovely restaurant right around the corner there, past the elevators. Perhaps if you'd like to wait . . ."

"Fine. Thanks." She should get some food into her system anyway. All she'd eaten was a miniature bag of pretzels on the plane, and she was a woman unaccustomed to missing meals.

Wheeling the navy case in the direction she'd been given, she found the restaurant. On the front of a scarred wooden podium hung a sign requesting that guests wait to be seated.

Yet after a few minutes, no host or hostess had materialized. Stepping farther inside, she looked around to see if she could catch someone's attention. She looked to her left and froze as her gaze landed on a familiar blond head streaked with distinguished silver. Allen! That was serendipitous.

His back was to her and he was leaning across a small two-person table in intense discussion with a striking redhead. Beth did a quick mental search, but didn't recognize the woman from any of the Virtu-tronix Christmas parties or company picnics. As she got closer to their table, she realized that Allen and the unknown female were arguing vehemently.

Beth's greeting came out shaky and uncertain. "Allen?"

His head whipped around. "Elisabeth!" The blood drained from his face as he glanced from her, back to the redhead, and finally to his wife again. His momentary uncertainty was replaced with an angry, granite-hard expression. "What the hell are you doing here?"

Two

Two

In the Unlikely Event

All of Beth's earlier buoyancy hemorrhaged out of her. "I-I came to see you," she stammered, trying to regroup. Trying not to flinch away from the uncharacteristically dark emotions her husband projected. "I thought . . . thought that we . . ."

Belatedly, she registered the redhead's expression, one of cool sympathy, as if the other woman simultaneously felt bad for Beth even while smugly assuring herself that *she* would never be in a comparable position.

Beth squared her shoulders. "Actually, I came with some news, which I'd rather discuss privately."

Allen's gaze snapped back to the redhead and he nodded quickly. "Let's go up to my room. If you'll excuse me, Jessica."

"Certainly. I'll just let the waiter know he can charge lunch to your room." There was underlying amusement in Jessica's voice. Though Beth didn't understand its source, she instinctively resented it.

You don't even know her. Disliking a woman just because she was a single-digit size and had been lunching with your husband was uncharitable. And illogical.

Beth didn't want to acknowledge the warnings her intuition was sending.

As she followed Allen through the lobby, she tried to tell herself that paranoia was not the same as intuition. She'd caught them having a public meal in the middle of the day, for crying out loud, not in flagrante. For all she knew, Jessica was an important client.

"I'm sorry if I interrupted your lunch," she said as the elevator doors closed.

Allen glared, the antithesis of every fantasy she'd had about surprising him. So much for grand romantic gestures. "I just don't understand why you're here. Is something wrong? Is it Joy? If there was an emergency, it would make more sense for you to call me than come—"

"No, no emergency." She swallowed, feeling childish. "I wanted to see you. I thought it might be nice for us to have some time away from home together." This didn't seem to be the right moment to break Joy's happy news. Beth was already deflated and didn't want to cheat them of their chance to celebrate the wonderful daughter they'd raised. Later, when he was no longer irritated by her unannounced arrival . . .

He ran a hand over his hair, barely disrupting the carefully gelled style. "This isn't like you." He sounded so disapproving, she could hardly answer *That's the point.*

"I won't get in the way of the expo, if that's what you're worried about."

"The expo?" He blanched, suddenly looking nervous but covering it with a defensive posture. "Elisabeth, are you here to check up on me?"

"Of course not." Those warning bells clanged again, loud in her skull and harder to ignore. "Should I be?"

"Tell me the truth—" His words were loud, too. Not quite a yell but close enough that he caught himself when the elevator stopped, lowering his voice as they stepped into the hallway. "Tell me the truth, did Ev call you?"

Everett Palmer, the service manager at Virtu-tronix, had worked with Allen for years. During Ev's marriage, the two couples had frequently socialized. After the man's divorce, however, he'd begun dating a woman who wasn't much older than Joy. Beth found it difficult to converse with his new significant other and equally difficult to like Everett as much as she once had, though it wasn't her place to judge.

"Did Everett call me about what? Allen, you're not making any sense." Her mind darted back to that redhead, nausea cramping her stomach.

"*I'm* not making sense?" Allen jammed his key card into a door, and she followed him into a generic room with a king-size bed. The red flowers on the comforter matched the drapes. An ugly painting of a mud brown calf bawling at its mother hung crooked on the wall. "You're the one who, on a whim, jumped on a plane. Just what did that last-minute ticket cost me?"

Beth gaped. Was he serious? They rarely traveled—except for his business-covered trips—and she didn't require designer Italian shoes or ask for jewelry on her birthday. Sure, Joy's college education and wedding had been expensive, but they had a nice income. Yet he was using the same derisive, accusatory tone he'd had when they were struggling newlyweds and Beth hadn't been able to breast-feed Joy; he'd pointed out more than once the money they could have saved on formula if Beth could just do what "came naturally." At the time, he'd been overworked, sleep-deprived, and generally stressed about being a brand-new father.

Now he had no excuse.

"Don't talk to me like that," she said quietly. "I flew all this way because I've been thinking about our marriage and thought it could use some improvement. I had some crazed idea about . . . about coming here and being a more loving wife. Instead, I find you cozy with a beautiful young woman, snapping all kinds of crazy questions at me. It occurs to me that maybe—" She swallowed back a vile mixture of her earlier anticipation and newfound fear. It would be so much easier to be back home, picking out a giant teddy bear for Joy, blissfully ignorant. "Maybe *I* should be the one asking questions."

Allen crossed the small room and took her hands, his salesman's expression radiating *damage control.* "Sorry. I didn't mean to snap at you, Beth. I've just been under a lot of stress lately."

Throughout their marriage, he'd used variations of that line, as if she couldn't fully appreciate the strain of outside work because she got to stay home every day. He'd reminded her of the tribulations he suffered—the commute, the office politics, the nights spent in econo motels instead of his own bed. For too long, Beth had felt guilty enough to buy into his attitude. Yes, he'd worked hard to provide for his family. But he was a jackass if he'd thought taking care of everything at home was simple and undemanding.

"Why don't you tell me about it?" She sat ramrod straight on the edge of the bed, which housekeeping had obviously made. It wasn't a chore Allen would think to do. "Explain what's making you so . . . manic. What are you afraid Ev told me?"

"I'm not 'afraid' of anything."

"I could ask him. I'll bump into him eventually while I'm here." At pretty much every company event she knew of, Allen's coworkers could be found at the hotel bar if one waited long enough. They often congregated together for lunches and dinners too, easily identifiable in their company shirts and convention badges—neither of which Allen currently wore, she suddenly noticed.

He shifted his weight. "Ev didn't come on this particular trip."

"Who did?" she wanted to know, her repressed intuition refusing to be ignored. "Where is everyone? When do you have to get back to the booth or to your next demonstration or meeting?"

"Damn it, Elisabeth, don't interrogate me. Insecurity in a woman is not attractive." He was looking at her with so much hostility that he appeared a virtual stranger.

But he's not. He's your partner, your lover. The man who took you on a cruise and asked the band to play your favorite song. On a more somber note, Allen had been the one who supported her through her own father's death.

They were talking in circles—he seemed more comfortable picking a fight right now than giving her a straight answer—but after two and half decades together, she *wanted* to give him the benefit of the doubt.

She stood. "Are you going to tell me the truth, or should I call the airlines and arrange a flight home?" She'd only bought a one-way ticket, hoping they could return together, maybe even stay an extra day once his business was concluded.

Allen looked pained. "How much *was* your airfare?"

The desperation in his tone made her think the question was more than a stalling technique. She thought back to her credit card being refused when she'd first tried to book an on-line reservation. "Allen, this stress you're under . . . is everything all right with your job? With our finances?"

He winced.

Beth's heart was pounding hard enough that her chest hurt. It had seemed so simple in Atlanta. Fly to Houston, go to her husband's room, slide into something slinky, the likes of which she hadn't worn in a couple of years, leading to a stunned but delighted spouse. She felt stupid now for her rosy scenario, humiliated. She hated him a little for that.

"Allen, *what* is wrong?"

He struggled to look composed and failed. "The truth is, we're having a small cash-flow problem, but you know I'll take care of it. It's nothing you need to get involved in."

"Maybe I could help," she said tentatively.

Could she really? It dawned on her that there was limited crossover involvement in their lives. She'd been the PTA president and currently served as the secretary for their home-owners' association. If it had to do with gathering old belongings to donate to the church, calling the gardener, or Joy's college forms, Elisabeth had been in charge. When it came to insurance, taxes, and their finances, Allen did the work. It hadn't bothered her much that she'd been the parent at all the pediatrician visits and teacher conferences—she thought of herself and Allen as a team, each with his own playing position. But now the division between them was striking. Should she have made more of an effort to include him in the domestic details of his own home, the parenting of raising their daughter?

"I have it under control," he said through gritted teeth.

"Allen, our Visa was turned down. Are you sure—"

"Get off my back."

She took a reflexive step away from him, the backs of her thighs bumping into the mattress. For a millisecond, she'd been afraid. Of her own husband. "I don't know what's going on, but I think it's best I leave."

There was a knock on the door, and she was glad for the interruption. She would even have welcomed that redhead right now, if the woman could provide some explanation. Allen shifted his gaze from the door back to Beth, obviously calculating his next move and not looking happy about his options.

"Are you going to answer that?" she asked.

He rubbed his forehead. "I thought we were in the middle of a conversation."

"We would be," she said, "if it weren't so one-sided."

"Al, you in there?" Definitely not the petite redhead from downstairs. This sounded like a large and somewhat annoyed man.

With a sigh, Allen went to answer the door. If she turned the corner to see who it was and eavesdrop on their conversation, would it be a complete violation of trust?

"This isn't—" her husband began, speaking over the other man.

"I got you what I could, but it won't—" The discussion ended abruptly; then the door shut.

They'd gone out to talk in the hall, she realized.

At a loss, she paced the room. If his laptop had been on, she might have succumbed to the temptation to study his desktop or even sneak a peek at his e-mail. There weren't any telltale clues lying about, only the smaller navy bag from the same five-piece set as her suitcase and a couple of books on the nightstand about Texas hold 'em strategy and probabilities. No lipstick-smeared shirts, no notes to himself on the hotel memo pad about what he might be keeping from his wife. His *wife*. She was supposed to be his helpmeet, his equal.

Feeling both guilty and desperate, she reached for the phone and pressed the front-desk button. When someone answered, she asked to be connected to Everett Palmer's room.

"I'm sorry. We don't currently have any registered guests under that name."

So Allen had been honest about that part. Beth tried another coworker she knew, although she wasn't sure what she'd say to the guy if he picked up. After two more names that didn't pan out, Allen had yet to return and the desk clerk had adopted a clipped, suspicious tone.

"Sorry for wasting your time," Beth said, the pit in her

stomach now a canyon. "I . . . I must have been confused about some arrival dates."

"No problem, ma'am," the woman answered, her tone evidence to the contrary.

The door opened, and Beth slammed down the receiver, as mortified as if she'd been caught taking dollar bills out of the collection plate. Allen's earlier question echoed ominously in her head: *Are you here to check up on me?* As of that call to the front desk, she *was* officially checking up on him. Even more worrisome, she'd racked up additional questions but no answers.

She rubbed damp palms on her skirt. "I don't suppose you'd tell me who was at the door?"

"Just a colleague."

"Here for the expo?" she prodded. "Allen, I love you. You know that. You're my husband. We're supposed to trust each other. But I can't shake the feeling you're lying to me."

He gauged her carefully. "Okay. You're right. I wasn't entirely honest. The convention *was* scheduled for this week, but it's been postponed until winter. I've made friends in the industry, people I see only once a year at these things. A few of us decided to go ahead and get together as scheduled even though the expo was delayed. Talk some shop, play a little poker. I should have told you, but I felt selfish."

"For wanting some R and R?" She frowned at him. "It's not as if I would have said no. I can't believe you didn't just tell me the . . ." Was he telling the truth *now*? If Jessica was merely some acquaintance who worked for a sister company, why the tense conversation in the restaurant? She glanced at the books on the table, guides to doing better at poker. If they were having financial difficulties, why was he playing poker? "You yelled at me for flying here when you paid to come for a boy's week away. The company's not putting you up in the hotel, is it? None of this is a legitimate business expense."

"Elisabeth, I've taken care of the family finances for over twenty years, and you've always had everything you need, so I don't think—"

"Everything I need? What about *honesty*? My husband is lying to me and taking one-man vacations with money it turns out we don't have." Rage rose within her, almost volcanic in force. She half expected to see lava pooling on the ugly carpet. If she were the dramatic type, she'd be throwing things by now.

Since she'd been raised to be meek and dutiful, she was at a distinct disadvantage for knowing how to behave. "I'm going." Anticlimatic, but the best she could come up with on short notice.

"Back to Atlanta?"

"Another hotel room." She couldn't handle a second flight today. Her nerves were officially shot. "Another hotel. I'm not sleeping here with you."

"Beth, you're over—"

"Shut up." Had she ever said that to anyone? She felt liberated and sick at the same time. "We can talk about this when we're both back home."

"But where—"

"I don't know. I just have to . . . I just—"

He came to her then, tried to put his arms around her. The

weak part of her wanted to lean into his embrace. But damned if she was going to be comforted by the person who'd lied to her and hurt her in the first place.

She pulled away. "Call me tomorrow. On my cell. Maybe we can talk then."

"You should stay here tonight," he cajoled.

Why, because he didn't want her spending the money on another room? She was glad she made it a habit to travel with extra cash but regretted tipping the cabdriver so much. Still, how bad could their monetary problems be if Allen was taking a week to lollygag around Houston, shooting the bull and playing cards with buddies?

"No." When she stalked toward the door, he made no further move to stop her, which surprised her.

Beth grimaced as she stepped into the hall. She'd had enough surprises for one afternoon.

Beth Overton hadn't known she possessed such a rebellious streak until she checked into an upscale hotel far nicer—and far more expensive—than Allen's. Seated on the white down comforter, she briefly considered ordering room service. Even stronger than the juvenile urge to pay twenty bucks for a hamburger was the impulse to pull the sheets over her head and sleep for the next twelve hours.

Tempting, but not productive. She retrieved her cell phone from her purse. It had been turned off since she boarded the flight that morning, a lifetime ago. When she switched it on, she expected half a dozen voice mails from Allen—scolding her for leaving or apologizing for his incomprehensible dishonesty.

Nothing. She stared at the screen in disbelief, then called the office number she knew by heart. When she was greeted by the automated menu, she spelled out Ev's first initial and last name on the number pad.

"Everett Palmer," the man answered.

She gulped air. "Ev? This is Beth Overton."

"Beth." He echoed her name warily. "What can I do for you, sugar?"

Not call me "sugar," for starters. But she'd never bothered to protest the habitual nickname. They lived in the South, for crying out loud. "Ev, we need to talk about Allen." She paused, hoping he would take it from there.

Allen had been worried about his oldest friend tattling on him. Why? Everett's loyalties to Beth weren't strong enough that he would call her about Allen hanging out in Houston on personal time. There must be something more.

Ev sighed. "My opinion? He needs help."

For what? "I think I agree," she said hesitantly.

"I told him it would be a mistake to participate in this tournament—"

The overall picture was suddenly clear, as if she'd been staring through the viewfinder at it all along but had forgotten to take off the lens cap until now. "The poker tournament." She'd had the presence of mind to wonder why he was playing poker if they were having a "cash-flow problem," but she hadn't bothered asking *why* they suddenly had such a problem.

Clutching a hand to her chest, she sank back into the pile of pillows. Her daddy had always said gambling was an evil vice, but then, he'd said that about a lot of things. "Allen's spent too much money. Playing poker."

"You want me to come over when he gets back from Texas and we can talk to him together? I've heard about stuff like that, where family and friends confront someone, but I'm not sure how helpful I'd be," Ev said. "I've already told him he needs to cut it out. The man owes me money from the last high-stakes game he entered. He borrows, with big plans to win it back, but he's been on a losing streak."

Which you enabled by giving him a loan. But it wasn't fair to blame Everett for this mess. She'd known Allen gambled whenever business took him to Reno or Vegas—he'd had a fantastic run of luck at the roulette table and blackjack on their cruise—knew that he liked to play cards with buddies, but . . . high-stakes, Ev had said. How high?

High enough that people who knew him well were talking interventions. Shouldn't Beth have known her husband better than anyone? If she hadn't taken this unforeseeable trip to surprise him, she *still* wouldn't have an inkling what was going on. Allen had made a fool of her.

"I—I'll think about what you said," Beth said. "Sorry to have troubled you at work."

"I do want to help." Ev sounded sincerely apologetic. "You and Allen got me through my divorce."

She felt terrible for every waspish thought she'd had about his youthful new girlfriend. "Thank you, Everett."

After disconnecting, Beth stared at the wall, losing track of time until her stomach growled. It was approaching evening, and she still hadn't eaten. She felt grimy, either from the travel or being lied to. Shower first, she decided; then she'd forage for food. Once she was clean and fed, she could try to determine the extent of her problems.

Crossing the room, she regarded the navy suitcase she'd naively assumed would be the heaviest load she'd have to bear today. She reached for the zipper on an outside pocket and opened the compartment, expecting to see travel-size bottles of her favorite shampoo and conditioner. Instead, she found a maroon blow-dryer she didn't recognize.

Perplexed, she flipped the top back, investigating the main contents. There was a built-in garment bag that someone had packed with gray slacks and a matching jacket, far more busi- nessy than Beth's suburban wardrobe. There was also a scoop- necked black dress in an impressively smooth fabric. She lifted the hanger and examined the garment. *I'd have to sell my soul to fit into this.*

She rezipped the suitcase and turned it over, locating a snapped rectangle the size of a business card. Inside was a name and phone number: DR. CARLY FRAZER. In her doomed eagerness to see Allen, had Beth swiped some other woman's baggage?

A few seconds later, a lady's husky voice answered the number in the suitcase. "Hello?"

"Carly Frazer? This is Elisabeth Overton—"

"Overton? The one with my bag! And lecture notes. I called the number on the ID tag but got your home machine. I thought I was screwed."

Beth frowned at the phraseology, but it could have been worse. "Sorry for the mix-up."

"Just let me know where you are, and we'll get them switched back."

They arranged to meet in the lobby of Beth's hotel, which was dominated by a bar with lots of peripheral seating. It was the perfect place to wait for the other woman, Beth decided. A sudden, perverse thirst eclipsed both her hunger and typical common sense.

She might have started the day as someone who rarely drank alcohol, but a lot could change in just a day.

Three

Beverage Service

I know her! Beth set down the now-empty glass that had held her rum and diet cola and watched the cool blonde stride through the lobby. It was the same woman Beth had almost bumped into at the airport—Dr. Frazer, judging by the navy suitcase rolling in her wake.

Long-legged with a firm chin and don't-mess-with-me posture, Carly Frazer was maybe late twenties, early thirties. Her pale hair brushed her jawline, straight and sleek, unruffled by Houston's spring humidity. Beth had pulled her own long dark hair back in a twist but was aware of tendrils frizzing around her face. She felt a spurt of envy for the other woman's smooth bob . . . for her youth, for her aplomb, for her ability to look like a runway model in what would have been merely a serviceable beige skirt on someone else. Beth was sure that *this* woman would have noticed her husband lying—assuming he was brave enough to try it in the first place.

Beautiful though she was, Dr. Frazer didn't look like the forgiving type. Holding a flaming sword instead of brand-name luggage, she could pass for an avenging angel. Beth scowled into her glass. Allen deserved to have someone do a little avenging on his butt. Unfortunately, she had been taught to forgive, to turn the other cheek. Even now, simmering just below her anger was wifely guilt that she should be with Allen, figuring out how to help him through this, not tossing back drinks.

Beth lifted her hand to signal the blonde, but she was already approaching, presumably having spotted the suitcase next to the table.

"Ms. Overton?" The younger woman stopped, brushing her bangs impatiently from her eyes. "I'm Carly Frazer. It took me longer than I thought—traffic's a nightmare."

Rising halfway, Beth offered her hand. "Nice to meet you. Please, join me for a drink."

Carly looked back over her shoulder toward the main doors and the congested street beyond. "I believe I will."

They waved over the waiter, who took their orders for another rum and diet soda as well as a vodka martini with extra olives.

"I deserve a drink after my week." Carly rolled her shoulders, somehow more human now that she was no longer looming. Even without the added height of her shoes, she had to be at least five foot nine.

"Man troubles?" Beth wasn't a cynic by nature, but she could probably pick it up with practice.

"In a manner of speaking." The woman's mouth compressed into a tight line. "My father died."

That announcement sliced through Beth's tipsy haze with surgical precision. Reexperiencing the pain of losing her own father, she jolted back. "I'm so sorry."

"Don't be."

How did one respond to that? At a loss, Beth nervously changed the subject.

"So, Dr. Frazer, what's your area of practice? My daughter used to talk about applying to medical school." Although Joy had always excelled at math and science, Beth had fretted that medical school would be too competitive and stressful. She'd been relieved when Joy became a math major at Kennesaw State and so proud she could burst when her daughter received her BS. Would Joy keep her job as an inventory analyst after the baby arrived?

"Actually, I'm a PhD. A history professor at Ramson Neil,"

Impressive in its own right. "That's supposed to be a fantastic college."

"It is." Carly paused as they accepted their drinks. "What do you do, Ms. Overton?"

"Beth. I stay dizzy. Busy," she corrected with a self-conscious laugh. She hesitated, reluctant to tell the PhD across the table about her amateur gardening efforts or socializing with her book club. "I volunteer with a Fulton County literacy program. And work through the church as a grief counselor."

"Noble."

Was it? Certainly she'd donated time and effort to some

worthy causes over the years. But was her motivation strictly philanthropic, or did it stem from trying to fill too many empty hours as Joy grew older and needed her less? The years had passed so fast. Beth had to blink back unexpected tears. *I should look for work.* That would help with the "cash-flow problem." With her organizational skills, she had to be qualified for something, despite her age and unimpressive educational credentials.

"I'm actually in the process of looking for a job," she said, enjoying the way it sounded out loud. Beth Overton, with a job. "At least, I will be once I get back to Atlanta."

"Oh?" Distracted, Carly traced a finger around her martini glass. "I'll be looking for someone to hire when I get back. I need someone to take care of my mother this summer."

"Like a nurse?"

"No." Carly refocused, as if she'd just remembered Beth was there. "Not a nurse, exactly, although Helene is injured. More like a companion. To keep her out of my hair while I'm writing."

Beth blinked. Carly wasn't merely a cool blonde—she was *cold.* As far as Beth could discern, the woman held no trace of familial affection for either of her parents. *So much for honoring thy mother and father.* Had they really done such a poor job? Carly was lovely, educated, and well employed.

The professor was still talking, nodding to herself. "That's what I need—an affordable part-time assistant who can help Helene so I'm not constantly interrupted."

She made the woman who'd presumably raised her sound like a burden. Worse, an annoyance, too trivial to qualify as a burden.

With a daughter of her own, Beth couldn't help the note of censure that crept into her voice. "I take it you don't get along with your mother?"

"We get along." Carly looked genuinely surprised by the question. "I don't think Helene's ever argued with anyone. She's just . . . She and my father were in a car accident. His death affected her deeply."

But not you?

"My mother's injuries include a torn MCL." At Beth's blank expression, Carly elaborated. "Medial collateral ligament. It stabilizes the knee. At least, that's what it does when it's healthy. Even with a brace and crutches, she can barely get around right now. In my parents' house, all the bedrooms are upstairs and there's only a half bath on the first floor. So she's staying with me while she takes physical therapy and recuperates. But I've got summer sessions to teach and a book to finish by the end of August." As she had earlier, she shoved at her bangs, tucking a few strands behind her ear.

Something about the movement hinted at a vulnerability Beth had originally overlooked, reminding her of Joy's angry-teen phase. Though it hadn't lasted much more than a month, praise the Lord, it had been a living purgatory for Beth. Her usually good-natured daughter had glowered and rolled her eyes as if everyone around her was just another fool to be suffered. During those moments when Beth had been tempted to smack her child, she'd challenged herself to look harder and see the confused girl beneath the self-assured sneer. Applying that principle now, she studied Carly again, paying closer to attention to the faint circles under her eyes—unusual eyes. One blue-green, the other light brown.

"Yes, they're two different colors," Carly said.

"Sorry." Beth lowered her gaze, chastened. "I didn't mean to be rude."

The blonde exhaled. "No worries. I'm rude a few times a day myself. At least, the TA who recently left me in the lurch seemed to think so. All I want is an assistant who's efficient, competent, and capable of following directions. Are those really such difficult requirements?"

The rum had kicked in, and Beth laughed without meaning to—she'd always thought a husband who told his wife the truth was a pretty basic requirement. "I'm not the right person to ask. I'm a little down on people today." Men people, especially.

"People suck." Carly raised her glass. "I can drink to that."

Beth frowned. She'd been raised to serve as an example, not perpetuate negativity. She should mitigate her earlier comments with something inspirational.

"People suck," she echoed, clinking their glasses together. She took a large sip, but her drink didn't taste as good as it had earlier. "I think you may be a bad influence. Or Captain Morgan is. Or Allen."

"The captain I'm familiar with." Carly had finished her own drink and was gesturing to the waiter, pointing at her empty glass and nodding. "Who's Allen?"

"My husband." She wanted to say something modern and cutting, skewer him with her wit. What was that word Joy used sometimes? *Snarky.* But nothing came to mind, just an aching sadness when she thought of the afternoon's discoveries.

Didn't he love her enough to tell her about his problem, to accept her help? Surely they could overcome this setback together. It was startling to be married for more than a quarter of a century and suddenly feel alone.

Carly leaned back as the waiter approached. After exchanging a ten-dollar bill for her second martini, she asked, "Did he cheat on you? From what I've seen on campus, most husbands do. Mine didn't, but—"

"You're married?" Beth couldn't imagine this woman exchanging vows that would bind her to anyone else.

"Not anymore." Carly bit into an olive. "So in what unoriginal, middle-aged way did yours sell you up the river?"

I don't like you. The knee-jerk reaction was surprising but forceful. This could be the perfect opportunity for female solidarity, venting to a total stranger about Allen's transgressions so that Beth could get the worst of it out before she tried to talk to him again. But she didn't want to confide in someone who immediately assumed her husband was a midlife-crisis cliché. Hearing him marginalized made her own existence feel small.

When Beth had first seen the professor, she'd envied the blonde's youth, but the bitterness emanating from her would age her before her time.

"This is embarrassing, but I'm not feeling well." Beth slid her chair back. "Dumb to drink on an empty stomach. I know I asked you to join me, but . . ."

Carly waved a hand, royally dismissing the help. "I'm secure enough to appreciate my own company."

That was fortuitous, because Beth doubted anyone else did.

Carly watched Beth Overton scamper off toward the elevators with her suitcase, darting one last glance over her shoulder, as nervous as a mouse evading a snake. *Which,* she supposed, *makes me the snake.*

Not the most flattering analogy, but she didn't hang her self-worth on being warm and fuzzy. Warm and fuzzy translated to getting eaten alive. Beth seemed like a perfectly nice woman, a community-oriented mom who'd let herself get screwed over. Although she hadn't spilled the specifics of Allen's crimes, the pain he'd caused had been evident in those big brown eyes. Yet the woman had continuously fiddled with her wedding ring, and she'd said "my husband" in an almost wistful tone. She'd been in a hurry to get away from Carly, but would she stand by the spouse who'd hurt her?

Spearing the last olive with a decorative toothpick, Carly tried to think of a couple she knew who had remained happily married. None came to mind. Daniel had done her a favor, bailing out and leaving her free to focus on her career.

Carly had big plans. One day, she would be the president of a university.

"This seat taken, ma'am?" drawled a male voice thick with cowboy.

Carly raised her gaze to the smiling man. *Too tall.* She didn't date men over six feet. Ever. But he did have blue eyes.

Against her will, she recalled Daniel's gaze. Not blue-green, like this man's, but vast undiluted azure, the horizon where it met the ocean.

"Feel free to sit wherever you like," she said, standing abruptly. "I was just leaving."

Traffic had abated since her cab ride across the city, and the trip back to her hotel was much shorter. In her room, Carly sat at the desk and pulled out her notes for the lecture. The words she should have known as well as her own name were as incomprehensible as an ancient dialect. Frustrated, she raked her fingers through her hair. *So tired.* She cast a glance at the bed behind her but felt no temptation to crawl beneath the sheets.

Relatively speaking, it was still quite early. Maybe she could just rest for a moment, then get back to work. She tilted her head against the forearm atop the desk, optimistic that the position was too uncomfortable for her to fall asleep.

She closed her eyes . . . and envisioned Daniel. Until her father's funeral yesterday, she and Daniel had successfully avoided each other for the better part of a year. Daniel held a master's in landscape architecture and had been working on campus when they met, but even before they split up, he'd taken over the family business from his retiring father. Stifling a yawn, she assured herself that his sudden presence back in her life had simply caught her at a vulnerable time. She didn't normally dwell on her ex.

Truthfully, when she looked back, it was difficult to process how they'd come together in the first place. So unlikely. *So mismatched.*

So . . .

Carly's eyes drifted closed, the memory of the day she'd met Daniel coming into focus as a vivid dream. She was en route to her car from the library, her self-assured pace unhindered by the familiar weight of books. In her shoulder bag were the textbooks she was considering for next semester; in her arms were the books she planned to peruse that weekend for additional research. She still needed to do some final cross-checking for her dissertation. She'd been hired at Ramson Neil ABD and she was eager to have the doctorate finished and defended in front of the committee. Though she'd only been here for a couple of months, she was confident that it was the right place for her. Her sections of Renaissance history and gender studies were both full. She'd initially hesitated in applying for the position, not sure she wanted to be this close to *him*—why not finish her PhD and move to the West Coast, far from the sphere of Dr. Samuel Frazer?—but that would be allowing her past too much power over her future. After all, Ramson Neil was a damn good school. And there was a certain deliciousness to the idea of succeeding here, on her own two feet, where he couldn't help but see. She'd already—

Her attention snagged on the dark-haired man ahead of her on the sidewalk. He was kneeling at the edge of the pavement, showing no concern for his khaki slacks or the crisp white shirt emblazoned with the college insignia. He seemed to be examining the flower bed nestled between intersecting paths, running his fingers over leaves and pale pink-purple petals.

As if feeling her scrutiny, the man rocked back on his heels and glanced her way. "Hi."

"Hello."

He shaded his eyes. "You're that new history prof, aren't you?"

His recognition startled her, especially since she couldn't place him. "Are you a faculty member?" She couldn't imagine him, with his deep tan and muscled forearms, cooped up in the classroom, but given his button-down shirt and the leather briefcase next to him, she doubted he was one of the maintenance crew.

"No, grounds supervisor." He stood—he was taller than she, but only by a couple of inches. "I helped Dr. Wexler redesign his backyard over the summer. We got to be friends."

Wexler had been on the hiring committee that interviewed her. "Ah. I'm Carly Frazer, newest member of the history department."

A rueful grin flashed white against his sun-kissed face as he turned his palms over for inspection. "I'm sure you'll understand if I don't shake your hand."

He had big hands, rough and slightly dirty, but she'd watched him brush those unmanicured fingers over delicate petals with concentrated care.

She shifted her tote bag. "So every plant on campus merits your personal attention? That's dedication."

"I'm gauging the effectiveness of a new organic treatment against powdery mildew. We're trying to phase out chemicals unless they're absolutely necessary. Do you know much about flowers?"

Raised in an environment where not knowing something was an invitation to being called stupid, Carly was never comfortable admitting any lack of expertise. She squirmed inwardly but kept her tone light. "Not at all. I can kill a silk plant."

His chuckle warmed her, turning her earlier good mood into a surprising playfulness.

"I had a roommate once who grew window-box flowers," Carly recalled. "She swore I destroyed her geraniums just by looking at them."

Daniel spread his arms out at his sides in a shielding gesture. "Ma'am, I'm going to have to ask you to back away from the zinnias."

She laughed, the warmth spreading. *God, his eyes are blue.* The uncensored thought embarrassed her. What was she doing? She'd hoped to get in an hour or so of work at home before she had to get ready for a reception this evening, so why was she wasting her time flirting with a glorified gardener?

She heard her father's mocking laughter. *Failed again, didn't you, Carlotta?*

Blinking, Carly jerked her head up, disoriented for a second to find herself in a hotel room but grateful it had taken Samuel Frazer so long to intrude on her dream. Part of her secretly hoped that once she got tenure, the nightmares that so often centered around her father would stop.

She wasn't exactly thrilled to be dreaming about her ex-husband either, but even that was preferable. Besides, it hadn't been so much a dream as a memory, so it shouldn't count. On that long-ago Friday afternoon, she'd felt foolish for staring into Daniel's eyes as if she were a hormone-addled freshman and she'd compensated by wishing him luck with the zinnias and bidding him a crisp goodbye.

They'd encountered each other several weeks later at a birthday party for Dr. Wexler in the man's home. Carly had found herself amid a small but vocal throng of sycophantic faculty, tripping over themselves to tell the new provost how much they applauded his new outreach initiative that would get community leaders more involved in the school. Personally, Carly thought the initiative was just begging for too many wannabe chefs to give uninformed input on an already damn good recipe. While she didn't plan on sabotaging her career by bluntly stating that, she wouldn't prostitute her self-respect for the sake of higher-ed politics. How many times had she seen her father fawn over a superior or someone with a say in funding, only to loosen his tie at home and start ranting about how the person was a moron compared to the Great Samuel Frazer? He'd be forced to play the subordinate to those he considered his inferiors, then would take his frustrations out on his wife and daughter behind closed doors. At Wexler's party, Carly had indicated her empty glass and excused herself, wondering if it was too soon to go home.

When she'd turned away, it was to see Daniel Cross approaching her with a smile.

"I come bearing martinis," he'd said. "I didn't know if you prefer vodka or gin."

"Vodka, please." Was the emotion buzzing through her at his appearance gratitude or something more?

He'd handed her one of the glasses and kept the other for

himself, though she later learned that Daniel preferred the occasional cold beer to liquor. They'd gone outside, under the pretext of his showing her some of the improvements that he and Wexler had made to the landscaping, though her interest in shrubbery was less pressing than her need to escape Dr. Saundra Arnold's nasal drone. Carly and Daniel had talked for nearly half an hour, and when she had bid him goodbye that night, she'd known it was a lie. They'd be seeing each other again soon.

In the months that had followed, Daniel had become her unlikely weakness. But Carly had always resented weaknesses, both real and perceived, and love hadn't come easily to her. She'd consoled herself with the knowledge that she wasn't the only one vulnerable. *He* loved *her*, too.

That was what she'd told herself right up until he'd asked for the divorce.

Four

❧

Turbulence

Beth woke up Friday dehydrated, with cotton mouth and a throbbing headache. It was the best moment of her day—because for that first second, her mind was too sleep-muddled to remember where she was and what had happened.

One glance around the hotel room brought her situation back into focus, though, and the pain in her skull only intensified as she checked out and hailed a cab. On the flight she'd booked the night before, she was unable to lose herself in the refuge of sleep. Instead, she squeezed her eyes shut and tried to sit as motionless as possible. Several rows behind her, an infant shrieked for the duration of the flight, karmic retribution for her irresponsible drinking.

She yearned to be curled up in own bed, preferably with all the shades drawn and something cold across her forehead. *I just want to go home.*

But when she turned into her driveway and punched the

button to open the automatic garage door, the two-story red-brick house in front of her appeared more mocking than comforting. It represented the life that she *thought* she'd had. A pretty illusion purchased with a hefty mortgage.

Too deflated to bother getting her suitcase out of the car—she'd triple-checked at the baggage carousel to make sure it was hers—she went through the interior door that led to the kitchen. It was one of her favorite rooms in the house. She sank onto the padded window seat. The beautiful stained-glass panels surrounding the breakfast nook filled her with a peaceful déjà vu, as if she were back in her father's church.

I wish you were here to talk to. It was a daughter's nostalgia, coloring reality as surely as the stained glass tinted the shadows across the table. The truth was, Reverend Howard hadn't been all that easy to talk to, holding his household to an even higher standard than the rest of his flock.

After Dana Howard drove off the road in a storm, leaving the reverend a widower and Beth motherless, he had counseled that Dana was in a better place and wouldn't want her loved ones to linger in mourning when they could be putting their energies into much needed good works. They should follow Dana's example; the night she'd died, she had been driving back from overseeing a dinner shift at a local soup kitchen.

Beth was supposed to be *happy* that her mother was in heaven? She'd wanted to do violence to someone, to throw things, to cry and yell and rage until her throat bled with the rawness of it.

The reverend had been disappointed in her displays of destructive emotion, insisting they should take comfort in a higher plan, in knowing that no one else had been injured and that the paramedics agreed Dana had been killed on impact and hadn't suffered. Beth had later regretted her outbursts, just as she'd regretted the pain she'd caused her father by getting pregnant as an unmarried teen.

Joy. Turning away from thoughts of both parents she'd seen buried, Beth clung instead to the daughter who had miraculously lived up to her name. *Did I do well enough by her, teach her everything she'll need to know?*

It suddenly struck Beth that she'd never told Allen that they were going to be grandparents. *Grandparents!* Didn't the very word connote maturity? She couldn't believe the man who'd once lectured her on buying the grocery store's generic brand of bread and milk so that they could save a few dimes was *gambling their money away.*

Restless, Beth stood. She definitely needed to talk to someone. Who? She rubbed her temples. Her pastor was an obvious choice, but her recent thoughts about her father and their difficulties in communicating had temporarily soured her on that option. Joy was out of town and not an appropriate person to burden with Beth's discovery. Later, when she and Allen had discussed the situation and reached some mutual resolutions, they could talk to her together. Or, better yet, they could get the situation under control without needlessly worrying Joy during her pregnancy.

So who could Beth pour her heart out to in the interim? She probably knew a hundred people in the community. Surely she had friends close enough to call in a situation like this. She loved Mitsi Lane, who lived two streets over, but poor

Mitsi couldn't keep a secret to save her life—not the best go-to confidante in a sensitive situation. Barbara Greyson was going through a divorce after thirty years with her lawyer husband, a "starter wife" being replaced by a woman not much older than her college-age sons. Barbara had enough on her own plate without Beth dumping on her. Besides, it was probably best if two recently scorned wives didn't lean on each other for emotional support. It might lead to one of those bizarre revenge-murder pacts that eventually got its own news special.

With a sigh, Beth forced herself to face facts. Her frazzled mind was bouncing from person to person like a nectar-drunk hummingbird flitting between flowers; she was avoiding the unpalatable truth. There was one person with whom she *should* be able to discuss anything. But they apparently didn't have the bond a man and wife were supposed to share. She stared down at her left hand, toying with her ring. When would Allen return home?

And what the devil would she say to him when he arrived?

⊰∞⊱

It was disquieting to be a guest in one's own home, Daniel Cross thought. Instead of spending his Sunday night watching football at a nearby sports bar with buddies from work, he was putting away dishes in cabinets he himself had refurbished. He'd replaced the previous warped doors with new ones, stained in cedar, and painted the surrounding woodwork a soft moss green. For years prior to its sale the two-story three-bedroom house had been a rental property for college kids, and it had needed significant repair—which was why he and Carly had been able to afford it. They'd been charmed by the graceful front porch, the genuine hardwood floors, the cozy potential of each room.

The ceilings were low—anyone over six feet would probably hunch nervously when passing from one room to another—and the storage space was limited. But what the house lacked in walk-in closets, it made up for with a stone fireplace in the living room and a bay window overlooking a small secret garden of a yard. He cast a wistful glance in that direction. *I had plans for that yard.*

They'd both been teeming with plans. He'd envisioned a side-by-side restoration, the two of them working together to create a lasting home. Dumb-ass romanticism on his part. Carly had no natural aptitude for wallpaper paste, installing dimmer switches or projects to modernize the plumbing.

During their engagement, she'd been defending her thesis and he'd seized that as the explanation for why she hadn't been as invested in their wedding plans as most brides. Aside from choosing her wedding gown, the part she'd seemed to care the most about was not utilizing the antiquated tradition of being "given" away. She'd even told Daniel that she would simply defer to his expertise when it came to flowers for the ceremony; he'd thought she was kidding at first. As much as he loved her and recognized that her drive was part of her, he'd assumed that she'd ease back a little once her PhD was official.

He'd been wrong. If anything, she became *more* intense as time passed, as if she were racing a ticking clock that only she could hear. Trying to get articles published in national journals, serving on committees that would count toward her tenure consideration, working—

"Daniel?" The fluttery voice that called from the front parlor was so insubstantial, it was like being summoned by a ghost.

He tossed the checkered navy-and-green dish towel on the counter. "Be right there."

Helene Frazer was situated on the white leather sofa. She wore the knee immobilizer that the doctors said they'd start removing a few times a day next week so that she could practice bending the joint. Daniel didn't envy her the rigors of physical recuperation, especially not on top of the devastating emotional blow she'd been dealt.

Looking at the sweet-faced woman, so fragile and feminine, out of place amid the room's stark colors and sharp angles, he was assailed by anger on her behalf. *Damn it, Carly, she's your mom.*

It wasn't that he minded adjusting his work schedule to be here for Helene. Since his father's retirement, Daniel had been the owner of Cross Lawnscapes, a company his dad had originally started in the late sixties as a basic mowing service but which had grown substantially, and was now flourishing under Daniel's leadership. He had good people working for him and could afford to take a few days off—more than could apparently be said of his ex-wife.

Until Daniel had impulsively offered to help his former mother-in-law at the funeral, Carly's plan had been to have her aunt Josie stay with Helene for the weekend; Josephine was seventy and about one optometry exam shy of being declared legally blind.

Working to keep his expression free of misdirected irritation, he smiled down at Helene. "What can I do for you?"

"Oh, Daniel, you're such a help. And I'm such a burden." Her eyes shimmered with unshed tears. "Can't even remember to take my pills. I should have with supper. They tear up my stomach somethin' fierce if I don't take them with food."

He reached out to squeeze her hand gently. The faded Southern belle was the kind of person who inspired tenderness in anyone who wasn't completely stone-hearted. "I'm sorry, I should have asked you about your medicine at dinner. I'll run get the pills and maybe a snack. What do you say, got room for dessert?" In the time he'd known her, she'd been tiny and birdlike, but since Samuel's death, she'd dropped weight she couldn't afford to lose. Daniel doubted she topped a hundred pounds soaking wet.

She leaned her head back, and as she closed her eyes, the beginnings of a dreamy smile played around her mouth. "We had a housekeeper when I was a girl, made the best homemade bread puddin' you ever had in your life. Drizzled in vanilla sauce . . . Decadent."

"Well, we don't have any bread pudding, but there's pecan pie."

She opened one eye. "Store-bought?"

"Afraid so, ma'am."

Her laugh was small and soft, easy to miss, but it gladdened him nonetheless. "Store-bought pecan pie—what's the world comin' to? But old ladies dependent on others can't be choosy."

"You are not old," he told her. "Middle-aged, maybe, and as beautiful as ever."

"Charmer." She let out a sigh, her expression solemn again. "I can't believe Carlotta let you get away."

He rocked back on his heels, the conversational terrain suddenly rocky and uncertain. Thirty seconds ago, he'd been exasperated that Carly hadn't changed in the year since their divorce was final, but it didn't feel right to find fault with her in front of the woman who'd raised her. Or to take verbal swings at Carly when she'd just buried her father. It was true that during family occasions, she'd seemed somewhat aloof with her parents, but then, that was just Carly. Losing her father had to be hard on her. If circumstances were different—if *she* were different—he would tell her that he was here if she ever needed to talk.

Daniel liked challenges. He'd transplanted trees and bushes that had seemed doomed, only to coax them back to blooming health. His work had taught him that hard work and patience cultivated beautiful rewards. He'd fallen in love with a brilliant woman with a capacity for humor and insight and unmatched heat in the bedroom. But he'd been arrogant to think that he could shape her passionate nature into a passion for *him*.

"I've made you uncomfortable," Helene deduced, sounding apologetic once more. "And after you've been so kind. It's just that a mother wants what's best for her child. I'm sure your parents feel the same way about you."

Daniel was an only child, one of the few things he and Carly had in common. "Yes, ma'am, I'm sure they do."

"I'm proud of her, of course. She's beautiful and bright. But my fear is that *you* were what's best for Carlotta and that she didn't realize it. Now she's all alone." Her face crumpled. "Just like I'm alone."

He reached for the box of tissues on the glass-top coffee table, feeling inadequate as he handed them to her. She'd lost the man she'd been married to for more than half her life; she didn't need the comfort of someone she'd barely seen for over a year. She needed her daughter.

Eerily on cue, the front door opened. Daniel jolted, turning to see Carly step into the tiny foyer just outside the sitting room. "You're home!" *Thank God.* He'd been expecting her in the next half hour, but traffic was always tough to predict.

Her face was a polite mask, her smile barely indicating that she knew him, much less that she'd ever been his lover. In multiple rooms of this very house. "Daniel, Mother. How's everyone doing here?" Her gaze had already moved to the entryway table, where he'd left her mail.

Reaching up, Helene patted his arm. "Daniel was just about to get us some pie. You should help him. And join us for dessert."

Carly glanced at her suitcase. Daniel remembered from their honeymoon that it drove her crazy not to unpack as soon as she returned. It drove her equally crazy when anyone else neglected to do the same, as he'd once learned when he'd come home exhausted from a late flight.

"All right," Carly told her mom. "Then I'm sure Daniel will want to get back to his own life. It was so generous of him to put everything on hold for us."

In other words, *Don't let the door hit your ass on your way out.* Still, it was progress that she noted his generosity. He'd been shocked that she'd accepted his help in the first place. Carly was self-sufficient to a pathological degree. The fact that she'd allowed him to step in and be here for Helene was a testament to how broken up she must be about Samuel's death.

Humoring her mother, Carly trailed him into the kitchen. She gathered silverware and boldly colored ceramic plates while he retrieved low-fat frozen vanilla yogurt. Apparently, Helene wouldn't have luck packing on much needed calories at Carly's house. Carly wasn't birdlike at all; she was tall and square-jawed like her father. But her runner's body was beautifully proportioned, her mismatched eyes mesmerizing. They weren't the only incongruous quality about her.

Realizing that he probably shouldn't be evaluating his ex-wife's physical attributes, he turned his attention toward slicing pie. "How was Texas?"

"Hot. Humid. My presentation was fantastic."

"Naturally."

"How's Helene?"

"Lonely. Scared." Two emotions he doubted Carly herself would ever admit to having. "It's good that you're back."

"You think I was wrong to go to the conference," she said flatly.

"I think everyone copes with loss in their own way. And work is yours."

She wasn't mollified. "If you disapproved, you didn't have to step in while I was gone. I made other provisions. I had it under control."

Josie was her idea of provisions? He wouldn't have left a dog in the absentminded elderly woman's care, much less his mom. Daniel shook his head. Carly was hurting and she was tired from travel. Why get sucked into an argument?

"I don't 'disapprove,' " he fibbed. "I just worry about both of you. You've had a huge shock. I was happy to help."

Maybe, deep down, he'd hoped that lending a hand in a time of crisis would mitigate some of his own guilt. He'd had plenty of time to review his decision to ask for a divorce and believed it had been the right thing to do—Carly certainly wasn't handicapped by a broken heart—but the way he'd left her had been an act of cowardice. He'd tried to apologize, only to have her interrupt with the clipped opinion that the separation had been inevitable and he'd spared her from being the villain.

Helene was easy to look after. Unlike her daughter, she accepted assistance with gratitude and shy smiles. She made a man feel useful.

Once the plates of pie à la mode were ready to be served, Daniel took a step back. "If you want to get her pills from the dresser in her room, I'll run upstairs and gather my stuff. From your office."

Helene was staying on the main floor in a minuscule guest room equipped with an en suite bathroom. Upstairs, Daniel had made use of the smallest bedroom, which Carly had converted to her office; it was furnished with a white metal daybed. There was also the master bedroom, with a much larger and more comfortable bed, but sleeping in the room and on the mattress he'd once shared with his wife would have veered further beyond bizarre than he'd cared to go.

The three of them ate their dessert in the parlor. Helene

was determinedly oblivious to the strain. With both Daniel's attention and her daughter back home, she was more animated than he'd seen her all weekend. It wasn't until he passed his empty plate to Carly's outstretched hand and announced it was time to leave that Helene's expression dimmed.

"You take care of yourself," he told her. "I want to hear that leg's recovering quickly."

"Promise you'll visit while it's healing?"

He was torn between the plea in her eyes and the waves of silent protest rolling off Carly. He didn't blame her for not wanting him here. It was awkward for both of them.

But the tears forming in Helene's eyes wrenched his heart. "I promise." He glanced at Carly. "You'll be going back into work this week?"

"I'm planning to grade final papers at home," she said defensively, "but there are some end-of-semester meetings I need to attend and I have time-sensitive undergraduate-advising responsibilities."

"I'm sure you're doing the best you can," Daniel said. "I just thought that on the days that require you to be away for long, I could swing by and check on Helene. Maybe bring her some lunch. You like barbecue, right?"

Helene was all smiles again. "What self-respectin' Southerner doesn't? Daniel, I just don't know how we can thank you enough. Isn't he wonderful to offer, Carlotta?"

"Yeah. He's a peach." Carly was careful to keep any sarcasm out of her tone, but Daniel heard it anyway. "Well, then, Daniel, I guess we'll be seeing you soon."

He glanced at his ex-wife, sitting so erect on an ottoman,

her body language screaming that she would never allow herself to graciously lean on anyone. "I guess you will." Difficult to say which one of them was looking forward to it less.

❧

It was Sunday evening when Beth heard the key in the lock. Seated in the glider that had been a Mother's Day present more than a decade ago, she immediately lowered her gaze to the needlepoint in her lap. Her reaction was reminiscent of those nights she'd stayed up waiting for Joy to come home from a date but did her darnedest to look nonchalant when her daughter came inside.

A moment later, an unshaven stranger wearing her husband's face and clothes entered the house. His laptop case hung from his shoulder, and he carried a bunch of despondent, cellophane-wrapped pink roses. Or maybe it was Allen himself who lent the air of despondency, his shoulders hunched inside his Windbreaker, his jaw neglected and scruffy. She wanted to believe his demeanor indicated he regretted hurting her and putting this strain on their marriage.

Please don't let him look like this because he lost money. When she'd left a voice mail on his cell phone that she was flying home, she'd desperately hoped he would follow right behind her. Surely, after what had transpired in Houston, he wouldn't actually stay until his allotted checkout time Sunday morning and play cards? But he hadn't come home. He'd let two days pass before he even returned her call.

She'd been furious, then panicked. She'd thought of Barbara Greyson, starting over at fifty, facing the prospect of being alone in her sixties. Beth had lain awake all last night, the same sentence chanting through her mind until the stars finally faded into dawn: *God, please don't let him leave me.*

She set aside the embroidery hoop. Pretending to be calm wasn't worth accidentally stabbing herself. "Hi."

"Beth." His tone held a wealth of tenderness.

She was absently reminded of last year's company Christmas party, when he'd had one too many whiskey sours at the open bar and had gazed at her in tipsy, uninhibited adoration for the rest of the night. Her heart had melted.

Right now, it sat in her chest, an unyielding lump. "Yes?"

He bent over, lowering his laptop to the ground. "You got my message, right? About expecting me home tonight?"

"I got it." Somehow, she doubted it was a coincidence that he hadn't bothered to contact her until the middle of the church service on Sunday. Fresh anger washed through her that he'd avoided her, on top of deceiving her, and thought a few limp roses would fix everything.

The dutiful-wife part of her, twenty-six years in the making, protested that she should be thrilled to see the flowers and the contrition in his gray eyes. This time yesterday, hadn't her greatest fear been that he wouldn't value what they shared as highly as she did, that he wouldn't be willing to work to repair the damage, that he might choose to start over somewhere else, as Jeff Greyson had? The cynical part of her, however, wondered if he valued her more or less than the poker tournament she assumed he'd been playing in all weekend.

When he came toward her to hand over the roses and place

a kiss on her cheek, she shocked them both by flinching away, her expression an automatic moue of distaste.

Allen straightened, his surprise at her reaction fading into something darker as he dropped the flowers on the end table next to her. "So you're going to freeze me out now? I fudge the truth about taking some time away just for me, and I have to be punished? I thought you were above that, Elisabeth. I didn't expect the cold shoulder from you."

She stood, pushing out of the glider with enough force that the chair rocked crazily. "I'd say you've fudged on more than your mini-vacation. The gambling, the poker playing?"

"What are you talking about? You know I play poker with the guys every wee—"

"You didn't empty our savings account through Wednesday-night poker with the guys!" She'd looked online at their credit cards, two of which were completely maxed out, and their savings account, which they'd dipped into for Joy's wedding but had been rebuilding, was down to a mere three hundred dollars. Beth had a long-held and somewhat girlish habit of keeping two twenty-dollar bills in her underwear drawer "in case of emergency." Forty dollars? *Good luck getting out of an emergency with that.* Given the economic climate of the last couple of years, they'd already lost money on some investments and she'd always heard that borrowing from or against your 401(k) should be a last resort reserved for extreme circumstances.

What infuriated her was how dire her circumstances had become *without her even knowing it!*

She should have spent more time figuring out what to say, because instead of offering to help him work through his problem, she was yelling. Having started, she felt powerless to stop the flood. Easy to see why wrath was one of the seven deadly sins. "Our savings, Allen! How could you blow that on ... on card games, for crying out loud?"

He'd gone pale, except for two blotches of hectic color in his cheeks. "That's a lot of righteous indignation when I don't recall you contributing to that account."

She reeled. He might as well have backhanded her. *All these years.* All these years he'd come home to a tidy house and warm meals ...

"I was raising our daughter," she said, lifting her chin. "You can't put a price tag on that."

At first, he didn't respond but the veiled contempt in his eyes threw her back in time. She'd seen that expression when he raged at her in college, nearly frightening her with the condemnation that was so different from her father's much quieter displays of disapproval. At nineteen, she'd been extremely new to birth control pills and hadn't realized that another medication she'd taken briefly could interfere. She had been naïve and sheltered, and it hadn't occurred to her, shortly before the AIDS-awareness boom, to ask Allen to use protection, too. He certainly hadn't volunteered.

Whatever he was currently thinking or feeling—or hiding from her—he wasn't so far gone that he tossed the pregnancy back in her face, pointing out that it hadn't been his idea to get married in the first place. Elisabeth didn't think she could have forgiven him that. It had been one thing to live under the shadow of his anger that first year, when he was finishing classes, starting a full-time job, and coming home to a new-born and a frazzled young mother, who was sure she was doing everything wrong. But in light of all they'd shared together since then and the incredible woman Joy had blossomed into, Beth knew she'd leave him flat if he dared imply that he re-gretted their daughter's existence.

He sighed, scrubbing a hand over his tired face. "I'm sorry. Is that what you want to hear? I am. I didn't come home want-ing to fight."

"What did you think would happen?" she asked, trying to keep her tone matter-of-fact instead of inflammatory. She fol-lowed him into the kitchen, trying to get him to see a per-spective besides his own . . . whatever that might be. "Wanting to be spontaneous and romantic, I flew to Texas to see you. And learned that you've been lying to me. That you're stealing money from us. *Then* you hang around another couple of days with your buddies."

Like Jessica? An unsettling thought. Now that Beth knew he was capable of lying to her, why should she trust him on anything? She took a deep breath, trying to wrestle her wrath into submission. How was it that after all the virtues her father had tried to drum into her, she couldn't recall a single one of them? "After all that, Allen, what did you think would hap-pen when you got home? I can't pretend it didn't happen. Ev said—"

"You talked to Ev about me?" He sounded nearly mur-derous.

Maybe it had been unwise of her to tackle this discussion

without reinforcements. Everett had broached the subject of an intervention, but who would she have asked to participate? Until this week, she hadn't even known there was a problem that required intervening. Should she have gone through the alphabetic directory at his office, asking whoever picked up the phone if they were aware that her husband was gambling too much? If they, in fact, knew more about her own husband than she did?

"Ev is your friend, and he's worried about you."

Allen snorted. "I owe him a few bucks and he's worried about getting it back."

"Just how bad is it?" she asked softly.

"You tell me." He slammed the gallon of milk he'd taken from the refrigerator down on the counter, sneering in her direction. "Checking into bank records, pumping my friends for information—you've been quite the busy little bee, Beth."

How many times, she wondered dispassionately, had he attacked her like this and *she'd* ended up backing down, apologizing? No, it wasn't a matter of "how many," she amended; they didn't fight often, especially in recent years. But there was definitely a pattern, a startlingly high percentage. Nine out of ten times, when they disagreed, Allen's default strategy was to bully her. Why had she tolerated it for so long? Because she'd been conditioned from adolescence to feel apologetic? *I confess that I have not been worthy.* Her father, for all his faith and gentleness, had always wanted just a bit more from her—or a bit less—than what came naturally.

She was overcome with an urge to call Joy, just to tell her daughter she loved her. *Please let me have given her the uncon-*

ditional affection she'll need in life. No woman should ever be someone else's doormat. Suddenly, Beth didn't know who she despised more: Allen or herself.

"This week, I'm going to start looking for a job," she heard herself say. "And I may ask around for the name of a good therapist—"

"Let's not overreact, Beth." He'd traded anger and accusation for his salesman's mask. Sweet-talking the client, anything to close the deal. "I'm sure we can work through this."

"I'm not." They were the most frightening words she'd ever spoken, and she paused, half expecting lightning from the sky or the earth to crack beneath her feet. But there was simply a raised eyebrow from Allen and the sense that she couldn't back down. Not this time. "I don't think you should stay here tonight."

"What? I'm tired, Beth. I want to sleep under my own roof." He switched tactics. "In the long run you know I'll take care of you financially. But for now, I got myself in too deep. A hotel is a gratuitous expense. There's more than one bed here."

Having solved the matter to his own satisfaction, he turned away from her and pulled a glass out of the dishwasher. She didn't bother pointing out to him that it was dirty. If he'd stopped for a second to look at the dishes, he could have deduced that for himself. But Allen was conditioned, too. Conditioned by her actions over the past twenty-six years to accept that the dishes would always be clean, that leftovers would always be available in the fridge to heat at his convenience, that his clothes would always find their way to the dry cleaner and back to his closet, as if by magic.

Conditioned to believe that he *was* worthy.

"You don't have to stay at a hotel. I'm sure Ev would be willing to put you up for the night. Or your parents in Gwin-nett. When was the last time you had dinner with them? Just leave Joy alone. She and Peter got back home tonight, and she's tired. She needs her rest." Beth paused, knowing it wasn't fair to tell him like this but feeling wrong about keeping him in the dark any longer. "She's pregnant."

"What?"

If Beth had been in a different mood, his expression of shock might have been comical. "Is it really that surprising? You know she and Peter want kids."

"But she's just a—" He broke off, glancing at his wife.

Just a baby? Beth felt that way, too, some days. As if she might turn around and see a drooling toddler in the doorway holding her favorite stuffed rabbit. But those days were long gone. As unbelievable as it seemed, Joy was older and better prepared to be a mother than Beth herself had been.

Nearly forty-five, Beth was still waiting to feel like she knew what the hell she was doing. "We're going to be grand-parents, Allen. It's probably time we grew up."

Five

Continue to Breathe Normally

Amid two e-mails in Carly's in-box from students preemptively protesting their final grades, which wouldn't even be posted until later that day—perhaps they should have shown such initiative *during* the semester—was a more succinct message from Dean Murrin that she wished to see Carly at her earliest possible convenience. Was the dean ready to make her tenure recommendations to the provost?

A ripple of apprehension stole past Carly's defenses. She tried to shake it off, to remind herself of all that she'd accomplished. Instead, she kept thinking of Dr. Saundra Arnold's smug expression at a department lunch yesterday. Saundra had been the one to steal Carly's TA—though, admittedly, that hadn't been much of a loss. While all the tenured professors, Saundra included, had their own TAs, it wasn't a guaranteed perk for junior faculty. Carly had rated an assistant mostly because of her book, but the kid hadn't lasted the year.

She'd been willing to overlook his indiscreet grumbling, but Saundra had made the case to Dean Murrin that an academic-assessment project based on students graduating this month was a top priority and needed extra manpower. Carly would bet her entire book advance that Saundra was the member of the tenure review committee who'd expressed "reservations."

One detractor, Carly told herself as she rolled her chair back from the desk and stood. One meaningless detractor against an exemplary record.

When Carly got to the dean's office, the secretary waved her in with, "She's expecting you."

Carly knocked against the frame of the dean's open door. "You wanted to speak with me?"

The older woman glanced up from her computer. "Dr. Frazer, good. Come in—why don't you close the door?"

A straight-A student, the top female track star in both her junior high and high school, Carly had never had cause to be called to the principal's office. She imagined it would have felt a lot like this. Drawing herself up to her full height—five foot eleven in the espadrilles she currently wore—she moved with unhurried ease.

She took a seat and waited, a pleasant smile on her face.

Beverley cocked her head, contemplative. "I haven't seen much of you since you got back from Texas. I've been busy with the president's new initiative and I'm sure you've been wading through final exams and papers. But I did want to mention that a friend of mine at Davidson, Dr. Regina Fine, attended your lecture. She said you were a credit to our institution."

Damn right I am. Carly inclined her head. "I appreciate your passing that along." But the dean wouldn't have called her in just for that.

"It's nice to be able to share good news." The older woman steepled her fingers. "I'm afraid some of the other items we need to discuss are less enjoyable."

Inwardly, Carly tensed. It took every molecule of discipline in her not to change her posture or drop her cordial expression. "Oh?"

"For starters, your class for the first summer session didn't 'make.' " That was the higher-ed term for a class that failed to meet its minimum-enrollment requirement and would therefore be canceled.

"Of course, we still wanted to find a place for you in the schedule," the dean continued.

While it wasn't uncommon for a professor working on a book to take a semester off, there was a strict policy here about untenured faculty only being allowed one sabbatical in a three-year period. Carly had used hers to go to Europe, so it made sense that they needed her to cover classes for other professors during a season when people loved having time away.

"I've slotted you for Western civilization."

Western civ? But that was a survey class! Full of freshman and sophomores who weren't even planning to major in history. Hell, they'd let an adjunct teach it last summer, and now they wanted to relegate Carly to academic Siberia?

"With all due respect, Dean Murrin, do you think that perhaps I might be of more use to the college in a course closer to my area of specialization? Understanding comparative history or even gender studies would—"

"Gender studies is being taught by Dr. Shapiro," the dean interrupted smoothly. "And it's my philosophy that going back to the basics is helpful for all of us from time to time. Don't you agree?"

No. While the crux of Carly's work stemmed from comparing different historical figures and civilizations, cramming everything from Mesopotamia to the European Renaissance into a six-week summer course would only provide a grossly superficial view of events. But Carly preferred to pick fights she could win. She smiled tightly, in acceptance if not agreement.

"While we're on the subject of classes, there is something else we need to discuss." The dean leaned back in her chair, removing her glasses and toying with the slim gold arms. "End-of-the-year evaluations."

Thinking of the two whiny e-mails she'd already opened, Carly wanted to roll her eyes. She could just imagine what discontent students might write behind the safety of anonymous evals. If she were in charge of the world, anonymous reviews and evaluations would be stricken from policy—you either had the balls to say something straight-out, identity known, or you didn't.

"I'm sure some of the undergrads are going to claim that I grade harshly," Carly conceded, "but—"

"This wasn't a random handful, Dr. Frazer. What alarmed me were the allegations of a specific group who accused you of gender favoritism."

"That's ridiculous. The number of male students that finished my classes with A's is roughly proportional to the number of females." The composure she'd been trying to maintain threatened to crack. Concealed in her lap, her fingernails bit into her palms. "If it was one evaluation, I'd say it was a bitter student who spent more nights partying than studying. If there are multiple claims, it's possibly a prank. It may not surprise you to learn that the students don't necessarily take the evaluations as seriously as we would like. I assure you, I'm no tougher on the male students in my courses than—"

"Actually, it's *female* students who complained. They say they're graded on a different standard and are derided during class discussions."

Carly went cold, completely flummoxed. "But that's . . . *I'm* a woman." Feeling stupid for pointing out the obvious, she bit the inside of her lip and tried to collect her thoughts.

"For the time being, there have been no formal complaints, and unless I find anything questionable in your final grades this semester, I think that we can file this under 'things to be aware of' and let it go."

Let it go? Hardly. College administrators were always hyperaware of anything that could lead to the threat of a lawsuit. Smile too broadly at a male student, you could be accused of sexual harassment. Withhold the broad smiles, you could be accused of gender discrimination. With everything in Carly's life that was actually deserving of her time and thought, now she had these inane evals hanging over her head like the sword of Damocles?

Her facial muscles spasmed, her grimace refusing to become a smile. "Well. If that's everyth—"

"There's also the matter of your being considered for tenure." Nothing in Dean Murrin's expression foreshadowed good news.

Carly's stomach dropped. *They have to give it to me. I've earned it.*

She could suddenly smell the nauseating fumes of the expensive whiskey her father had favored, hear his gravelly voice: "You watch your tone with me, girl. You think you're smart, acing a few fluff classes, but you're never gonna be anything in the brains department compared to your old man. So you just watch. Your. Tone."

"Dr. Frazer?"

With embarrassing effort, Carly jerked herself from the past back to her meeting. "I apologize. I . . . I was thinking about my father." *May he rot in hell.*

"Of course." The dean's expression softened. "Such a well-respected man. He must have been a great influence on you."

"It was my dream," Carly said, "for him to see me tenured at a first-rate college like Ramson Neil."

Beverley faltered, looking uncertain for the first time. "You're aware that at least one member of the tenure review committee had concerns about collegiality?"

An official-sounding term that really meant "popularity contest."

Carly was a credentialed professional seeking the acknowledgment due her, not a damn sorority pledge trying to make friends during rush week. "I saw the report, yes." She managed not to point out that lawsuits were cropping up against universities all over the country over the "collegiality" issue. In her opinion, the administration should be far more worried about *that* than occasionally threatened student cases that would mostly be laughed out of court if they ever made it that far.

"I'm supposed to make my recommendations to the provost," the dean said. "But he's agreed that, in light of my leaving the country for a month, I can have some extra time this once."

The president was sending Beverley abroad to pursue an international relationship with another institution. Carly didn't dare breathe, wondering if the extra time was going to help her or hurt her in terms of Beverley's endorsement. The provost tended to agree with the dean; after him, there was only the rubber stamp of the board between Carly and her goal of tenure.

"I just thought you should know," Dean Murrin continued, "since normally I would be handing in my write-up any day now."

"Well." It was hard to speak with so many thoughts churning through her brain, a welling sense of unfairness—*I've earned this, goddamn it*—inside her. But Carly kept her voice level, sensing that she was being tested. "I appreciate your keeping me in the loop. I don't take any of the committee's concerns lightly." No, indeed.

"Good." The dean studied her closely. "Good. We're certainly aware of your speaking and publishing credentials, not to mention the extra hours you've given in service to the institution—search committees, curriculum review and planning, campus beautification. But, going forward, keep in mind that annual events like the pie pursuit that might seem frivolous are part and parcel of the traditions that individualize Ramson Neil and make it a great college."

"Of course." And what, Carly wondered, did the dean have to say about the annual kilt-inspired dare, an irreverent homage to the founders' Scottish ancestry, in which graduating seniors tried to get one member of their class to go commando beneath commencement robes? Maybe if Carly started the rumor at this weekend's ceremony that she was au naturel under her faculty regalia, she'd be a shoo-in for tenure.

"I see a lot of potential in you," the dean added, her expression annoyingly maternal. Carly was seeking career recognition, not a second mother. "And I hope that potential can be realized here at Ramson Neil in the years to come."

Carly stood, knowing they were done. "That's my wish as well."

Stay calm, she told herself as she passed the secretary and walked down the hall. *Don't let the bastards get you down—or see you sweat.* On the return trip to her office, she went by Professor Saundra Arnold and managed not to lunge for her throat. *Okay.* Okay, she would handle this. Dean Murrin had all but admitted that she was buying Carly some time. So, starting this June, she would be the best Western civ instructor and the most *collegial* fucking prof Ramson Neil had ever seen.

"No, I—" Beth's grip constricted around the cordless phone, but she kept her voice sunny. "No, of course not, Barb. I understand. Please tell your nephew I said thanks anyway."

She hung up the phone, having exhausted another avenue

of potential employment. *This is ridiculous.* She'd lived in the same house for almost twenty years, knew a lot of people. Yet neither diligent perusal of the *Atlanta Journal Constitution,* nor networking with her friends, nor Web sites with names like Monster or Work Wiz had netted her any promising leads. All she wanted was a regular income, a modest one that didn't involve flipping burgers. Granted, this was only Thursday afternoon, but she didn't see her prospects getting brighter in the immediate future.

She was competing with college students less than half her age—and with twice her education—who were out of school for the summer and looking for jobs that would allow them to pay for textbooks next fall. Come to think of it, even if she included burger flipping in her revised job search, she'd still be competing with plenty of younger applicants who'd had the good sense to begin seeking seasonal employment weeks ago.

In Beth's defense, she hadn't *known* weeks ago that her life would be falling apart, or she would have planned accordingly.

Allen's voice rang in her ears, his parting words as he'd tossed some clothes in a duffel bag before leaving for Ev's: *I can't talk to you when you're like this, Beth. I don't even know you. Call me when you're ready to face reality.*

Reality or defeat?

If she begged him to return, they'd never grow any stronger. Looking back now, she realized there were dysfunctional habits in their relationship that she'd let take root as a new and insecure bride. She'd chosen to overlook the small fissures in their marriage rather than make waves. Maybe Allen's gambling problem was a warped blessing, a way of making her face the truth. They hadn't really been living as two equals who shared their lives and feelings. Though she wasn't ready to give up on their marriage, she was no longer willing to pretend or settle.

Brisk tapping against the front door shook Beth from her reverie. She slid from the window seat, clinging to wry hope. Maybe it was opportunity knocking.

Or her husband? That would be a good sign. She'd had the sense that he was waiting for her to crack, to beg him to come home. What he didn't seem to realize was that, after years of his traveling—sometimes prolonged trips to visit European companies—she'd gone more than a week without seeing him many times in their marriage. While it had been her suggestion that they spend some time apart to clearly evaluate the situation, she hadn't meant they should stop speaking. The gauntlet he'd thrown when he'd left had discouraged her from calling him more than once during the past few days.

Fingers mentally crossed, Beth reached the front door. And saw her daughter waiting on the other side.

Flinging open the door, Elisabeth ushered Joy into the house. "Oh, baby, I'm so happy to see you. How are you?"

"I've been better." Joy was dressed far more casually than Beth was used to seeing her, huddled in an oversize T-shirt that no doubt belonged to Peter and a baggy pair of khaki shorts. Her dark hair, Beth's genetic contribution, hung in a limp ponytail and her gray eyes were troubled.

"What's wrong? It's not the baby, is it? Is everything all right with the pregnancy? With Peter? I know some men can react strangely to fatherhood. Just be patient with him, honey. Or is it your job?" Beth asked, belatedly realizing that Joy should be at work right now. She was an analyst for a national retail chain headquartered in Atlanta; she was on a team that charted product gains and losses, predicted trends, and reported to territory managers.

"One thing at a time, Mama!" Joy held up her hands as if warding off any more questions, and Beth was relieved to hear her chuckle. "My short-term memory is Swiss cheese these days. I can barely answer the first question before I forget what the second question was."

"Here's an easy one, then. Can I get you a drink?"

"Filtered water, thanks. I'm trying to cut back on sugar and caffeine." Joy sighed as they went back to the kitchen. "You'd be surprised by how little that leaves me."

After Beth had filled two glasses with water, she carried them to the table, where her daughter sat. "Have you lost weight?"

"Morning sickness." Joy pulled a face. "And midmorning. And afternoon. And occasionally evening."

Though sympathetic, Beth couldn't help laughing. "Ah, yes. It's coming back to me now. When I was carrying you, I could barely keep down water for the first four months." Then again, that could have been from stress as much as hormones. She hesitated.

Was it time for them to finally have the conversation? Joy was a mathematician, after all! She'd known perfectly well when her parents had celebrated their twenty-fifth wedding anniversary, compared to her own birth date. Yet the inevitable question, or at least comments, Beth had braced herself for over the years had never come. *The elephant in the house.* It had been there for so long that mostly Beth just dusted it, vacuumed around it, and let everyone pretend it didn't exist.

"You're probably wondering why I'm here," Joy said, unknowingly helping Beth once more postpone the awkward discussion.

"You're welcome any hour of the day or night," Beth said. "With or without a reason."

"I know. I love you." Joy sipped her water. "But I need to talk to you about Daddy. He said you threw him out!"

"What?" Beth began making immediate plans to break a major commandment. If Allen walked through the door right now, she could calmly kill him with her bare hands. Well, maybe not *calmly.* "I can't believe he told you that."

"I can't believe you didn't!" Tears spiked Joy's lashes. "We always said we could tell each other anything."

Yes, they'd said that. They just didn't always practice it.

"I didn't want to upset you, especially in your first trimester. Besides, he's exaggerating. We had a disagreement, and I suggested that maybe he stay with a friend while we both cool down and think over each other's points of view." Beth congratulated herself on sounding reasonable, well-adjusted, and not at all murderous.

"He seems wrecked, Mama. Told me that he screwed up, lost too much money in a poker game, and that you were justifiably furious with him."

If Allen had verbally attacked Beth, their daughter would have automatically defended her mom. But he'd appealed to

Joy's soft heart and sent her as his emissary. If he thought this was the way to sway Beth from her anger, he really didn't know her.

"It wasn't just one poker game." How could Beth admit that she didn't even know the extent of the losses? "You remember Ev, right?"

"Uncle Everett? Sure." Joy smiled fondly. "My pregnancy memory loss isn't *that* bad."

Beth chose her words carefully, not wanting to overdramatize the situation but at the same time wanting to be as honest as possible now that Joy had learned what was happening. "Ev and I spoke last week, and he's worried that, maybe, your father has a gambling problem."

"You mean like an addiction?" Joy frowned. "In that case, he needs you even more than I thought. Aren't there . . . I don't know, programs or something that we should enroll him in?"

"It's something I'd like to discuss with him, along with a marriage counselor, but he has to be ready for it. I can't make him do anything."

Joy nodded. "I know this must be hard on you, Mama. But you can't abandon him. He needs us. You aren't going to stay angry with him, are you?"

While Beth frequently gave her daughter advice, she tried never to tell people how to feel—or not feel. It brought back too many reminders of letting down Reverend Howard. "I want to forgive him, but that's not going to happen overnight."

"Of course you're right. I'd be mad, too, if I were you." Joy's facial muscles twitched as though she were attempting to conjure a smile. It didn't take. Her shoulders hunched, and her hands were already rising to cover her face when the first tear fell.

Beth had seen this exact same body language sequence many times before: when Joy was in fifth grade and her long-time best friend had moved away; when Joy made it to the state spelling bee in junior high, only to stumble over a word she knew and get eliminated in the first round; when Beth's father had died and fifteen-year-old Joy had regretted being so petulant about spending the previous summer with him on a missions trip. Now Beth did what she had on those prior occasions. She moved to her daughter and embraced her silently, waiting for the cleansing tears to pass. She hated that she and Allen had upset Joy during such an emotional time, but she couldn't help the spark of gratitude she felt when her daughter leaned into her. *All grown-up, but still my baby.*

Joy sniffled. "I feel like an idiot. No wonder you didn't think you could tell me you and Dad were having problems. It's these damn hor—*darn* hormones."

Beth laughed. "I think you're past the age where I can send you to your room for bad language."

"I didn't mean to start blubbering. It's just . . . I love you guys so much. I want you to be happy. Like Peter and me."

"We'll be fine." *I hope.* "Every married couple encounters a few rough patches—even you and Peter someday."

"Bite your tongue!" Joy's eyes were round with mock horror. "Well, if that ever does happen, at least I know I can always come to you."

Beth kissed the top of her head. "Yes, you can."

"You'll talk to Daddy, won't you?" Though Joy had subdued the sobs quickly, genuine fear lurked in her eyes. No child liked to think about her parents having troubles, even an adult child.

"I'll speak to him soon." Beth took in her daughter's shaken demeanor, cursing Allen's selfishness for having caused it. "You can count on that."

⊰❦⊱

Once she'd watched Joy's car drive down the street, Beth grabbed her purse and shoved her feet into a pair of pumps. She was so enraged by Allen's end run, using their only child to try to guilt-trip Beth into contacting him, that the drive to his office building passed in a red haze. On autopilot, she flicked her blinkers on at the appropriate times and turned on the appropriate streets, noticing little more of her surroundings than the streetlights and occasional stop signs.

It wasn't until she caught the alarmed expression on Allen's administrative assistant—a kid named Kirk, no older than Joy—that she realized how she must look, barreling down the carpeted hallways so fast she was probably throwing sparks off her Nine Wests, homicide in her chocolate eyes.

Kirk half rose behind his desk outside Allen's office. "M-Mrs. Overton?"

Taking a deep breath, she slowed. Out of the blue, she recalled that moment in the Houston hotel bar when she'd first seen Carly Frazer, striding purposefully, the look of an avenger about her. Maybe they *did* have something in common besides look-alike luggage.

"Afternoon, Kirk. I don't mean to interrupt whatever you're working on. Is Allen in?"

"Yes. No. He's in today, but he's not currently at his desk. If you'd—"

"Kirk, my man." A tall gentleman with a garish green-and-yellow tie and equally ostentatious handlebar mustache rounded the corner at a clip. She recognized him vaguely from office parties but wasn't sure they'd ever been introduced. "Are you the one to see about the pool?"

"I am." Kirk cut his gaze back to Beth. "Give me just a sec, Mr. Chase."

Mr. Chase stopped, taking his demeanor down a notch. "Mrs. Overton. I apologize for interrupting. Didn't see you there."

"I was just explaining that Mr. Overton has stepped out of his office for a moment, but should be back shortly. Would you like to wait inside?" Kirk invited her. "I'd be happy to grab you a cup of coffee or something."

"Thank you, but that's not necessary." Beth took a step closer, surveying the papers on Kirk's desk. "So, office pool, huh? What are you boys betting on this time?"

For a second, Kirk fidgeted. Companies all over the city held sports pools and lotteries, but strictly speaking, the betting wasn't legal. Then he relaxed, shooting her a grin. "PGA. The U.S. Open's in a few weeks." He pulled out a clipboard and handed it to Mr. Chase.

Along with names of famous golfers, Beth made out OVER-TON in black marker. A social activity for fun, not meeting a bookie in a smoke-filled after-hours club, but still . . . "Kirk, I believe I will go wait in my husband's office."

He nodded. "Holler if you change your mind about wanting a drink."

Even though she knew it wasn't the type of drink he meant, her mind flashed again to that Houston lobby bar. Not that rum had given her anything but a headache, and Allen was capable of providing that without chemical assistance.

Inside Allen's office, she slid into one of the visitor's chairs, her legs shaky. Entry in the pool was probably only five or ten dollars, so was she overreacting to this latest instance of gambling? If he'd been at his desk when she stormed in, riding her earlier fervor, this would have been simpler. Now, newly concerned about how deep his troubles ran, she couldn't help reflecting on what Joy had said: Allen needed their help and understanding now more than ever.

"Beth?"

She started in the chair, turning to see her husband hovering in the doorway, hesitant to enter his own office. "We need to talk." All week she'd felt it was important for her not to call him first, but now that seemed juvenile—a game with jumbled rules that paled in comparison to the blessed institution of marriage. She was ashamed of herself.

Shutting the door behind him, he joined her, choosing the seat next to her rather than the chair on the other side of the desk. "Okay."

"Joy came to see me," she said, watching his face. "You spoke to her?"

"I'm her father. I wanted to congratulate her and Peter on the baby." He paused, his expression wistful. "She sounds so happy."

"I'm glad you called her, but I wish you hadn't bothered her with our difficulties." Her jaw tightened. "You told her I threw you out?"

He squirmed. "I'm not sure that's how I put it. Look, I didn't have the specific intention of telling her all that. She asked about you and the conversation got away from me. It was refreshing to have a sympathetic ear," he added balefully.

Unlike the last two times they'd spoken, she refused to let him bait her. "You're right. I wasn't very sympathetic. I was too busy being hurt and confused. You haven't been honest with me, Allen. And when I tried to talk to you about what's going on, you lashed out at me."

Fiddling with an ink pen, he avoided meeting her eyes. "Ev told me I'm being an ass. And that if I don't beg your forgiveness, he's giving you the name of his divorce lawyer."

Divorce. The word froze the blood in her veins. Divorce was unthinkable. It was something other people did. "Allen, you know that's not what I want."

"I hope not." He still didn't look at her. "But I wouldn't entirely blame you if you did."

"I love you." The admission didn't come easily, not after everything he'd put her through, but it was true.

He reached across the space between their chairs, taking her hand. "I love you, too, Elisabeth."

"Then come home," she said. "Come home and let's sort through this."

"You mean it?" He smiled, the slightly lopsided beam of pure charm that had transfixed her as a college coed. After her sheltered, small-town upbringing, the college senior had seemed so worldly. She'd been dazed that he was attracted to *her*. "Thank God. Ev snores and he's a lousy cook."

"I don't suppose it occurred to you to cook for yourself?" she asked, the words out before she could censor herself.

But he didn't take offense. "Oh, it occurred to me. In fact, it was forcibly suggested. As it turns out," he admitted with a laugh, "I'm even worse than he is."

She laughed, too, letting herself be won back. "How about you pick up some Chinese on the way home tonight? We'll talk, and neither of us has to cook."

"That sounds—" His phone rang, cutting him off, and he cast her an apologetic glance. "I may need to take that. I've been waiting on a call."

"Go. I'll see you tonight." She left feeling lighter than when she arrived, but also deeply tired. She hadn't realized how draining it was to be so angry.

Tonight she'd revisit the idea of a therapist and perhaps, when Allen was relaxed and not feeling under attack, ask him if it was wise to participate in social activities like office pools. She simply had to convey she was on his team, not on the attack. Life—marriage, even—was looking brighter.

Just the same, Beth found herself pulling into a bank parking lot. *Still fifteen minutes before closing.* Feeling breathless and slightly traitorous, she went inside.

She took her driver's license and Social Security card from her wallet and opened a checking account for Beth Howard Overton, relieved that she only needed a twenty-five-dollar deposit to do so. It was the first time in her life she'd had an account under her name only, without her father as a cosigner or Allen as a joint holder. When she unlocked her car door, she was flushed with equal parts guilt and giddiness, like a teenager who'd just gone to second base with the hottest guy in school.

If she was trying to get her marriage back on track, was it wise to have secrets from her husband? And where was she going to get the money to build up her account? Forty dollars had been more than enough to make a small strike for self-reliance, but it wouldn't get her much further. She rested her head on the steering wheel. When she straightened again, her gaze caught on the cellular phone she'd left on the passenger seat. Carly Frazer had talked about needing to hire someone for the summer. Had she already filled the position with one of the seemingly thousands of students looking for work? *You didn't even like her.*

No, not in the traditional sense, but Beth had glimpsed some admirable qualities in the younger woman. Besides, God didn't want her to judge others, especially those she barely knew.

Could there be a reason God had placed Carly and Beth in each other's paths?

All right, that was reaching, but she *really* didn't want to spend the foreseeable future flipping burgers. She picked up the phone and scrolled through the call logs for outgoing numbers. Before she could talk herself out of the impulsive act—not wanting to think about how her *last* spontaneous decision had turned out—she dialed. A cool, cultured voice informed her that she'd reached Dr. Carly Frazer's mailbox.

Beth squeezed her eyes shut as she spoke. "Good afternoon, this is Elisabeth Overton. As you recall, we recently met in Houston, where you made a passing comment about needing to hire someone? I don't know the specifics of the job, and I'm not sure I have the required experience, but I'd like to find out."

Six

Exits Are Clearly Marked

After a person divorced you, he should have the common decency to go away. But while some couples shared custody of a beloved pet or, far more complicated, children, Carly Frazer was sharing Helene with her ex. It was disorienting to come through the door and hear Daniel's booming laugh from the back of the house, accompanied by her mother's more genteel titter. Still, it was *almost* better than when two other Emory faculty wives had visited Helene and they'd spent the entire time reminiscing about how great a man Samuel Frazer had been, how with a bit more time, he surely would have received the Presidential Green Chemistry Challenge Award in Academics.

Samuel had been nominated for a great many awards, but won few. The first time he'd ever slapped Carly was after an award ceremony. He lost his temper with her, a smart-mouthed eleven-year-old, in only minutes although he'd no doubt reined himself in for two hours while performing the role of gracious loser. Strangely enough, Carly's first date with Daniel had been to one of those damn award banquets.

"I have to get to class," she'd said, wondering if he'd noticed that she was always the first to end their conversations.

If he did, he was not bothered by it. "Go, shape young minds."

"Not that young," she chuckled, thinking about a few of her non-traditional students.

"Carly."

She'd already turned to leave, but he stopped her with a hand on her shoulder. His fingers, gentle but in no way soft, brushed skin exposed by her boat-neck sweater. A shiver that owed nothing to cool November temperatures rippled through her. "Yes?"

"What are you doing tonight?"

Any other time, her answer would have been "working on my dissertation." But that particular night her presence was expected downtown. Her father was up for an award in research application; the provost from Ramson Neil and others from her academic circle would be attending. "I have a dinner to go to that will be deadly dull." She flashed a wry smile. "Don't suppose you want to come with me?"

Daniel had agreed easily, although she'd had immediate reservations. While he might hold a master's degree, he wasn't exactly part of the Ivory Tower crowd. Her worries had proved unfounded. He was a man comfortable in his own skin and that put others at ease. The only person to exhibit any trace of snobbery was Samuel Frazer. Perhaps affronted that someone who did manual labor was dating *his* daughter, Samuel had asked one or two pointed questions about Daniel's job. If it had been a ploy to make the landscaper feel inferior, it had backfired when several faculty wives began swapping stories about their gardening clubs. Even Helene cooed over Daniel. Carly deduced from the icy gleam in her father's eye that Samuel was displeased with his wife's temporary defection. He was used to being the center of her universe. No, he was used to being her *entire* universe.

It was odd—for years, Carly had hoped her father would slip up in public, lash out and reveal his ugly second face. Yet rather than hope his disdain for Daniel would grow more pronounced, she found herself wanting to spirit Daniel away . . . feeling almost *protective* of him.

She asked him to dance, murmuring an apology once they were swaying to the music. "You're probably having a terrible time," she said, looking up into those blue eyes.

He'd bent his head and kissed her, shooting sparks through her as if she were the living embodiment of July Fourth. She'd managed to keep her footing, if not her balance, as her tongue tangled with his. The kiss had been powerful, but not forceful, and she'd known they would become lovers. And that it would be *good*.

"On the contrary," Daniel had said when he pulled away, resting his forehead against hers, "I'm having a wonderful time."

The other outcome that night was that Daniel seemed to assume he was partly responsible for the coolness between her and her father. A better wife wouldn't have let him think it.

And yet he'd not only tried to be a worthy husband—he'd also come back to offer his assistance even now that the marriage was over. Daniel's visits were no doubt the highlight of Helene's recovery.

"Hello," Carly called out, making her way down the hall. Most days, Daniel dropped by so early that she didn't see him, but Helene had had an appointment with the physical therapist that afternoon and had specifically requested her ex-son-in-law's assistance. She claimed it would be easier for him than Carly to help move her around, but Carly didn't believe it for a moment. Given the difference in size between Helene and Carly, Carly could probably bench-press the woman.

Carly found them sipping iced tea on the back porch, a screened-in space that was so narrow there was barely enough room for the ceiling fan spinning lazily overhead. Carly didn't see any crutches, so Daniel must have literally carried Helene there. Carly frowned, hoping her mother wasn't getting too attached. It was good that Carly had two more interviews this week with potential companions.

They'd better be more promising than last week's. Carly had spoken with a licensed home care professional who'd scoffed at the proposed salary. Then there was the applicant Helene had offended when she'd whispered loudly enough to be heard by neighbors down the street that she wasn't sure she wanted to spend her days in the hands of "that colored girl," since she worried they wouldn't have anything in common. Finally, there had been the aborted meeting with a grad student who, halfway through their discussion, blurted, "Ohmigosh, you're *that* Dr. Frazer? I dated a guy who was a TA of yours. Briefly." The girl had developed a sudden pressing need to be elsewhere.

Watching Helene smile up at Daniel, Carly wondered

what on earth those two had in common. Besides, perhaps, disapproval of her. *Too bad dear old Dad's dead. The three of them could have formed a club.* Of course, Helene and Daniel thought Carly's priorities were skewed, placing too much emphasis on her work, while Samuel had maintained that no matter how hard she worked, she'd never be good enough.

Her fingers clenched at her sides, today's meeting with Dean Murrin having done nothing to improve her mood.

"Carly." Daniel swept her in a once-over, seeming as aware of her body as he had been when they were lovers. "You're tense."

"Long day."

"Why not go upstairs and take a bubble bath?" he suggested. "I can stick around a bit longer."

For a second, the temptation of the claw-footed tub filled with eucalyptus bubbles beckoned her. One year, Daniel had created a Valentine's Day "bouquet" for her made up of assorted floral bath gels. Sweet pea, magnolia, white cherry blossom, gardenia. *He's a good man.* The thought slipped easily into her tired mind. She straightened abruptly. Too good for her, apparently.

"I appreciate the offer, Daniel, but I need to get dinner started. And you don't want to get stuck in rush-hour traffic."

The friendly, open expression in his blue eyes dimmed. "Of course."

Carly got out of the way so he could assist Helene back to the sofa in the parlor, her preferred resting place until bedtime.

As he helped her settle comfortably, Helene called plaintively over his broad shoulder, "Any chance we could have chicken-fried steak and mashed potatoes from scratch?"

Carly leaned against the archway between the rooms, repressing a shudder at the thought of all that cholesterol and starch. "Grilled chicken salad. You didn't stay that size your whole life by eating a steady diet of fried foods."

"Comfort foods," Helene said dolefully. "Dr. Rylan insists I take it easy while I recover. Not just by keeping my weight off the leg, but by being good to myself in other ways. He calls it the spirit-body connection."

You have a handsome man carrying you from room to room and I'm doing all the cooking. How much easier could Helene possibly take it?

"Oh, you must think me ungrateful," Helene fretted. "You know that if I could, I'd hobble right in there and make dinner for both of us. Just like I always did for your father, God rest his soul. I know you have more important things to do than take care of a decrepit old lady."

"You're not old or decrepit," Daniel said. He shot Carly a reprimanding glare.

"Really, Mother, it's no trouble to fix dinner. I'd have to do it for myself anyway." Carly sighed, trying to dig deeper. She was better at studying how relationships unfolded throughout time than actually having her own. "This weekend, I'll make mashed potatoes. Okay?"

Helene beamed, almost childlike in her immediate delight. She was so taken with simple pleasures. Why didn't Carly indulge her more often? Normally, she wasn't one for a lot of self-analysis and second-guessing. Perhaps Dean Murrin's words had left her more rattled than she'd realized. Issues of collegiality was higher ed's fancy term for "We don't like you." While Carly didn't suffer from the misconception that she was full of gushing geniality, she was hardly the only professor on campus with an exacting nature. And she *certainly* wasn't a chauvinist!

Daniel was grinning at Carly's promise of potatoes, too, his approving gaze warm on her skin. She turned away, a lump in her throat. She was an educated adult. She didn't *need* anyone's approval. Well, not anyone who couldn't secure her tenure, anyway. In the house where she'd grown up, everyday life had been shaped by the threat of Samuel's disapproval.

Your father's reading, Carlotta. Practice your piano later.

Go wash your face. If your father says it's inappropriate for you to wear eye shadow, then I agree with him.

No, you can't have a drumstick. I save the dark meat for your father.

Had Helene Frazer once been a more vibrant woman—with her own opinions—only to be bullied into meek colorlessness? Possible, but difficult to imagine. In contrast to her blustering husband, Helene had been such a quiet background character, it had almost been easy for Carly to forget her mother was in the house. Carly had resolved early in life that she'd never succumb to such a fate. In everything she'd ever done, she made her presence known—winning track medals, graduating valedictorian, even challenging her professors during her university years.

As Carly pulled vegetables out of the crisper bin in the refrigerator, she heard Daniel and Helene exchange their farewells, then the creak of the front door as he left. Suddenly, the air in the house was easier to breathe. Being around Daniel made her . . .

Never mind him. Concentrate on dinner.

She chopped with methodical strokes, the knife's rhythm on the cutting board reminding her of when she ran, the way her shoes sounded slapping against the concrete. There was nothing better than running. She'd taken piano because her parents insisted, she'd joined the student council board because it looked good on college applications, but her years of track had been for *her*. Sprinting full out with her lungs on fire and the wind rushing over her, she felt euphoric—free and invincible and strong.

But only temporarily. She'd never found the cure for the inevitable letdown that followed.

"Carly?" Her mother's voice came from the other room so faint that Carly went to the doorway rather than try to make out the words from the kitchen.

"Yes, Mother?"

Helene pointed to the black lacquer table in the foyer. "Your purse is buzzing."

My cell phone. She crossed the quiet room, where Helene sat alone with a silent television. Earlier that week, she'd tried to get Carly to watch game shows, cop dramas, and the evening news with her. But Carly wasn't much of a TV person, especially when she needed to catch up on work. Now, instead of viewing the shows by herself, Helene simply left the set off. Years ago, she'd given up watching soap operas during the day because Samuel had declared them "moronic."

At least I fought back. Helene had faded until she was damn near transparent.

"Are you sure you wouldn't rather watch something?" Carly asked, gesturing toward the remote control easily within her mother's reach. *He's dead. You can do whatever you want.* "The background noise wouldn't bother me."

"That's all right," Helene said. She smiled, but it was a pale imitation of what had been on her face when Daniel was there. "I'm enjoying the peace and quiet."

No, you're not. So why say she was? Because she thought it was what Carly wanted to hear? Truly, Helene Frazer was like an alien being to her. There was nothing in either woman's temperament or appearance that offered up proof of shared DNA. Shaking her head at the vagaries of genetics, Carly pulled her phone from her purse to check messages.

"Good afternoon, this is Elisabeth Overton ..."

The mousy older woman she'd met in Houston? Carly was startled to hear from her. She'd had the distinct impression when they parted that Beth found her abrasive. Either Carly had misread her or Beth *really* needed a job. Carly cast a speculative glance in her mother's direction, replaying her recollections of the housewife. Maybe someone like Beth Overton, who could play gin or watch episodes of *Deal or No Deal*, would be a better companion for Helene than a college kid who would probably spend half her time plugged into an iPod and perusing Carly's fridge for free food.

Carly came into the parlor and perched on the arm of a chair. "That was a message from a woman I recently met. She's interested in coming to work for us."

"Oh?" Helene didn't meet her daughter's eyes. "I hate that on top of everything else you're having to do for me, it's costing you extra money. I should be getting stronger soon, and in the interim, Daniel doesn't mind—"

"I mind," Carly blurted. Pushing aside the unsettling way Daniel Cross had once stolen through her defenses—and how she'd later been hurt for allowing it—she continued in a no-nonsense tone. "I realize that you and Daniel are close, Mother. He always liked you. But he runs his own business, has his own life, and we can't take advantage of him."

Helene's sigh rattled in her throat. "Of course you're right, dear. I was being selfish. It's just … I'm used to having a big strapping man around. I miss Samuel. I loved him—still love him—so much."

No, you don't. Carly recoiled from the very thought. What her mother and father had shared couldn't possibly be love; it was more the upper-class version of Stockholm syndrome. But even discussing Daniel was preferable to having *that* conversation.

Carly and Helene had never been each other's confidantes, and Carly had no desire to change that now. "I'm sure Daniel will still come visit you, but we need someone here to officially help. And it won't just be for you. If I'm going to concentrate on writing, on top of teaching, it will be immensely useful to let someone else worry about the little chores like breakfast dishes and returning library books."

If Beth Overton could cook chicken-fried steak, she had a job.

"This is nice," Beth murmured, stifling the insecure impulse to add, *isn't it?* Ever since Allen had arrived home with a half dozen white take-out boxes, they'd been smiling and chatting. She couldn't remember the last time two people had been so determinedly amiable.

If it also felt a bit artificial and forced, well, maybe she should keep her expectations more realistic. They were both trying. That was the important part.

"Mmm." Glancing across the table, Allen smiled in the candlelight. "Is there any more of the pork?"

Beth reached for the wire-handled container, glanced inside, and shook her head. "No. But there's still some of the shrimp and plenty of tangerine beef. Honestly, you got enough for a small dinner party."

"Trying to cover my bases. I wasn't sure what you'd like," he confessed.

It was endearing the way he said it, as if he wanted to bring her the best possible selection. But it made her a little sad, that her husband of twenty-six years couldn't look at a menu and pinpoint her favorites. She opened her mouth to tell him that, for future reference, she was quite fond of garlic chicken, but she checked herself, not wanting to seem unappreciative of the dishes he had selected.

She tried with marginal success to scoop up some rice with her chopsticks. "Speaking of dinner parties, what do you think about inviting Joy and Peter over this weekend? We've yet to celebrate their news as a family. And it might ease Joy's mind if . . ."

"Yes."

"She was really upset by what you told her." Beth tried to stifle her resentment from this morning. The memory of her daughter's tears made it difficult.

Allen paused, a forkful of lo mein halfway to his mouth. "I said I was sorry for that."

Actually, he hadn't.

She cleared her throat. "Allen, can I ask you something?"

"Of course."

"While I was waiting to speak with you this afternoon, I noticed . . . Well, there's an office pool on an upcoming PGA tournament."

"Yeah." His expression was shuttered, and she suddenly regretted the candles, which had seemed a cozy touch earlier. The dim light made it too hard to read him.

"And you're participating in it," she prompted.

"Pretty much everyone is, right down to the mail room. We did one for the Super Bowl, too, and will probably have one for baseball play-offs this fall. Good, clean fun."

Illegal, addictive fun. "Are you sure it's wise for you to participate?"

He set down his fork. "It was only a few bucks. I know I temporarily cut into our savings, but I'll put money back when I get the quarterly sales bonus."

"And you'll repay Ev, too?"

"Jesus, what did he do, come to you with an itemized bill? He's like an old woman, nagging me to death."

It was disturbing to see how quickly he turned on the friend who'd been sheltering him for nearly a week. "He was just—"

"It's a crummy sports bet, Elisabeth. Not the World Series

of Poker. Would you feel better if I went to Kirk and got my cash back, told him my wife won't allow me to participate?"

"I . . ." *Why didn't I leave well enough alone?* Before she could figure out how to restore the peace they'd previously enjoyed, the phone rang. If the conversation had been going well, she would have let the machine answer.

She vaulted out of her chair and lifted the receiver before the second ring. "Hello?"

"Ms. Overton? Carly Frazer. I'm calling about the message you left me earlier."

"Oh. Thank you for getting back to me so quickly. I don't know if you're still looking f—"

"I'm looking. Are you free to meet my mother tomorrow afternoon?"

Beth's pulse pounded with excitement. "Y-yes."

"We're in Decatur. I can give you directions to the house if you need them." Carly quoted her a salary that wasn't much, but far more than no paycheck at all. "The position includes—requires, really—that the caregiver stay here for the next five weeks or so, accessible during various hours of the day. The only spare bed is in my office. I can work on my laptop from any room in the house and will move my files out of the way, but I may need to come in to use the printer or retrieve something I didn't realize I needed. I'll do my best to respect your privacy. Does all of this sound doable?"

Beth stole a glance in Allen's direction, then decided to seize the moment. "No problem." After all, it wouldn't be much more than a month and it wasn't as if she'd be living on the far side of the moon. Decatur was roughly half an hour away. The important thing was that she might actually get a paying job—her first as an adult if she didn't count the disastrous year when she'd tried to sell skin-care products—and she'd accomplished it on her own.

By the time she hung up, she was almost vibrating with exhilaration. "That was Dr. Carly Frazer! She was calling me back about a job."

Allen hitched an eyebrow. "You're going to be working in a doctor's office? What the heck qualifications do you have?"

She ignored his lack of faith. "Different kind of doctor. She's a college professor who needs help with her mom for a few weeks. The woman was hurt in a car accident." Her tone grew more somber. Though she'd long since dealt with her mother's death, there were still moments when she yearned for a mother's patience and advice. She would have loved for her mom to know Joy, and felt the maternal loss more strongly now that Joy was going to become a mom herself.

As if he knew the direction of her thoughts, Allen stood and patted her shoulder on his way to the sink. He set his plate and fork on the counter. "Beth, I meant what I said about restocking the savings account. You don't *have* to get a job."

"Yes, I do. Maybe not for that reason, but trust me, this is something I need." She waited a beat, then spilled the rest of the news. "The only thing is, I'll need to move in with Carly and her mom while her mother heals."

He frowned.

She began speaking more rapidly. "It will be around a month, maybe a month and a half. You'll probably be traveling part of the time, anyway, so why does it matter if I'm here?"

She was actually more concerned that she wouldn't have as much time to donate to the literacy center over the next month, but the disconcerting truth was she'd probably needed them as much as they'd needed her.

"Beth, I don't think now is a good time for . . . What about us? You told me you wanted me to come home, said you wanted us to be together."

"I do." She stepped closer, pressing against him in an embrace he was slow to return. "Allen, this isn't me leaving you. This is just me taking a part-time job. Besides, it could do us some good. You know, like long-distance couples who don't take each other for granted because they don't see each other every day? This might be fun. We can date."

"Date?" He regarded her blankly. "You want me to *date* my wife? Most men would consider that a step backward."

"This is important to me."

"Okay." He smoothed a hand over her hair. "Okay, if it really matters that much to you, we'll try it out. Who knows? Maybe you won't even get the job."

⁓❦⁓

Beth found her way with minimal difficulty to Carly's Decatur home. Set on a magnolia-lined street, the house had an old-fashioned porch with columns and a white railing. The paint was peeling in a few places and one of the steps was cracked, but the porch still looked like a perfect, well-shaded spot to while away summer afternoons with a pitcher of lemonade and a good book. If Beth were recuperating from a leg injury, she'd spend her convalescence here.

Carly answered the door immediately and ushered Beth inside. "Thank you for being so prompt. I must say, I'm glad you called me. I have a feeling this could work out well."

Really? "I hope so." Beth followed her through a foyer with hardwood floors into a well-decorated but perplexing little sitting room. Since Carly was a history professor who lived in a house that brought to mind mint juleps and bygone eras, Beth was taken aback by the white sofa and contrasting black chairs, the framed splotches of red and purple that hung on the wall.

Tearing her gaze from the angry-looking abstract art, she studied the woman seated on the couch. Helene Frazer was every bit as beautiful for her age as Carly was, but there was absolutely no resemblance between the petite senior citizen with the pale eyes and the Amazonian blonde. "Good afternoon, I'm Beth."

Helene's mouth quirked. "Please forgive me for not standing to make your acquaintance." She indicated the knee brace that protruded from beneath loose walking shorts.

Beth smiled, leaning over the table to shake the woman's hand. Her grip was delicate. "It's nice to meet you." She regarded the two rectangular-shaped chairs in the small room. They had such low backs she was afraid she might fall out of one if she sat down.

"I can scoot over and make room for you here," Helene volunteered. "I'm afraid I'm not sophisticated enough to appreciate Carly's furniture, either."

"Oh, the furniture is striking," Beth said hurriedly, thinking it was probably best not to offend her potential employer in the first five minutes. "The room looks almost like a maga-zine layout! I guess I just expected something . . . else."

"Such as?" Luckily, Carly seemed more curious than in-sulted.

"Well, given that your profession is based on history, an-tiques maybe?"

Carly stiffened instantly.

What did I say wrong? Beth was aware that the vibe in the room had changed, but she had no clue why until Helene sighed.

"Samuel had an impressive collection of antiques. He and I were picking up a new piece the day of the—of the crash."

"I am so sorry for your loss," Beth said. Should she share that she'd lost a loved one in an automobile accident as well, or would that be a self-absorbed way to respond to Mrs. Frazer's too-fresh grief?

"Thank you." Helene sniffed. "They tell me that missing him will ease after time, but how is that possible? He was so . . . big. Tall and important and on the verge of some major break-throughs in his research. There seems to be a gaping hole in the world where he's supposed to be."

Was this why Carly had stiffened? Because she, too, missed her father? That seemed contrary to the picture Beth had painted for herself in Houston, but people reacted differently to tragedy. Maybe her sarcasm had been born of pain.

Rather than go to Helene and comfort her, Carly cleared her throat. "Beth, how about I show you the rest of the house now?"

Was isolating herself Carly's method of coping with her

father's death? Surely she was educated enough to know that denial was only one stage of bereavement and not a long-term solution.

Aware that raising one child did not qualify her as a psychoanalyst, Beth pushed her musings aside. She nodded politely to Helene, hating to leave her alone when she still looked upset, and followed Carly to the second story. The staircase was narrow and creaky and led up to two bedrooms and a master bathroom in the middle of the hall.

"That is my room." Carly pointed to a closed door on her left. "This one's the office I mentioned."

They walked into a shoe-box room flooded with sunshine from two big windows. A desk was pushed against a wall, facing away from the windows, so that anyone working there would be staring at the pale textured wallpaper instead of the wild profusion of climbing roses out back. Beth swore she could smell honeysuckle from just outside the window.

Carly looked down at her. "Your husband—Allen, wasn't it? He would be all right with you staying here?"

"Um, sure." Not that he was winning any supportive-husband awards for it. *Maybe you won't even get the job.* Beth squared her shoulders. "You know what? It's my decision to make. He can adjust." Just as *she'd* done with his every promotion or travel assignment.

"Well." Carly's expression softened, and a fleeting smile graced her lips. "I may have misjudged you, Mrs. Overton."

"For the record, you misjudged my husband as well. The last time I saw you, you made the assumption he was cheating on me."

Beth wasn't sure why she was bothering to make the correction. Was it to protect Allen's good name, so to speak? Or was it her pride balking, wanting to let the other woman know that Elisabeth wasn't the doormat of a philandering husband?

Carly waited, as if curious to know what exactly Allen's crime had been but not willing to lower herself to actually asking. After a moment passed, she dropped the subject and began outlining the caregiver's duties. The official job description seemed to include anything Helene needed and anything Carly thought of at a later date. Beth could imagine what a taskmaster the other woman could be.

Still, the position was expected only to last from five to eight weeks—an addition to what she'd been told on the phone, depending entirely on Helene's recovery. Beth had managed a house for years, meeting the needs of a traveling husband and a teenage daughter. This job would be a walk in the park.

"I'm sure you want to make sure your mother's in good hands," Beth began, trying not to sound too hopeful, "and I understand if you need some time to think it over. But I brought along the names of a few character references who—"

"The job's yours if you want it."

"Oh." Beth was so nonplussed that, for a moment, she forgot to be excited.

"You *do* want it?" Carly prodded.

"Yes. Yes, I do. I have a family event this weekend for my daughter—she's expecting her first baby—but I can start on Monday, if that—"

"Splendid." Carly turned toward the stairs. "Let's go tell Helene, shall we?"

Helene seemed as delighted by the turn of events as Beth was. She told Beth warmly that it would be nice to have her company around the house. "And I'll feel much better, knowing you've relieved some of the burden from Carlotta's shoulders. I've been such an imposition."

A statement that Carly did not, Beth noted, contradict. It wouldn't surprise her to learn that the professor was adopted. Or maybe switched with another baby at the hospital.

"I'm sure you and Beth will be fast friends," Carly said. "The two of you have a lot in common."

Beth blinked, curious what Carly was basing that assessment on since the woman barely knew her. But since Helene was looking at Beth expectantly, she offered, "I, um, I have a grown daughter, too."

"Really?" Helene looked genuinely interested. "Do you have a picture with you?"

The only thing in Beth's purse was a wallet shot of Joy's college graduation. "Nothing recent. I'll bring some when I come back next week, maybe a few from her wedding. She was a beautiful bride."

"She's married?" At Beth's nod, Helene smiled, one mom to another. "That must put your mind at rest, knowing she's taken care of. I hate that Carlotta's all alone now, but—"

"Mother, I'm sure Beth's not interested in the sordid details of my personal life."

"Of course not," Helene said obediently.

Actually, Beth found herself very inquisitive about Carly, but held her tongue. There would be plenty of time to snoop later. It would give her something to think about besides worrying about the sordid details of her own life.

∽❦∽

Since the "wine" was really sparkling grape juice, Beth was making free with the toasts Saturday night. She sat at one end of the table, Joy and Peter on either side of her, Allen opposite. They'd toasted the baby news first and Peter's recent raise, which couldn't have happened at a better time.

"We've been looking into nursery stuff," he said with a grin, "and it turns out having a baby ain't cheap."

"I have one last toast," Beth said, still jubilant over how quickly she'd gone from no prospects to gainfully employed. "To me! I have a job."

Beth had created a lot of different scrapbooks over the years, both as gifts and for organizations. The ones she'd put together for her daughter had always been broken into phases: the baby book, toddler and preschool years, an entire album tracking Joy and her three best friends through high school. Beth always loved preparing to start a new book, picking out a color scheme, the acid-free stickers she might use, buying new die-cut shapes. Now she felt that same buzz, only magnified. *She* was about to enter a distinctly new phase.

"Congratulations! What kind of job?" Peter asked.

"I'm going to be a temporary companion to this very sweet lady who's just lost her husband and is recovering from an injury."

"That's wonderful, Mama." Joy bit her lip. "About the job, obviously, not the other stuff. It sounds perfect for you. You've always been so good with people."

"So how much does this gig actually pay?" Allen wanted to know. "I don't think you've mentioned."

Without even thinking about it, without having any idea she was going to do it, Beth lied. She opened her mouth to answer the question, but the response that came out was only about sixty percent of what she'd be making. Beneath the table, her palms grew clammy. *I can't believe I just lied to him.* For a second, she quailed, nearly backtracking and telling the truth. But she didn't.

With sudden clarity, she realized she'd be depositing the difference in the account she'd started.

Immediately she began worrying about the consequences of her fib. Wouldn't he need to know all her income for tax purposes? Or was she making so little that it wouldn't matter? Were you supposed to put your bank account information on taxes? That probably wasn't the best way for him to find out about her tiny strike toward independence. It was a bit embarrassing that, as a grown woman, she knew so little about how all this worked. *Half your friends don't either. Barbara and Jeffrey used an accountant. She probably wouldn't know a W-2 if she saw it.*

Would Joy? Beth glanced at the table, wondering about the division of labor that was none of her business.

For years, Beth had believed herself content with her life, raising a child any mother would be proud of and keeping a lovely home for her hardworking husband. She hadn't seen it as a source of shame for either of them that he'd be hard-pressed to name his daughter's pediatrician of fifteen years or that Beth herself was foggy on the details of all their insurance policies. She'd simply viewed the two of them as separate but equal in terms of family management.

But now . . . Getting this job, reevaluating how her husband treated her, Beth realized that perhaps she should have gone after more in her life. She took hope in the nonchalantly affectionate way Peter had said *we've* been looking into nursery stuff. *Maybe they'll get it right.*

Like mother, like daughter, Beth thought wryly as she and Joy dried dishes together later. While Beth had been silently hoping that Joy and Peter had a bright marriage ahead of them, Joy had apparently been worrying about the state of her parents' union. She started her gentle interrogation as soon as the two of them were alone. The men were shooting pool in the refinished basement. Allen had bought the secondhand table years ago, and it had always been a hit with Joy's high school and college friends.

"I'm glad Daddy's back home," Joy said, almost shy—a little girl afraid of the divorce monster in her closet rather than an adult with her own marriage and opinion. "Aren't you?"

"Yes, of course. I told you, honey, we just needed time to cool down."

"So you're not mad anymore? About the poker thing?" A cup slid from Joy's fingers and clattered against the tile floor, the noise not quite masking her muttered curse.

"Butterfingers," Beth teased. She retrieved and rinsed the cup. "I know glass is fancier than plastic, but I've never regretted using these instead."

Joy waited a few minutes, then tentatively broached the subject again. "You never did tell me . . . how you and Dad left it with the gambling. Is he going into rehab or something? Do they even have rehab for Texas hold 'em?"

Beth gnawed on the inside of her bottom lip. "We talked more in general terms than specifics." Was she giving her spouse the benefit of the doubt or avoiding conflict? "He knows I'd rather he not gamble anymore, and he's already talked about how he's earning back the money he lost. He's just waiting for a bonus to kick in—I should have known he had a plan to cover it. Still, we won't be hosting any poker nights here anytime soon."

"Glad that's settled, then. And I'm tickled to hear about this job of yours. Is the lady you're keeping company old? Maybe she has lots of friends with upcoming knee replacements or something to whom she could recommend you."

Beth laughed. "Helene's not old, although you may have a different definition than I do. She's fifty-nine, a comparable age to most of my friends."

Among the women in her book club who were empty nesters, Beth was the youngest. But she felt at home with them, which was something she couldn't have said for her acquaintances when she was in her twenties. By the time her girlfriends could drink legally, Beth was already bleary-eyed from taking care of a baby. Even if she could have afforded a sitter, she would have been more interested in catching up on sleep than barhopping. It wasn't unusual for her friends to study with their boyfriends; while Beth had helped Allen prepare for exams, she'd simultaneously folded laundry and fretted about Joy's dependence on the pacifier. Beth had actually experienced neurotic daydreams about her daughter as the only adult in the state with a "binky."

Recalling what had seemed perfectly rational terror at the time, she laughed.

Joy glanced up with a puzzled smile. "Did I miss a joke?"

"I only have one big piece of surefire mothering advice," Beth said. "Want to hear it?"

"Sure." Absently, Joy rubbed a hand over her still-flat abdomen.

"This, too, shall pass. Obviously, it's not the most original thought, but trust me, it will be applicable. I once almost hyperventilated in a grocery store because I was convinced I would have to send you to kindergarten in training pants. One week in winter, when you were miserable with an ear infection and determined to shatter the eardrums of everyone around you, I was convinced neither you nor I would ever sleep through the night again."

Shifting her weight, Joy grimaced. "Boy, don't sugarcoat motherhood for me. It's not like I'm, you know, already scared to death."

Laughing, Beth hugged her daughter. "Trust me, I was terrified. And I probably screwed up a dozen times every day. But look at you! I'm so proud of the woman you've become. For all those frustrating moments when I just wanted to scream—no offense—you've given me a thousand memories I wouldn't trade for anything."

"Oh, Mama." Joy hugged her back fiercely.

"But it can be tough," Beth admitted as she pulled away.

"Have you thought about what you'll do after the baby's born?"

"You mean other than call you on a near-daily basis for advice?"

"I meant as far as work goes. Do you plan to keep a full-time job?"

Joy nodded. "I'll take some time off at first, of course, but I don't think it will be a problem. I can occasionally work from home. Plenty of other women in the department have kids and seem to balance everything."

"Well, if anyone can do it, you can," Beth encouraged. "Just remember there can be a big difference between *seeming* to balance it all and actually doing so. Don't buy into the perception that you have to be a superwoman. Promise?"

"That's an easy promise to make. In no way do I feel like a superhero. Actually, I'm starting to fall asleep on my feet," Joy admitted.

Beth called down to Peter and soon the young couple had left for home.

After the shared family evening, Beth felt enveloped in a warm glow. She found herself singing in the shower as she got ready for bed. After Chinese last night, Allen had fallen asleep almost immediately—he'd been snoring by the time she finished brushing her teeth. Maybe now, with the house to themselves, they'd have a chance to consummate their reconciliation. Her pulse thudded a bit faster.

Wrapping herself in a towel, she wished she'd grabbed something more alluring to wear than faded pink cotton. She still had that lavender number Allen had yet to see.

But recalling the garment she'd bought in anticipation of her Houston surprise, she lost some of her siren's drive. She'd flown on a *plane* to seduce him, despite every fiber in her being not wanting to be there.

She wanted her husband, but pride forbade her from expending a major effort again so soon. Why couldn't he try to entice her?

No harm in nudging him in the right direction, though. She smoothed some flavored balm over her lips and dabbed a fingertip of the perfume he loved at the base of her throat.

When she reemerged in their bedroom, she found him shucking off his belt and polo shirt. He turned to her in his pants and white undershirt. "All done?" he asked. "I wanted to hop in the shower before I boot up the computer."

"Computer?" She felt deflated, although it wasn't quite fair to blame him for not meeting her expectations. Again.

He nodded. "I have some work to catch up on." Her expression must have betrayed her, because it suddenly occurred to him to ask, "You don't mind, do you?"

"Of course not." At least, she never had before. But it struck her as ironic that the man who hadn't wanted her to take a job that required spending nights elsewhere would be spending one of her nights here at his laptop.

She could protest. She could demand his attention, tell him she needed to be held. *You want me to* date *my* wife?

Forget it. She wasn't desperate. "I'm just going to watch TV for a little while," she told him. If she was still awake when he came to bed, they'd see what happened, but Beth wasn't needy.

She lay in bed channel-surfing late-night talk shows and syndicated sitcoms for nearly an hour before admitting that she was only killing time in the hope that he'd come back to her. *I give up.* She punched the button on the remote, savagely glad to silence the laugh tracks and host-guest banter.

It took her longer than usual to fall asleep, and her eyes felt grainy when she opened them to stare at a bleating alarm clock the next morning. Sunday. Early service. Stifling a yawn, she snuggled back under the covers, stopping when she realized that the other half of the bed was cool and unoccupied. Had he fallen asleep in the living room?

Trepidation rippled through her as a thought occurred. Was Allen deliberately avoiding intimacy with her? And, not knowing the answer, did she have the courage to ask him the question outright? Automatically, she reached for the ring on her left hand, only to discover that she hadn't put her rings back on after showering and moisturizing last night.

A few minutes later, with fresh breath and a replaced diamond-set band, she padded down the hallway toward the living room. As she got closer she heard computer clicks and the faint hum of Allen's laptop motor. The knot of dread in her stomach loosened. If he had a work project so important that it had kept him up all night, then he was simply preoccupied, not dodging his marriage.

"Hey," she said from behind him as she entered the room.

He was leaning back in his recliner, his laptop propped across his legs on a breakfast-in-bed tray. "*Shh*—just a . . . God-damn it."

"Allen!" Had she disrupted his work so badly, just by saying good morning? She peered over his shoulder, even though she wasn't expecting to understand whatever she saw. Virtutronix manufactured communications software, and most of the technical aspects were lost on her.

But she wasn't looking at a page of programming code or columns of numbers detailing quarterly projections. She—

Darting a quick glance over his shoulder, Allen slammed the folding top down. "Sorry about cursing at you."

That was the least of her concerns. "You're playing poker? On a Sunday morning?" It was a stupid qualifier—vices and deception were wrong all seven days a week.

"I'm entitled to take a break from my work," he said. He was floundering in the chair, simultaneously trying to right it from its reclined position and set down the tray.

An unforgiving chill swept through her. "You were on that computer all night."

"Time got away from me." He stood. "Now that you've pulled me back to reality, I realize how tired I am. I wish you'd come and gotten me hours ago."

She might have, but she'd mistakenly assumed he was smart enough to prioritize basic biological needs like sleep over poker. "How long was your break?"

His eyes were bloodshot. He rubbed one of them, then the small of his back as he stretched. "Huh?"

Skirting him, she picked up the laptop. "You said you were taking a break. From work, presumably. How long did you work, and how long did you play poker?"

"I didn't time myself. I would have if I'd known there was

going to be a quiz." He frowned. "What the hell are you doing with my computer?"

She might have smashed the thing over his head, but she didn't trust herself not to kill him with it. Georgia was a death-penalty state. "No, Allen, what the hell are *you* doing with your computer? This is why our credit cards are maxed out, isn't it?"

Naively, she'd considered the gambling a situational problem—office bets and scheduled tournaments, the occasional Reno or Vegas binge. But gambling was available twenty-four hours a day anywhere he had a modem connection. It was always there, tempting him—far more than she did, evidently.

"I told you I would replace that money." He rocked on the balls of his feet, gesturing manically toward the computer. "For your information, I was winning."

"That's not the point! You shouldn't be gambling at all. I think . . . I think you have a serious problem."

"You let Ev put some bug in your ear just because I owe him a few bucks. Give me back my computer."

"No." She held it in front of her like a shield. "Not until you promise me that you're not going to gamble anymore. I mean it, Allen. Not even slot machines or office pools."

"Stop issuing ultimatums and give me the damn computer."

Tears filled her eyes. This was Houston all over again, but worse. "Do you know, last night I wanted to make love? We haven't in too long."

"You should have just told me that," he said impatiently. "Is this why you're busting my balls over a little online gaming? I can't read your mind."

"I shouldn't have to tell you to want me! I'm your wife. The one you're supposed to be working things out with, remember? Yet you ignored me to keep spending more of our money."

"I told you, I was *winning*. I'm on a hot streak, Beth. If you'd just—"

"You are not winning! Not at the stuff that matters." She tossed the laptop then, but intentionally dumped it into the recliner and not on the floor, where it slid anyway. "You've lost money. You've lost the respect of others. And if you're not careful, you could lose me."

"Is that a threat?" he asked coldly.

She put her arms across her chest, hugging herself. "I'd prefer you think of it as a wake-up call. Allen, you have a problem."

"My only problem right now is being nagged to death by a wife I never wanted in the first place!"

Beth reeled, nearly doubling over from the assault. When she finally found her voice, what she gasped out was, "I want a divorce."

Deafening silence crashed around them, neither able to undo what had been said. *OhGodohGodohGod*. Did she really want a divorce?

As recently as last night, she would have dismissed the idea out of hand. But she couldn't imagine staying married to this loathsome stranger who glared at her from behind Allen's silvery eyes. She'd vowed to love him until death parted them, but she could easily hate him. More easily than she'd ever realized.

"I'm going for a drive," he said stiffly. "I'll have Ev call you this week with the number of that lawyer."

Common sense dictated that an angry man working on no sleep shouldn't get behind the wheel of a car, but before she could gather her wits enough to make that point, the door to the garage had already slammed shut.

Her movements so stiff and unthinking she might have been an automaton, she returned to her room. *I have to get out of here.* From sheer force of habit, she started toward Allen's closet. It was where they kept their luggage set, the different-size suitcases nested inside one another. But she recoiled at the thought of his space, his things, the rack of ties she'd helped pick out. She whirled away, grabbing her vanity chair and hoping it was sturdy enough to support her weight.

At the top of her closet was the vintage burgundy alligator train case that had been her mother's—politically incorrect, but beautiful. Beth had never actually used the case for travel. By the time she'd placed a few essential items inside, however, she felt much calmer. Packing was purposeful. It was *doing*. She went into the bathroom to grab some toiletries, glanced at the anniversary band Allen had given her—gallantly replacing the hastily purchased ring he'd jammed on her finger on their wedding day—and walked back out of the room without it.

When she slid behind the wheel of her own car, she was almost serene. Or maybe that was only the contrast between how numb she was now compared to the anguished chaos that had been screaming through her earlier. She didn't even question where she was going—she merely drove.

And was unsurprised to find herself in front of Carly Frazer's soothing house on its picturesque, tree-lined street. Case in hand, a grim anti–Mary Poppins, Beth made her way up the weathered stairs. She was just reaching the front porch when the door opened.

Wearing shorts, sneakers, and one of those tiny athletic tops that was supposed to be both bra and shirt, Carly stepped outside, shading her eyes against the sun as she stared. "Mrs. Overton?"

Beth nodded crisply. "I'll be starting work a day early."

Seven

For the Comfort of Fellow Passengers

Carly Frazer was not easily startled—spending one's formative years being yelled at by a six-foot-three petty tyrant tended to harden one. Even Ramson Neil's recent campus politics were more maddening than surprising. But finding Beth Overton on her doorstep early Sunday morning was a bit of a shock.

For starters, the woman was nearly unrecognizable at first, so alien was the blazing anger stamped on her features. It wasn't irritation or injured indignation; it was cold fury, an aura of "I will no longer be fucked with." A sentiment Carly recognized and instinctively admired.

"Something happened with your husband," Carly deduced.

"Yes." Her brown eyes narrowed to slits, but Beth stopped, took a breath, and spoke again with composed precision. "So I'm here a day early, if that's acceptable to you. Other than that, my marriage is none of your business and I don't wish to speak of it."

Stepping up to the porch rail to stretch her calves, Carly nodded. "Understood. I don't suppose you run?" she asked as an afterthought. Beth wasn't glaringly out of shape, but there was a certain doughiness about her that suggested physical fitness had fallen off her to-do list.

"No."

"You should." Carly could sense the vibrating tension in the other woman and knew from her own divorce how important it was to have a physical outlet.

Beth shot her a withering glance. "Is it a job requirement?"

"Of course not."

"Then I'll pass." Ending on that, Beth went into the house, the screen door clattering behind her.

Carly watched, bemused. She tended to quickly categorize people, reevaluating later if it became necessary. It rarely was. The only person who'd ever truly confounded her was Daniel. He'd been full of surprises that had been both beautiful and painful.

But she might have to revise her first impression of Beth Overton. Initially, Carly had seen shades of her mother in the Alpharetta housewife—a meek, stand-by-your-man type. Today, in a not entirely comfortable way, Carly had also glimpsed shades of herself.

⁂

It was a relief to Beth that both Helene and Carly accepted her unexpected arrival so easily. When Carly returned from her run, she went straight up for a shower and then stayed in her room, typing a mile a minute. Helene was thrilled to see Beth again, chattering so happily throughout breakfast that her poached eggs must have turned cold long before she finished them. She regaled Beth with anecdotes from her long-ago debutante days and more recent campus stories from when Samuel was alive.

"Being with him in public, I still felt like the belle of the ball," she admitted. "But it was even better. It wasn't based on my smile or my dress, but his brilliance. I knew when I met him that he had the ability to really make a difference in the world. Some of his theories allowed other chemists to make significant breakthroughs! It's all interconnected, you know, not as if one person discovers something in a single inspired moment. He uses years of careful research done by others in the field. Samuel was a *part* of something."

"He sounds like an amazing man, one I'm sure won't be forgotten anytime soon," Beth added. It seemed to be the reassurance the other woman was looking for. "Now I want to hear more about you. What kinds of things are you a part of?"

Helene blinked. "I don't understand."

"Clubs, charities, hobbies?"

"Oh, sure. But that was all trivial compared to the contribution of being Samuel's wife. You've heard the saying about the woman behind every great man?"

Beth smiled weakly. Though she was familiar with the saying, Helene's attitude was unsettling. It sounded almost as if she'd pinned her entire self-worth on her husband's achievements. That couldn't be healthy. And what happened to her self-worth now that he was dead?

Beth rose from the table, eager for something to do. A quick peek inside the dishwasher confirmed that it had already been run and that the plates were ready to be put away.

Beth lifted the basket holding forks, spoons, and knives. "So where does the silverware go?" she asked Helene.

"The drawer to the left of the stove?" It sounded more like a question than an answer.

Close. Beth found the flatware in the drawer to the right. Helene was similarly confused as to where the cups, pans, and bowls belonged. It became easier to search through trial and error than to keep asking. Helene seemed visibly upset that she didn't know her way around Carly's kitchen.

Beth and Joy had suffered a few rough patches, when Joy had felt she was being treated too much like a daughter rather than an adult, or when she'd gotten in trouble as a teen, but they'd always been close. They laughed and shopped and gossiped. Even during that horrible first year when Beth was convinced that her husband resented her and that she was doing everything wrong with the baby, Joy had been her touchstone, the person who made her smile throughout the day, the reason Beth kept trying harder. Eventually she'd become a stronger mother and a model wife.

Now she was far more sure of her relationship with Joy than of her relationship with Allen. She couldn't imagine living with her daughter and being as distant as Carly and her mother seemed to be.

"I'm sorry." Helene twisted a tissue she'd plucked from the box in the center of the table. "I'm just not any help, am I?"

"That's all right. I'm supposed to be earning my keep,"

Beth reminded her teasingly. "Speaking of which, what can I do for you today?"

"Oh, I don't want to be a bother. We don't have to *do* anything."

Beth started to insist that surely that wasn't true; Carly hadn't hired her merely to sit around. But then she had a vague recollection of her first conversation with the professor. Hadn't she said something about finding a person to keep her mother out of her hair? Beth preferred to view it as providing beneficial companionship to a woman going through a difficult time.

Setting the dish towel on the counter, she took the chair across from Helene. "Just so you know, I'm here if you ever want to talk about the accident." Perhaps the reason Helene was obsessing over Samuel Frazer's life was because she hadn't accepted his death.

Unfortunately, even Beth's invitation seemed to agitate her. "I don't know what to say."

"Whatever you're comfortable with. Or nothing at all, if you're not ready." There was something she should probably find out before she had to take Helene somewhere, though. "Does it bother you to ride in a car now?" For nearly a year after her mother's crash, Beth had eyed vehicles with loathing and fear, opting to walk to school and church whenever the weather allowed.

Helene looked away. "It wasn't the car that killed him— it was me. I was annoying him, blathering on about how we might rearrange the furniture to make room for the desk we'd bought. He turned to point out why my idea didn't make sense, why certain pieces needed to be where they were, and then we were spinning through the intersection. He didn't see the light change. His neck broke because he was looking right at me, not facing ahead. Carlotta must hate me. I'm the reason her daddy's dead."

"No. I can't imagine that . . ." Beth drew up short. She'd been about to say that no one with Carly's intelligence and reason would draw such a conclusion. But that argument would be insulting to Helene, who was obviously not in a rational place right now. "The accident was just that, an accident, with no one to blame." Except maybe for the driver himself, who hadn't been watching the road and had run the red light.

Helene blamed herself because the last conversation she'd had with her husband had probably been bickering, typical marital fare over whether to do X or Y. You never thought that, after building a life together, your final words to someone would be something so trivial, so petty. Beth swallowed, thinking of the horrible exchange between herself and Allen early that morning. What if that was it, all they had?

She'd told her husband she wanted a divorce! How would she feel later if those were the last words she spoke to him? It didn't take a huge stretch of the imagination to picture him, angry and tired, running a red light or not staying safely in his lane, ending up as roadkill on some Atlanta highway. The violent morbidity of her thoughts suggested that her anger hadn't abated any since she'd arrived here.

If something happened to him, would she still feel justified in that anger? Or would she simply regret that they hadn't done more to foster a closer union?

"I don't think Carly blames you at all," Beth said. "What you're feeling is called survivor's guilt. And it's perfectly natural, but what happened isn't your fault. Have you talked to Carly about this?"

"No. She deals with her emotions her own way." Helene's face twisted. "She's so like him. There were days I would almost feel like an outsider if I weren't so proud of them both. Samuel was not . . . easy, but he was a great man. He shaped her in that image. Even as a baby, she had no patience for me cuddlin' her. She never really crawled, went straight to walking. We raised her to be strong and independent. I'm glad she is."

But you wish she needed her mother, too. Beth thought of the moment in her kitchen last week, when Joy had cried and accepted Beth's hug of solace.

"If Samuel had lived, instead of me, he would have handled everything so much better," Helene said. "I've leaned too much on Carly."

"Nonsense. That's what family and friends are for." Beth tried to smile, despite the turbulent jumble of emotions she was suppressing and the overpowering melancholy of Helene's feelings. "I know we've just met, but I'd like to be a friend."

"Thank you." Helene sniffled into a fresh tissue. "I would be honored."

"So." Beth injected brisk cheerfulness into her tone. "What kinds of activities do you enjoy doing with friends? It's going to be a beautiful Sunday afternoon, if you're interested in being outside. Or if you'd rather just go in the other room and watch television—"

"Oh, I'm comfortable here," Helene said. "We could maybe play cards, if Carlotta has a deck around somewhere."

Beth couldn't help noticing that her charge preferred to remain stationary, in no hurry to utilize her crutches. She could only imagine the difficulty of physical therapy and the pain of a long-term injury, but Helene wasn't going to heal without some concerted effort on her part. Beth wished she could suggest something that would get them out of the house, but Helene probably wasn't up to big excursions just yet. *Well, that gives me something to work toward this summer.* A clear direction—professionally, at least.

When it came to her personal life, Beth was wandering in the wilderness.

It wasn't until that evening, when Beth prepared to take a shower—Carly was cloistered back in her room writing again, and Helene had turned in for the night—that her cell phone chirped from inside the open train case. She'd left the device on in the event that Joy needed to reach her. All day she'd been half braced to hear from her daughter, wondering if Allen had gone tattling to her a second time. But the other half of her knew he couldn't possibly do that. Joy would press for details, and he wouldn't want his only child to know what he'd done. Or said.

Wary, Beth picked up the phone and looked at the incoming number. PALMER, EVERETT. She closed her eyes briefly. Had Allen really followed through on his dispassionate promise to have Ev call with the name of a divorce attorney? Squaring her shoulders, she punched the ACCEPT button.

"Hello?"

"Beth." Ev's voice was a warm balm meant to soothe. It drove her closer to tears than she'd been all day. "How are you holding up, sugar?"

"I'll be fine."

There was a pause. "Allen isn't. He's a wreck. Called me earlier from some sports bar, and asked me to meet him for a beer. He spent the entire time ranting that he'd lost you and Joy forever."

"What happens to his relationship with him and his daughter depends entirely on him." She elected not to comment on her own relationship with the man. "Look, Ev, if you've called to put in a good word for him, to tell me how sorry he is—"

"No. I called to check on you. He didn't get into the nitty-gritty specifics, but I gather he was a real bastard."

"You gather right."

"For what it's worth, he told me repeatedly that he wanted to call you, but that you probably wouldn't pick up."

And here she'd thought Allen liked taking gambles.

"I poured him into a cab and advised him to sober up before trying to contact you," Ev said. "I figure you've been through enough lately without wading through his drunken rambling."

"You're a good friend to him. He doesn't deserve you," she said without thinking. *Spiteful.* The truth was, Allen needed close friends now more than ever.

Ev returned the compliment. "You were the best thing that ever happened to him. You and Joy. You said their relationship is up to Allen? I doubt that's entirely true. Marissa and I never wanted kids of our own. We both traveled a lot and liked our corporate lifestyles the way they were, but she told me once that the closest she ever came to changing her mind was after watching you with Joy. You could poison her against Allen, and he knows it."

That Allen might suspect her capable of such a thing stung. The fact of the matter was, tarnishing Allen in Joy's eyes would be just as damaging to their daughter as to him. With a lump in her throat, Beth thought of her own father, who'd never planned to be a single parent, and how he'd clumsily done the best he could after his wife's death.

Important as the mother-daughter relationship might be, girls needed their daddies, too.

❧

Beth expected that with everything on her mind and sleeping in a strange bed, it would take her forever to drift off. But sheer emotional exhaustion kicked in, dragging her under into a black, dreamless sleep. Until a shriek jolted her awake in the middle of the night.

Years of motherhood had conditioned her to wake quickly in crises—slumbering with half an ear out for a baby's cries, a kid's sleepwalking or a teenager's infrequent attempts to slip in past curfew—so she sat bolt upright. As her eyes adjusted to the darkness in Carly's office, she held herself still, listening for whatever unidentified noise she'd heard the first time. The digital clock read three fifty.

She picked up her light robe from the floor and shrugged into it. What if Helene had been trying to move around and had lost her balance or otherwise injured herself? But as Beth headed for the top of the stairs, she heard a second, softer noise. Not shrieking this time, but whimpering. From behind the closed door of Carly's bedroom.

Compelled by the anguished sounds, Beth moved down the hallway but stopped at the door with no idea what to do next. Given the time and the uncensored cry that had woken her, nightmares were her guess. She wanted to knock, wake Carly, and help her escape whatever altered reality tormented her, but would the professor appreciate the help? Or, once awake, would she resent her new employee having seen her so vulnerable?

Beth was still undecided when a ray of light shone beneath the door—a bedside lamp, given its dimness. A floorboard creaked, and she returned hastily to her own room. Minutes later, she heard the sink running in the bathroom, followed eventually by the whirr and beep of a computer booting up and staccato typing. It would seem that Helene Frazer was correct: Carly could take care of herself.

But the sound of that night-splitting shriek lingered in Beth's mind for hours.

❧

By nine thirty Tuesday morning, Daniel Cross was already off schedule. He was meeting with potential clients, the Jensens, to quote them an estimate on landscaping. But no sooner had he arrived than he realized Mr. and Mrs. Jensen had two very different ideas for the yard. If he wanted the job, he would first need to mediate their arguments about what to do with their acre and a half.

Forty-five minutes and one spousal concession of a koi pond later, he excused himself to his truck and called Brad, his second-in-command. "Hey, it's Dan. You remember the Fiorellos that we worked with two summers ago?"

"How could I forget? They scarred my psyche."

Daniel glanced back at the three-story home. "Well, my nine thirty prospectives turned out to be a couple who make the Fiorellos look agreeable and well-adjusted."

"Dude, get in the truck and drive away. I'm begging you."

"Doesn't your kid need braces?"

Brad sighed. "Point taken. What can I do to help?"

"Handle my eleven? Looks like I'll be here for a while. If you can't fit it in, maybe delegate it out to Trey."

"Taken care of, boss."

By ten fifty, Daniel had a raging headache and the beginnings of a blueprint for a one-month project. After leaving the Jensens, he decided to grab an early lunch and, at the drive-through, impulsively made it an order for two. With his next appointment passed off to Brad, Daniel had a gap in his schedule he could fill by checking in on Helene.

Helene or her daughter?

Since running into Carly last week, he hadn't been back to the house. But thoughts of her had persisted, like Georgia red clay you couldn't quite wash out. He kept recalling the obstinate set of her jaw, at odds with the faint purple smudges beneath her eyes, bruises of fatigue on her delicate skin. In her maddeningly complicated way, she was the most appealing woman he'd ever met.

Daniel was drawn to her independent strength even while

wanting to shelter her. She evoked protective instincts she'd never entirely welcomed—her nightmares, for instance. She'd gone through spells of disturbed dreams, waking him with smothered yelps but yanking out of reach and insisting she was fine when he'd tried to hold her.

There was only one method of comfort she'd consistently allowed, preferring to lose herself in athletic sex rather than cry on his shoulder. His hands gripped on the steering wheel as he tried not to remember. Making love to Carly could be really good—damn good—but, at times, disconcertingly impersonal. As if his wife were no more emotionally invested in the connection of their bodies than she would be in a pounding run meant to relieve the day's stress.

That had been the crux of their marriage. Daniel had wanted to get personal; he'd refused to stay on his side of her invisible boundaries.

Every time he pushed in some small way, she'd retreated in an equally subtle but undeniable manner. Over time, it had eaten at him, to be so in love with a woman who was so incapable of letting herself be loved. When she'd gone to Europe, he'd realized that he didn't miss her so much as he was relieved that there was an ocean between them. Spurred by self-preservation, he'd gotten out of their marriage while he could. And he'd told her over the phone because he didn't think he would have been able to look her in those beautiful mismatched eyes and tell her goodbye.

He was ashamed of his actions, but they'd ultimately allowed him to go back to the easygoing person he wanted to be. After five more years with Carly, he would have become a very bitter man. Would he have eventually turned to another woman, one who welcomed his affections more readily? He didn't think that was in his nature, but it was scary how unsure he was. Leaving was arguably nobler than staying married and coming to hate his wife, punishing her for her own nature.

He'd tried to find a way to tell her that when she was in Europe, but all she heard was criticism.

"If you see me as cold and remote," she'd said curtly, "I'm surprised you stayed this long. By all means, follow your bliss."

"Carly—" How should he respond? Certainly her tone could be used as an argument that she was emotionally withdrawn. But did the aloofness stem from not caring about him or the opposite? Was she abrupt because he'd hurt her? He definitely couldn't have separated from her in person because even over the phone, with the barrier of an ocean between them, he found himself backsliding. "I should probably give you more time to think about this. When you get back we could—"

"You've obviously given it plenty of thought." For a moment, her voice had gentled. "I'm not so buried in my research that I haven't seen you're unhappy. We're so different, Daniel, this was probably inevitable."

If that was how she felt, why had she accepted his marriage proposal? He wanted to call her bluff, but he was tired. He shouldn't have to constantly push her to admit her feelings, to admit she *had* feelings, to care about him more than she did women who had been dead for three centuries. Hell, maybe their divorce truly had been inevitable.

Daniel was so preoccupied with Carly that he didn't think to call Helene to let her know he was coming until he was already parking his truck in the driveway. No matter—he had the spare key Carly had given him before her trip to Houston, and Helene liked happy surprises. He scooped up the drinks and the white paper sack full of food.

Taking the steps two at a time, he frowned at the condition of the stair rail. Back when he'd thought he had years ahead of him to complete projects on this house, he'd wanted to renovate the front porch, replacing some of the tongue-and-groove wooden boards that were vulnerable to rotting. Looking at them now, he itched for his circular saw and locking pliers. Not that the porch was collapsing beneath anyone's feet yet, but it would probably come to that before Carly noticed. His wife was more interested in the collapse of royal monarchies than in her own home.

Daniel stumbled over his own thoughts, almost dropping the drink carrier in his left hand. *Ex*-wife. Very ex. He needed to work harder to remember that.

He'd viewed assisting Helene as a mild form of penance, being here for Carly now after the way he'd abandoned her a year and a half ago. But maybe this was a bad idea, spending time in the home they'd shared, stirring up emotions he'd tried to put to rest, potentially raising Helene's hopes for a reconciliation. During the marriage, he'd been frustrated by Carly's boundaries, but perhaps he should try harder to maintain his own now that they were divorced.

Something to ponder for the future. At the moment, he had lunch to deliver. He unlocked the door and called hello as he stepped inside. Helene wasn't in the front parlor, so he followed the sound of music back toward the kitchen. A modernized gospel hymn played on the radio and an unfamiliar female voice was harmonizing with the band. A plump brunette was standing at the kitchen counter.

"Hello," Daniel began.

She whirled, her face pale. "Wh-who are you? How'd you get in?"

"Daniel Cross. I have a key." He held up the paper bag and plastic cups of sweet tea. "I brought lunch for Helene. Are you a friend of hers?"

Pressing a hand to her heart, she took a deep breath. "I work for her. Her and Dr. Frazer. I'm Elisabeth—Beth—Overton."

"Nice to meet you." He set the food on the kitchen table and extended a hand. "I didn't mean to scare you. I didn't realize Carly had hired anyone yet." He'd assumed she would let him know when she found the right person.

Beth shook his hand, smiling and exposing dimples that instantly took years off her face. "Sorry if I overreacted. Helene has mentioned you several times. You're her ex-son-in-law? With the radio playing, I didn't hear you come in. Helene's sleeping now. We had an active morning."

"Oh? Sounds like progress."

"I hope so. We worked on the knee bends Carly told me she should be doing, although Helene wasn't . . . She isn't a difficult patient. Quite the opposite, in fact. But her heart doesn't seem to be in it. I managed to get her outside on the porch for a little while, because it was such a pretty morning."

"The fresh air will do her good." He grinned. "I was outside all morning, too, but, trust me, you were in better company."

Beth stood behind one of the chairs, looking uncertain. "Should I wake her? I know she'd hate to miss you."

He was working on a retaining wall this afternoon, but he didn't have to leave just yet. "Maybe I could stick around for a bit," he suggested. "Give her a little more time to rest before we wake her. That is, if I'm not in your way."

"Not at all." She pointed to some open books on the counter. "I was using the downtime to try and find a good chicken-fried-steak recipe and making myself hungry in the process. Feel free to eat while I fix myself lunch. Would you like a plate?"

"Nah. I'm not too civilized to eat from the wrappers." He sat, opening the bag. "There's plenty to share. I got a couple of different kinds of sandwich so that I could give Helene a choice. Why don't you take one?"

"Thank you." She hesitated before choosing a chicken club sandwich. "Would you mind terribly if I asked you a few questions?"

"Depends on the questions," he said with a friendly wink.

Accepting the iced tea he handed her, Beth chuckled shyly. "You're exactly how Helene described you."

"And Carly?" *Damn.* The words were out before he could stop them, an undisciplined by-product of his earlier distraction. He pushed the carton of French fries to the center of the table, trying to look nonchalant. "Does she ever mention me?"

Beth's look of sympathy was all the response he needed. So it was no surprise when she said softly, "Not really."

Well, you had that coming, you dumb ass. He'd known the answer even before he asked the question. He forced a smile for Beth's benefit, sorry he'd made her uncomfortable with his own wishful thinking. "So what were those questions you had?"

"Medical stuff. I know Carly was at the hospital with Helene right after the crash and took her to the first appointment once she'd been released, but you've actually been taking her since then, haven't you?" Her voice was admiring.

Helene already viewed him with something akin to hero worship, and he didn't want Beth to see him that way, too. He squirmed in his chair, thinking again of the way he'd ducked out of his own vows. "It's no trouble. Like you said, Helene's not a difficult patient and she's practically family. Or was. And I own my business, so I have some pull with the boss."

"I know Helene appreciates it. And I'm sure Carly does, too," she added in a prim tone, obviously not sure of any such thing. "I had some questions about Dr. Rylan's recommendations. Helene tells me what she remembers, but it's always good to have a second pair of ears when a doctor's throwing suggestions and medical jargon at you. I learned over the years at my daughter's pediatrician visits that getting the most out of the appointment depended in part on knowing what to ask."

"Oh, you have a daughter?" He'd been under the impression that Carly wanted live-in help, but maybe the kid was in college by now.

Beth nodded, soft pride filling her features. "She's twenty-five and expecting her own child now."

Twenty-five? He blinked but said nothing. Beth Overton was obviously older than Carly—and probably himself—but she didn't look nearly old enough to have mothered a full-grown adult.

"Congratulations," he told her.

"Thank you! I still can't believe my hus— I mean, I still have trouble envisioning myself as someone's grandmother, but I couldn't be happier." Her thumb rubbed over the base of her ring finger, where a pale indentation marked a band that was no longer there.

Divorced or widowed? he wondered. Had this become a houseful of halves who used to be wholes? Maybe that was why Carly had never taken to marriage, because she was more secure than most in her own self-identity, her own totality.

"You know, I was planning to take Helene again to the doctor's this Friday," he said, "since I didn't know someone had accepted the position yet. Why don't I come along anyway? Even with the progress she's made, maneuvering the steps and car and hospital corridors isn't easy. I can help with that and transition Dr. Rylan over to you. Unless Carly can spare the morning from work to go with you," he added, "which is unlikely."

Beth frowned at the bitterness in his tone. "It wouldn't be a good time for her to ask off. She starts class this week, and they changed her schedule around. She wasn't expecting to teach in the mornings."

He was both amused and intrigued by the mama-bear protectiveness in Beth's tone. He was aware of the reputation Carly had among TAs, so it was a noteworthy change of pace to hear an employee defend her.

"Do you enjoy working for her?" he asked.

"Some parts of it. I wish there was more I could do," she admitted, setting down her sandwich. "Even if Helene is technically making strides in her physical progress, as I mentioned before, her heart doesn't seem to be in it. She may be depressed. Understandably so, given the circumstances, but that must slow down her recovery. And Carly . . . Should I be discussing this with her ex-husband?"

Hell, no. She'd probably fire you. But the concern in Beth's gaze had roused his own. "I care about Carly. And I want to help, too. Trust me, I won't tell her we had this conversation."

"Well, there's nothing much to tell—it's not as if she confides in me. But she doesn't seem to be sleeping, outside of afternoon catnaps. I often hear typing when I go to bed and again when I wake up. I know she has a deadline at the end of the summer and is trying to make the most of my time here, but it's almost as if she deliberately avoids sleeping at night. A couple of times, I thought I heard . . . I just don't think she's coping with her father's death as well as she would like everyone to believe."

Nobody could be handling it that well. It would be unnatural.

He hazarded a guess. "She's having nightmares?"

"So that's happened before?"

"In spells," he recalled. She would go for weeks sleeping like a baby, but then the bad dreams would hit in batches.

They both turned as a thump came from the other room: Helene trying to position her crutches.

"I'll go let her know you're here," Beth said, "and that you'll be joining us on Friday. That should brighten her day!"

A few minutes later, Beth returned with his former mother-in-law and the three of them enjoyed a friendly lunch. He spent only about fifteen minutes visiting with Helene, but he left feeling that she was in good hands. From his brief interaction with Beth Overton, it would seem that Carly had chosen well. The woman was nurturing and coaxing, openly softhearted. Everything Helene—and maybe Carly herself—needed right now.

As he merged with northbound traffic, he thought about Carly and her nightmares. It had scared the hell out of them when, shortly before they got engaged, she'd screamed in the middle of the night. When he'd sat up next to her, groggy and scanning his dark apartment for an intruder or other visible crises, her eyes had been wide-open. He hadn't immediately realized she was asleep. She'd calmed herself down and slipped into easier slumber by the time he'd grasped the situation. When he'd asked her about it the next morning, she'd shrugged off his questions, claiming not to remember her dreams.

After that, at least two or three times every few months, Carly would wake him with nightmares. He'd tried to pull her close the first few times, only to have her forcibly shove him away, once crying out, "Don't touch me!" in such a broken tone that he'd felt ill. In all the years he'd known her, she'd never once talked about it.

It had become another one of those areas where he'd initially tried to push, only to have her retreat. Daniel had told himself that as bright as she was, maybe it wasn't unusual for her mind to stay more active than most people's in sleep. Not for the first time, he wondered what haunted her when she closed her eyes.

Would a better husband have pressed the issue?

⊰❦⊱

"Shall we bless the food?" Beth asked, glancing curiously at Carly. Every night so far, Beth and Helene had dined alone in the kitchen while Carly took a plate to her room. Although Helene always lowered her head for an automatic grace at mealtime, Carly didn't seem the most worshipful person Beth had ever met.

But the blonde shrugged, lowering her chin and closing her eyes as Beth said a few words. Then the three women dug into the pot roast Beth had prepared.

After her first bite of food, Carly stared at Beth, looking taken aback. "Damn, that's good. You undersold your culinary skills when I interviewed you."

"Oh. Thank you."

Helene glanced between the two of them, smiling tentatively. "Beth promised to try her hand at chicken-fried steak later this week. Can we invite Daniel to join us?"

Carly paused, and at first, Beth was certain she would say no. But then she gave another quick lift of her shoulders in a what-do-I-care gesture. "Why not? I just hope you'll all overlook my lack of hospitality if I eat at the computer."

Helene's eyes were huge pools of disappointment, but she said nothing to argue with or reprimand her daughter, merely went back to her food.

Seconds ticked by, dragging into long minutes, and Beth

set her fork down. "I've had an idea, Helene. What if I took you to your house tomorrow?"

The woman peered at her. "Oh, but we can't stay there. The stairs—"

"Not to stay, just to visit. I thought it might . . ." *Cheer you up* wasn't quite the right phrase. But perhaps Helene would derive a certain comfort in being around her own things, in her own environment, where she knew where the cups and plates belonged, instead of feeling an interloper on someone else's turf. Maybe enough time had passed since the funeral that Helene could feel closer to her husband in the house they'd shared without the pain overwhelming her.

Come to think of it, there were some items Beth would like to get from her own home, now that a few days had passed since her angry flight. She could swing by while Allen was at work. Thinking of her scrapbook supplies, she wondered if it would help Helene to put together a memory book of her husband and his accomplishments. Maybe in another week or so, when the grief wasn't so fresh, Beth would ask her about it. For now just getting her to a destination other than the doctor's would be a victory.

"What do you say?" she asked Helene. "Would you like to go out for a bit tomorrow? We could make a girls' day of it, maybe even have lunch with my daughter. You mentioned you wanted to meet Joy."

"All right," Helene agreed. If she wasn't overcome with enthusiasm over the prospect, at least she didn't seem to hate it.

"Or"—Beth swung her gaze to Carly—"we could wait until after lunch if you'd like to join—"

"No. Thank you. You two have fun."

They finished the meal in silence. Carly carried her plate to the sink and was halfway out of the kitchen when the phone rang.

Beth tilted her head. "Would you like me to get it?"

But Carly was already retracing her steps and caught the receiver on the next ring. "Hello?" Her forehead compressed into a series of perplexed wrinkles. "She is here. Just a moment. Elisabeth? It's for you."

Feeling as puzzled as her boss looked, Beth took the phone. "Hello?"

"*Beth*. Lord, it's good to hear your voice."

Allen?

When days had passed after Ev's advice to Allen to sober up and then call his wife, Beth had wondered if her husband was on one hell of a bender or if he'd simply decided he had nothing to say to her. Given what he had said last time they spoke, maybe the latter would have been just as well. "How did you get this number?"

"Information. You told me who you were working for, and although it may not always seem like it, I do listen."

He really *had* worried, then, that she wouldn't take his calls if he tried her cell. "This is my job now, Allen. You can't phone here and bother Dr. Frazer."

"You flew all the way to Texas, planning to interrupt my job. I didn't mean that disparagingly," he added. "I meant that, when something's important, like we are, like our marriage is . . . I'm so sorry, Beth, for saying I never wanted to marry you in the first place."

It was the worst thing anyone had ever said to her. She couldn't think of a description for it that didn't sound melodramatic.

"You know it wasn't true," he said.

"Do I?"

"We should talk about a therapist, like you suggested before," he said. "Maybe we need help."

"*You* certainly do. Are you ready to admit that you have a problem?" She was suddenly aware that she was still in Carly's kitchen and that neither Carly nor Helene was trying particularly hard to hide her interest in the conversation.

"I'll stop playing poker while we work through the other—"

"That doesn't sound like an admission." She sighed. "Allen, you need to quit for good. For yourself, if not for me. Don't call me back until you're ready to face that." Without waiting for a goodbye, she disconnected.

"Was that your husband?" Helene asked as Beth hung up the phone.

"Yes. Now what would you like to watch tonight? We can get you settled in the den, and I'll join you when I'm done cleaning up in here."

Ever compliant, Helene allowed herself to be relocated without asking further questions. But when Beth returned to the kitchen, she wasn't shocked to find Carly lingering, rinsing the dishes.

"Alcoholic?" Carly asked without raising her gaze.

Not yet, but I could become one if things don't start getting easier. "Compulsive gambler."

"Ah." Carly turned then, her expression almost friendly. "It takes a real strength to end your marriage. Especially after so much time."

Deep down, part of Beth still hoped it wouldn't come to that, that Allen would seek the help it had become apparent he needed. She thought of the divorced couples she knew—the Palmers, the Greysons. Carly, herself, with a handsome and kind ex-husband who obviously cared about her.

"Thank you," Beth said quietly. "But it takes real strength to try to save one, too."

Eight

❧

Rerouting

Normally, Beth would look forward to coffee and shopping with her daughter. But what had been normal in her life lately?

Joy glanced up from a rack of lullaby CDs. "What's wrong, Mama? Are you worried about leaving Helene alone?"

Since the house that Helene and Samuel Frazer had shared wasn't far from where Joy worked, Beth's original idea had been all three women meeting for lunch. But Helene had timidly requested having some time alone in her house, so Beth had instead asked if Joy could meet her at a nearby shopping center that boasted a bakery Joy loved and a store that catered to new parents. It was probably best that mother and daughter had this time alone, but Beth was dreading their necessary conversation.

"I told Helene that I would only be a few minutes away and that she should call me if she needs anything. But I definitely don't want to stay gone long. Is there anything here you want to buy?"

Joy shook her head. "Just looking, mostly."

"Come on, then. I'll buy you one of those black-and-white cookies you love."

Joy grinned. "Oh, all right, if you insist."

Soon, they were seated in a two-person mini booth with a cup of tea and cookies for Joy and a decaf coffee for Beth.

She stirred in far too much sugar and thought, inexplicably, of Carly's suggestion that she should take up jogging. The only thing that sounded worse than being middle-aged and single again was being middle-aged, single, and *fat*. Maybe she could start running—or at least walking. After all, it would hardly be the most radical change in her life recently. In a weird way, she found herself excited, wondering what other changes were still in store. She would be starting a whole new chapter of her life when she turned forty-five next week. Living under her father's roof, she'd always felt as though her activities and his expectations were clearly mapped. She'd only had a brief taste of independent freedom in college before she found herself pregnant and settling down. Even though part of her still ached over the tenuous state of her marriage, it was exhilarating to feel as if she were standing at a crossroads and, for the first time, could pick from a limitless number of paths.

Unfortunately, her excitement didn't make telling her daughter about the changes any easier.

"Have you talked to your dad lately, honey?"

"Mm-mm," Joy said from around a mouthful of cookie. "Why, is something . . . What is it, Mama?"

Beth had been dealt some hard knocks in her time, most of which she hadn't seen coming. She'd always wondered which was worse: the shock of something painful or the dread of knowing something bad was going to happen and not being able to change it. She so desperately wanted to prevent the anxiety creeping into Joy's gray eyes but knew that she was about to make it worse.

"Honey, first of all, promise me you'll keep in mind how much your father loves you. He always has." In utero didn't count, she told herself, even as Peter's happy paternal anticipation flashed through her mind.

"Mama, you're scaring me."

"Sorry. I don't want to sensationalize this, but I wouldn't be doing you any favors by downplaying it either. I know we talked about it a little before, but I believe your father has a real gambling problem. Worse than I'd originally realized. He's making financially irresponsible decisions, borrowing from friends, lying to me to go off on poker trips, staying up all night to play. . . . When I confronted him about it, he got angry, defensive. He said some things that will be hard for me to get past."

"But you have to try," Joy implored. "You will try, won't you?"

Beth didn't know. *I got married for you, honey, but I can't stay married for you.* It seemed such a selfish thought. She'd based so many of her decisions on how they would affect her daughter, but this was Beth's life. Reminding herself of that left her feeling both liberated and oddly guilty. Reverend Howard's daughter had been brought up to think about how she could be of service to others.

Well, then. She would use this opportunity to be of service to her daughter by setting a strong example and not being anyone's doormat, even Allen's. *Especially Allen's.*

"Joy, you're a wife now," she said gently, "and you know a marriage takes two people to make it work. I will support your father if he gets help, but he has to make that choice. He's still resisting it. I'm telling you all this not only because I love you but because I respect you as an adult, one who's capable of handling the truth."

Was now the time to admit that harder truth: that Allen Overton had never planned to marry Elisabeth in the first place? Or would it be cruel to dump that on her already upset daughter?

Joy sat back against the vinyl padded booth, stricken but dry-eyed. "I don't know what to say. You—you told me everything was all right."

"That was before I caught him playing poker online when he said he was working." She said it without malice and without getting into the awful encounter that had followed. "Joy, I truly wanted to believe that things *were* all right. But I was in denial. I'm not anymore. With luck, your father won't be for much longer, either. I can't control that, though."

Joy swallowed. "Should I talk to him?"

"Maybe that would help. But, honey, this is a sensitive subject for him and he's lashing out like a wounded animal right now. I would hate for—"

"It's okay," her daughter assured her in a wobbly voice. "I'm a big girl."

Because Ramson Neil's summer courses attempted to squeeze preexisting curriculums into much shorter semesters, the hours of the classes themselves were twice as long. Western civ met twice a week from eight in the morning until eleven, with a fifteen-minute break in the middle. Carly was not, by nature, a morning person, but she had the fortitude to overcome. Noticing a few blank faces, she concluded that the same could not be said of everyone else.

While there were numerous students with notebooks, laptops and Alphasmarts, ready to note her every pearl of wisdom, two or three seemed less intent on their academic development. In the middle of the room, a petite girl in a tank top was flirting with the guy behind her, oblivious to the fact that someone was trying to pass her copies of the syllabus. All the way in the back, a man-child with unnaturally black hair, shining violet under the fluorescent lights, was resting his head on tattooed arms. Bored or hungover? At the end of that same row was a young woman whose wavy strawberry blond hair hung in her face in a mass that made it impossible to tell if she was even awake.

In the event that they failed to live up to her expectations, Carly would be sure to flunk them both so that no one could accuse her of gender bias.

At the opposite end of the spectrum were the painfully eager. While she herself had been an overachiever, she hadn't sucked up to her professors. A kiss-ass student sitting front and center said that he'd heard she had a book coming out and he looked forward to reading it. She considered telling him he wouldn't get extra credit for doing so, but figured her "no extra credit" policy was already clear in the syllabus.

By the time midmorning break rolled around, Kiss Ass had interrupted four times to ask questions that were barely disguised attempts at showcasing his own intellect. Carly actually empathized with the two or three who were staring out at the summer sunshine, looking bored. Most of the history students she dealt with in higher-level courses never even took Western civ because they'd exempted out of it, just as she had more than a decade ago. She cheered herself out of the doldrums by planning to spring a pop quiz on them tomorrow.

Since she was already feeling grumpy, Carly decided she might as well cap off her day on campus with a stop at Saundra Arnold's office.

A faculty e-mail had gone out naming Saundra this year's pie-pursuit coordinator; she would maintain the sign-up list and appoint the "clue" committee. Each summer, incoming freshmen were invited to a three-day orientation. Activities were designed to familiarize them with the college and to help them get to know their future classmates. The annual highlight of these activities was a clue-based scavenger hunt that sent four-person teams all over campus, solving puzzles and meeting faculty personnel. The first ten groups to solve the location of the "finish line" received a homemade pie, baked by one of the professors or administrators.

"Hey." Carly poked her head inside the open door but didn't actually walk into Saundra's office. "Got a minute?"

"No, but I'll make one. What can I do for you?" Saundra asked, her voice butter-smooth. As if haf the campus hadn't figured out that she'd been the one to try to sabotage Carly's tenure.

No one would know until after Dean Murrin's return whether the attempt had succeeded.

Carly bared her teeth in what might have passed for a smile. "Actually, it's what I can do for you. I wanted to sign up for a pie. French silk sound good?"

"*Actually,*" Saundra volleyed back at her, "Dr. Weisman has already signed up for that."

"All right. Key lime?"

"Dr. Shapiro."

"Apple?"

"I'll be doing that one myself," Saundra said, her voice saccharine sweet. "I don't mean to be difficult, but the pie pursuit *is* a tradition. Most people knew what they'd be baking even before the e-mail went out this morning because it's what they always make. I only have two slots left. Dean Murrin will naturally be making her lemon meringue, and the head librarian's sweet-potato pie is the best in the South. Here at Ramson Neil, pies are a form of legacy."

Carly almost snorted. She preferred her legacy be based on a brilliant research perspective or, in her later administrative years, policy. Not a nine-and-a-half-inch dessert with a flaky crust. *Collegiality, collegiality. Focus, Carlotta.*

"In fact." Saundra tapped her finger against her lips. "Maybe I should reserve the next to last slot for Genevieve Baker, as a welcome gesture."

Right, because when you were busy unpacking and moving into a new city, nothing said howdy like giving you more work to do. Genevieve had been hired away from a university in Texas to come work as the assistant dean of academic administration. She was due to arrive shortly before Dean Murrin's return, giving her the rest of the summer to ease into the job before the busier fall semester.

"Even if you leave a slot open for Genevieve, that still leaves you one to fill?" Carly prompted, impatient with the petty way her colleague was making her work for this. "Just tell me what you have a need for."

Saundra pulled a spiral notebook out of the top drawer of her desk and made a show of studying a small handwritten list. Carly considered suggesting that if it took Saundra that long to read through eight volunteers and their contributions, then perhaps it was time for higher-powered glasses.

Finally Saundra glanced up. "You know, this is odd. Georgia's the Peach State and no one has come forward yet with a peach pie."

"I'll take it."

"I'll make a note. You do realize these are homemade pies, not store-bought?"

Carly wondered how the committee felt about homemade pie in a store-bought crust, then decided not to find out. "Of course."

Saundra cocked a brow, her beady little eyes flashing. "Just between us girls, I have to say I'm surprised. I certainly don't remember your being interested in participating *before*. And I thought that this summer, you'd be even less invested." She paused a beat. "Since you have that important book to write, I mean."

No, what she'd meant was "since you won't be getting tenure and may already be out the door." Faculty at Ramson Neil seemed to have an unwritten six-year expiration date. The ones who didn't secure tenure shortly thereafter usually found positions elsewhere.

Carly couldn't take it anymore. Though she hated giving anyone the emotional upper hand, she *refused* to be bullied. She edged closer, looking down at the other woman. "While we're talking, just us girls, do you want to tell me why you dislike me so intently?"

Flustered, Saundra dropped the notebook. As she bent to get it, she stammered, "I'm sure I don't know what you mean."

"You can tell me. I'm not thin-skinned," Carly assured her. "And it just makes sense for me to try to rectify the situation, since after Dean Murrin makes her tenure recommendations, I suspect you and I will be colleagues for a long, long time."

Saundra's jaw clenched as if she were barely biting back a retort. In the end, however, she remained silent, face-to-face forthrightness not being her style.

Which could be why the Saundra Arnolds of the world don't like me, Carly thought.

In retrospect, the encounter probably hadn't gone very far to establish Carly as someone who played well with others. On the other hand, Carly decided as she unlocked her car door, it had been more fun than she'd had in ages.

Beth knocked, then let herself into the two-story house where she'd left Helene. While she would never say as much to the other woman, Beth didn't like the home. She'd already known that Samuel Frazer and his wife collected antiques, but they weren't homey Duncan Phyfe pieces or heirloom quilts. These were heavy, ostentatious pieces of furniture—mahogany and cherry with brass and gold scrollwork. The cumulative effect was a bit overwhelming. Almost . . . forbidding.

Overactive imagination. Was she simply reacting to the fact that the man of the house had died?

Actually, maybe her emotional reaction stemmed from everything screaming Man of the House. There was no feminine touch, no sign that Helene or Carly, who'd grown up here, had ever been in residence. In Beth's own home, she'd had to make decorating compromises based on Allen's tastes, but there were still the pretty stained-glass panes, the pastel throw pillows, and ruffled ties on the curtains. This place was . . . bleak. Perhaps bringing Helene by hadn't been the best idea for perking up her charge.

"Helene?" She walked toward the back den, where she'd last seen the woman and found her in the center of the room, legs stretched out in front of her, framed pictures on the floor around her.

Even with the lines around her eyes and silvery-white hair, the woman looked young and vulnerable as she held out a gilt-edged portrait. "Doesn't he look strong? So vital and *alive?*"

Beth glanced down at the proffered wedding picture: Helene smiling and delicate in her gown, a tall groom towering over her in a tux. Vital, perhaps, but not altogether cheerful. "The two of you made a lovely couple. And a lovely daughter," she added, trying to help the grieving widow focus on what she still had.

"It should have been more," Helene mumbled. "He wanted sons, but I didn't . . . I couldn't carry full-term. We had one miscarriage before Carly and two after."

Beth couldn't imagine how awful that must have been; she personally had never been given a chance for more children. With no intention of being caught unawares twice, Allen had talked her into letting him get a vasectomy early in their marriage. She'd been almost too tired from the demands of a toddler to argue in favor of having more children. Besides, she'd suffered enough guilt during her pregnancy with Joy to ever again carry a baby she wasn't certain her husband wanted. If he ever *did* want one, well, she'd heard that vasectomies were reversible.

Later, as Joy grew into an inquisitive child with an enchanting smile, Beth had told herself that one healthy, beautiful daughter was more than many people got and was more than enough to ensure Beth's happiness.

Helene's smile was bittersweet. "You're so lucky, a grandchild on the way! I thought I'd have more children, thought Carly would have children of her own by now. She's so brilliant, like her father. How could she have let Daniel get away?"

That was one relationship Beth had trouble envisioning— Carly with flirtatious and laid-back Daniel. Beth guessed, from the way Daniel's blue eyes gleamed when he talked about her, that Carly had been the one to do the leaving. Was Daniel helping now because he was angling for a second chance, or was he simply that decent a human being? Beth hoped, for his sake, it was the latter. Even if Carly regretted the dissolution of her marriage, which Beth had seen no evidence of, she didn't seem the type of person who could admit she was wrong.

Then again, as Beth thought about her own life and the tiny ways Allen had subconsciously made her pay for "trapping" him into marriage, there was something to be said for standing up for yourself and not allowing someone else to make you feel you'd done something wrong. The unspoken prevailing assumption in the Overton household had been that if someone was in error, it was Beth, that her time or efforts or opinions were somehow less valuable than Allen's.

At times—like when Joy had looked across the table with those heartbroken gray eyes twenty minutes ago—Beth couldn't help asking herself if she'd done the right thing, taking this job and leaving her gambling husband to his own devices. Twenty-six years they'd shared, much of it good. She'd meant what she'd said to Carly, even if her employer hadn't appreciated the unsolicited advice, it *did* take strength to commit yourself to repairing a broken marriage. So was escaping to Carly's house when marriage got rough the cowardly route?

Was it Beth's duty to cleave to her husband and stick it out, or was that just habit talking, just Beth once again placing herself in the wrong?

Beth and Helene were watching an afternoon talk show when Carly entered the house. Even though Beth had grown more accustomed to her employer, she still marveled at the woman's purposeful stride—as if she were on her way somewhere important and wouldn't tolerate anyone getting in her way, even when she was simply walking through a door.

The professor nodded crisply to each of them. "Mother. Elisabeth. I don't suppose you have a convenient recipe for a peach pie? I could just Google one," she added almost to herself, "but your cooking has been impressive so far."

Beth was flattered. She couldn't remember anyone ever using the word "impressive" to describe something about her. "There's a peaches-and-cream pie I've baked before, with cream cheese and cinnamon. I don't have the ingredients to make it tonight, but—"

"Oh, it's not for me." Carly waved a manicured hand. She grimaced. "It's for the pie pursuit."

"Pie pursuit?"

"A number of colleges have their own version of a freshman 'cake race,' " Carly explained. "Georgia Tech, AU, Davidson. It's a literal race, once upon a time used to help coaches designate potential track stars."

When she mentioned track, her face softened subtly, her gaze more affectionate than it ever was when looking at her mother. But then she was scowling again.

"At Ramson Neil, we have a variation, challenging students to use their brains and learn about their chosen college. It's a scavenger hunt, and the win— What the hell is that doing there?" She froze, her eyes locked on the mantel across from her.

Following her gaze, Beth saw one of the mementos Helene had rescued from her empty house. A framed eight-by-ten of Samuel Frazer. It had probably been taken no earlier than the nineteen eighties, but it looked much older, done in sepia tones and shot in the historical, unsmiling tradition. Beth had seen similar somber expressions on grandparents and great-parents in formal photos.

"I brought it back from the house today," Helene said. In the most censorious tone Beth had ever heard from the woman, she added, "I noticed you didn't have any pictures of your father."

In Carly's defense, there were hardly pictures of *anyone* displayed throughout the house. There was high-end abstract art, and in the upstairs hallway hung framed photos of places that Carly had visited in Europe. Those seemed the sole concession to sentimental memories.

Could that be because the memories were too painful? Beth had never seen anyone turn as pale as her employer was now without passing out.

Instinct propelled Beth forward. "It's hot out today, and you're looking peaked." She laid a hand on Carly's arm, barely conscious of her action until the younger woman jerked away. "Let's get you a glass of water, okay?"

Carly's gaze swiveled to Beth. "Actually, if you could fill one of those sports bottles in the kitchen with water, I'll take it with me. I was planning to go for a run." She disappeared up the stairs and returned in record time, her blond hair tied back in an elastic band. It was really too short for a ponytail and stuck straight out in a little point at the back of her head. She barely paused on her way out the door to accept the bottle before the front door slammed shut behind her.

Seemingly oblivious to her daughter's taking flight, Helene had gone back to watching the talk show. Beth sat next to the woman, disturbed by the brief and bizarre encounter. Even more disturbed because Helene seemed so unfazed. Surely she'd realized that Carly was upset?

"Did Carly and her father get along?" Beth couldn't keep herself from asking. It was none of her business, of course, but it was difficult to share a house with two other people and not feel caught up in their lives.

Helene glanced away from the television for only a second, and if Beth didn't know the placid woman better, she would have said her set expression was angry. "What a question! Did she say something to you that might make you think otherwise?"

No, she took one look at his photo, then fled. Beth knew that Carly routinely ran, but now she had the nonsensical thought that the woman was actually running from something. Had Helene not noticed, or was Beth reading too much into the situation? "It wasn't anything Carly said."

"Good." Helene let out a breath. "I'd hate to think she would speak ill of the dead. I told you before, Samuel was demanding. But if she doesn't understand that he made her who she is, then she's being plain mule-headed. She owes everything to that man. We both do. He took such good care of me."

Beth frowned at the sentiment. She couldn't put her finger on exactly why, but for the first time since she'd met Helene, she found herself deeply annoyed with the woman. *Perhaps because she reminds you of yourself?* Had Beth depended on Allen taking care of her to the exclusion of reality, content to trade housework for mortgage payments and health insurance, and pretending he loved her more than he had?

Beth had already started cooking dinner by the time Carly came into the kitchen, sweaty but serene, to put her water bottle in the sink.

"You look . . ." Beth studied her. "Zen-like."

Carly pursed her lips. "Appropriate, I guess, since running's the closest thing I've ever had to a religious experience. Well, that and—" She broke off with a brief shake of her head. "So, what's for supper?"

"I found some great tomatoes at the farmers' market, and I'm stuffing them with tuna salad. I thought we'd have mixed berries and fresh cream for dessert."

"I'm going to shower. Feel free to eat without me if I'm not back in time for dinner."

You mean, feel free to give you more time to be antisocial. For herself, Beth didn't care. She was hired help.

But the odd disconnect between Helene and Carly . . . It was unnatural, even more so because neither mother nor daughter seemed to think anything of it. They barely looked at each other, barely spoke, yet neither seemed to believe they had a bad relationship.

"Speaking of dessert." Beth seized the conversational gambit, determined to better understand this enigmatic young woman. "You never did finish telling me about the pie pursuit."

"Oh. It's a scavenger hunt that's a college tradition. Part of the tradition is that the faculty makes the pies given to the winning freshmen. Some of my colleagues take it pretty seriously." Carly shook her head, damp wisps giving up the ghost of her ponytail and sticking out in clumsy and endearing spikes. "Way too seriously, if you ask me. Baking is not my strong point. But since you know a recipe, maybe you can—"

"Talk you through it?"

"I was going to say, cook it for me. We'll file that under the miscellaneous column of your job duties."

Beth was tempted to point out that her baking the pie was tantamount to cheating, just as she'd explained to a nine-year-old Joy that she had to solve her own math problems, not ask her mother to do it for her. But what Beth actually said was, "All right. I'll make it. In exchange for you eating dinner with me, your mom, and Daniel Friday night." *Where did that come from?*

Carly laughed incredulously. "You're blackmailing me with pie?"

"It's really good pie," Beth promised. "Rich and gooey, with cinnamon and nutmeg balancing the sweeter flavors."

Eyes narrowed, Carly considered the offer.

While Beth didn't doubt the other woman was capable of following a recipe well enough to produce a single pie, she wondered if Carly could do so well as to uphold her own perfectionist standards. The bigger question was whether she would consider the effort worth her limited time.

"All right," Carly conceded. "But you won't use a store-brought crust, will you? That's part of the deal."

A laugh burbled up in Beth as she thought about the "crustless" recipe but she swallowed her humor, projecting earnest-ness as she said, "Of course not."

"Then we have an agreement." Her own expression metic-ulously neutral, as if she didn't care where or with whom she dined, Carly shrugged one shoulder. "You bake. I get dinner on Friday. A friendly word of advice? Work on your negotiat-ing skills. I came out the clear winner here."

Satisfied with the outcome, Beth turned back to slicing the tops off tomatoes. "Does there have to be a winner? I would have said we reached a mutually advantageous arrangement."

Carly snorted. "No. There's always a winner."

As she listened to Carly's footsteps on the stairs and then above, Beth reconsidered her own life. Raised by a father who professed we were all sinners and, shackled by our very hu-manity, that we could never live up to Christ's example, she'd felt like a failure since childhood. Nothing she ever did would be good enough. Her early years of marriage had confirmed that.

Which did not add up to stellar self-esteem.

But now she thought that it could have been worse. She couldn't imagine the unrelenting pressure of thinking, instead, that every situation and event had a clear victor, and that she must be that person. *I'd have snapped years ago.*

Of course, Carly was still young. She might be firmly on the path to neurotic self-destruction and not even realize it.

Nine

❧

If You Look Out Your Left Side

Daniel had just walked into his house when the phone started to ring, shrill in the dark. He flipped on an end table lamp, trying not to notice how blandly Spartan the room looked in the dim light. He'd poured so much energy, so much of himself, into that house with Carly. This new place... The very fact that he still thought of it as the "new place" underlined that he hadn't truly settled here. Would he ever recapture his enthusiasm for building a home? He would have simply rented a furnished apartment if he hadn't needed the accompanying garage and storage space for landscaping supplies.

The truth was, he'd lost his enthusiasm for a lot of things, as tonight had awkwardly demonstrated.

Banishing the well-intentioned double date from his mind, he reached across the back of a blue plaid sofa to get the phone. "This is Daniel."

"H-hi." The female voice sounded jittery and vaguely apologetic.

For a second, he thought it was Brad's wife calling to apologize for dinner. Not that it was *her* fault these setups never led to anything deeper.

"This is Beth," the woman said. "Beth Overton. I work for Carly?"

He almost chuckled at her hesitance. "Yes, of course." His amusement fled. "Is everything all right? Is Helene—"

"Oh, she's fine. Looking forward to seeing you for her appointment on Friday. We all are." She paused. "That's actually what I'm calling about. To invite you to dinner. On Friday."

Daniel was nonplussed. Was Helene's caretaker asking him on a date? He found that hard to imagine, but he wasn't sure why she sounded so nervous. "Dinner?"

"Here at the house, with us," she clarified, sounding more sure of herself now. "I'm making chicken-fried steak."

"Oh, dinner with you and Helene." He felt stupid now for not having understood that in the first place. Maybe Carly had some faculty event that—

"And Carly. All three of us. We'd love for you to join us."

We would? Skepticism filled him. "Beth, does Carly know you're calling me?" It was beginning to sound like Helene, blindly optimistic, had put her unsuspecting new employee up to this.

"She doesn't specifically know that I'm on the phone," Beth admitted. "She's closed up in her room working at the moment. But she promised to take Friday night off and eat with all of us."

"Including me?"

"That's the idea." She sounded impatient now, exasperated with a slow-witted male.

Carly was willingly sacrificing an evening of work on her manuscript? His ex-wife was on deadline, and he knew more than most how driven she could be under those circumstances. When she'd been writing her doctoral thesis, he'd had to interrupt her with reminders to eat. She'd once retorted that sleep and food were for lesser mortals than herself. She'd grinned when she said it and he'd laughed at the time, but there had been too many later instances when he felt she saw him as "lesser." *And now she wants to have dinner with me?*

He was confused and, on some level, insulted that no one thought he might have plans already. Just because he was making extra time for Helene in his schedule didn't mean he had nothing better to do with his time than pine for his ex-wife.

But his mixed feelings weren't enough to keep him from blurting, "I'll be there."

What is wrong with me? He hung up the phone and leaned against the couch, wondering at life's irony. In the past year, he'd gone out with a number of sweet, uncomplicated women. Outdoorsy types he'd met at the park or the occasional good-natured single mom Brad and his wife knew. Daniel hadn't been a monk. He'd taken women to dinner, to the theater and, on a few rare instances, to bed.

Yet despite the time that had passed and the assurance he'd given himself that the divorce had been right for both of them, the one woman he couldn't stop thinking about was the one he'd left.

❦

The classroom was silent except for the scratch of pens filling blue books. Carly had waited until Friday for the first quiz, but the four essay questions covered a substantial amount of material. Periodically, she glanced up to monitor progress and make sure no one appeared to be cheating—although this wasn't the sort of assignment where you copied down multiple-choice answers. It caught her notice that the scraggly strawberry blonde in the back—Leslie? Laurie?—was staring out the window across the campus lawn. Searching for inspiration? Collecting her thoughts?

Judging from her vague expression, that would be a pretty small compilation. After another moment's observation, Carly realized the girl had set her pen down and showed no signs of reaching for it. Her only movement was to every so often rub absently at a spot above her elbow.

Ten minutes later, the student Carly had dubbed Kiss Ass walked to the front of the room, his smug smile making it clear that he equated finishing first with scoring the best. Two other people followed, exiting the room as they turned in their quizzes. Finally, the girl with the pale red-gold hair stood and came to the front, placing her exam book on Carly's desk.

Knowing the girl hadn't written anything in at least fifteen minutes, Carly asked, "All finished?" She glanced down and saw that the girl's name was Laurel. *Well, I was close.*

"Yes, ma'am," the student said, her voice barely audible, her gaze meeting Carly's nose rather than her eyes.

From her sitting position, Carly could see a bruise high on the girl's arm, almost covered by the oversized lime green T-shirt she wore. Carly picked up the book and rifled through the first few pages, which were filled with neat penmanship and coherent thoughts. It appeared that Laurel had indeed completed the questions and might even have earned herself a decent grade.

"You were the first one done," she said softly. "Why'd you wait until someone else turned in his quiz?"

"Um . . ." The girl's eyes widened and she glanced toward the door as if she wanted to flee. "I was j-just thinking over my answers," the girl said.

Bullshit. Carly wanted to shake the girl's shoulders for the disservice she was doing herself, hiding her light beneath a bushel. Or baggy cotton shorts and stringy hair, as the case may be. There were always people out there who tried to make your achievements seem smaller—why do it for them?

Deciding it was none of her business, Carly sighed. "Have a good weekend."

Laurel nodded and practically tripped over her own feet in her haste to exit. Horses during a thunderstorm weren't that skittish.

When Carly returned her gaze to the remaining students, she caught one preppy guy in a polo shirt staring after the retreating Laurel with yearning. His name escaped her, but he'd made a mildly insightful observation earlier in the week about the Roman Empire. Carly wasn't sure what he saw in the skinny young woman.

Forget it, dude. That one's damaged.

Making chicken-fried steak was messy business, and Beth's hands were coated in flour when her cell phone rang. She had it clipped to her slacks because she was waiting to hear how Joy's OB appointment had gone. Rinsing off the worst of the mess as quickly as she could, she managed to answer partway through the digitized "Let It Be" ring tone before the phone kicked over to voice mail.

"Hello?" She smushed the phone between her ear and shoulder, still wiping one hand on a piece of paper towel. "Joy?"

"It's Allen. Were you expecting her? I could . . . call back if this is a bad time."

She paused, not sure what to say. "How are you doing?"

"My wife left me, my colleagues dislike me, and I'm a gambling addict," he said drily. "Other than that . . ."

Straightening, she gripped the phone tighter. Was he ready to face up to his problems?

Almost as if he'd heard the unspoken question, he told her, "I went on the Internet. There's this . . . There's a directory of meetings in the Atlanta area. You wouldn't believe how many there are. I called for some information. I'm going tomorrow, Beth."

"Oh." She wanted to say *That's wonderful*, but it seemed inappropriate under the circumstances. "I'm so glad."

"I . . . I wanted to ask you to go with me," he said in a shy voice she'd never heard from him before. It could have been reminiscent of hearing a nervous young man ask a girl out for the first time, but when Allen had asked her on their first date, they'd both known her answer would be a surprised but delighted yes. Neither of them had that certainty anymore.

"But," he continued, "it turns out that only the addicts themselves are allowed. It's part of respecting everyone's privacy. There are peripheral groups, though, for family and friends. If you or Joy ever . . ."

Moved by his blatant vulnerability, Beth tossed him a rope. "Down the road, if there are opportunities for us to participate that would be helpful to you, please let us know. We're both worried about you."

"She called me yesterday. Gave me an earful," Allen confessed. "It was along the lines of 'How dare I have a midlife crisis when she's carrying her first child because pregnant women don't need this kind of stress?'"

Beth smothered a bark of laughter. Joy was a good girl, growing into a good woman, but it was a mark of youth that she'd somehow managed to make this all about her. "She's upset. She loves you, though. You'll work through this and win her back."

"What about you?" He asked it so softly that she intuited the question as much as heard it. "Do I have any chance of winning you back?"

Don't put me on the spot.

She supposed that, since she was legally his wife, he had every right to ask. But she was elbow-deep in chicken-fried steak for a dysfunctional family other than her own and had been caught off guard by Allen's call and his gratifying announcement that he was seeking help. They said that admitting the problem was the first step, but weren't there eleven more? It seemed premature for either of them to be making guarantees.

"Go to the meeting tomorrow," she said. "Focus on yourself, and give us both time."

"I don't want time. I want *you*."

"How sure are you of that?" She lowered her voice, looking over her shoulder to make sure she was still alone in the kitchen. Helene and Daniel were playing gin on the front porch. They'd come home from Dr. Rylan's to a note on the fridge that Carly was running but would be back for dinner. Only Beth knew that the woman's presence would be the result of mild extortion.

"Allen, habit isn't love. You're used to me being there for you, used to me doing things for you—"

"You're not a maid service—you're my wife! I do know the difference."

Yeah. Maids got paid. "I'm not trying to start an argument. I'm just saying that . . . twenty-six years ago, we didn't feel we had a choice. Maybe this time, if we choose to stay together, it will be because we both *want* to. Not because we have to."

He was silent for a moment. When he spoke again, she sensed that he was making an effort to keep his tone light. "So, is it too late to ask what you want for your birthday?"

A month ago, she might have said that anything he picked out specifically for her would make her happy. Or encouraged him to write a check to the literacy program in her honor. Now she turned over the question in her head. What *did* she want? Oddly, she doubted it was anything he could give her. She'd just have to find it herself.

"Your going to this meeting is enough for me," she said.

"Do you have special plans?"

"Joy, Mitsi, Barbara, and I are going to a six o'clock chick flick. Then Joy and I are having a late dinner together." It would be easier that way. Although she'd told both of her friends that she was staying somewhere else as part of her temporary employment, she'd downplayed the marital-separation angle. Going to the movies would give her a chance to see them without leaving a lot of time for sensitive discussion she didn't want to have in front of her daughter.

"Can I call you after the meeting?" He sounded completely unlike the confident husband she'd known.

"Please do. And if I can ask one other favor? Let Joy know that you're going."

"What do I tell her about us?" he challenged.

"The truth. That we're both figuring things out the best we can, which may take a while."

❧

Usually, the metronomic rhythm of her running shoes against the concrete soothed Carly. This evening, however, she couldn't find her cadence. The staccato of her footsteps seemed jerky and uneven, mirroring her thoughts. She pushed harder, trying to reach that trancelike zone, but peace refused to be forced. Her efforts gained her a stitch in her side and a throbbing left calf.

Stop. It was the logical, intelligent decision. *Go home.* Where Daniel was.

She'd assured herself several blocks ago that her jog wasn't avoidance. After all, Carly ran every day, and cowardice wasn't in her nature. But the longer she ran, frustrated and sweaty, the more she was forced to ask: *Was* she deliberately staying away from the house because her ex-husband happened to be there?

It was becoming nearly impossible not to roll her eyes whenever Helene waxed rhapsodic about the man, silently blaming Carly for not being a better wife. Why did that seem to be the pattern with Helene? Reproaching her only child, no matter the circumstance. Carly might not have much in common with her new domestic help, but she found herself developing a grudging respect for the older woman. Though Beth Overton came across as meek, she'd walked away from her husband rather than act as a doormat. And it was clear that Beth thought the world of her own daughter and would go to great lengths to protect Joy. In theory, most mothers naturally felt that way about their daughters. But Helene—

Is a frail woman, old before her time. Not an adversary worth angst and animosity. Carly would do her duty in helping the woman recover and be glad that *she* possessed a stronger nature. She wasn't going to waste time and energy playing the what-if game when it came to her family or childhood. She had a PhD in history. The most one could do was learn from the past, not change it or relive it.

As she wheeled around, circling the cul-de-sac back toward her house, she found that it was more difficult to avoid the what-ifs when it came to Daniel. What had she told Beth? That it took courage to walk away from a bad marriage? Carly had always taken comfort in telling herself that while the marriage might have failed, *she* wasn't a failure.

She hadn't quit.

The contempt she'd felt for Daniel's slinking off while she was away had helped keep other, more painful, emotions at bay. But it was difficult to maintain that cool disdain while praising Beth for being smart enough to get out. Had Daniel been acting in wise self-protection, just as Beth was? *Totally dissimilar. I'm not a gambling addict who lied to my spouse and jeopardized our financial standing.*

Rather than clear Carly's head, this run seemed to be unpleasantly mixing her thoughts—a bunch of incompatible ingredients thrown into a blender and pureed into a noxious pulp. In her mind's eye she saw the face of Laurel, from her class, a young woman perhaps too damaged to live up to her potential. *Is that why Daniel left?* Was Dr. Carly Frazer, a successful and respected academic who'd made a point of excelling her entire life, too damaged to love?

Daniel knew better than to try to pretend he *hadn't* been watching the curved street for Carly's appearance. Of course he had. Even on her worst days, she was compelling. And for all that she might be sweaty and disheveled, he'd always enjoyed seeing her run. Her carefully paced strides notwithstanding, it was Carly at her most uninhibited. There was a . . . freedom in her expression he rarely glimpsed.

Today, however, her controlled gait seemed off. Jerky.

He frowned. Carly could be awkward emotionally, but almost never physically. Daniel found himself tuning out Helene's words in order to better study her daughter. Truthfully, he was glad for the disruption, as he'd been on the verge of curt impatience with the older woman.

She was a delicate female who naturally evoked sympathy or at least protective instincts. Lord knew she'd been through a lot during the past month. But he couldn't shake the feeling that she wasn't really committed to doing her physical therapy or getting well and returning to her own house. While she hadn't argued outright with Dr. Rylan or refused to do any of the exercises, she acted as if every move or small accomplishment required a team of cheerleaders. Daniel had understood during those first few visits how difficult the therapy regimen must be, but didn't she want to get better? She should have progressed by now beyond range-of-motion development to actively strengthening her hamstring and quadriceps. Yet she passively resisted most of the doctor's and therapist's suggestions. She was so different from Carly, who was never passive about *anything*.

"Daniel?" Helene asked plaintively, apparently realizing that she'd lost his attention. She followed his gaze. "Oh. Carly's back. How nice."

Was it? Daniel shot his former mother-in-law an appraising glance.

It was no secret that Carly and her mother didn't share a close bond. He'd largely laid the blame for that at Carly's feet, knowing her tendency to prioritize success above personal relationships. But perhaps that was an unfair assumption. He couldn't help noticing the way Helene's mouth thinned when she saw her daughter approaching. As if Helene were a coquettish debutante unhappy to see a rival. Was Helene jealous of her daughter? It had never before occurred to him.

"Hey." Carly spared minimum energy to acknowledge them, jerking her chin toward them in an almost masculine gesture. A reverse nod, as far removed from delicate and coquettish as he could imagine.

"Hi." He stood, leaning against the rail instead of giving in to the inclination to meet her on the stairs. It wasn't healthy to seek out close contact with his ex-wife. "How was the run?"

She scowled, then dismissed his question with a shake of her head. "Everything go all right at the doctor's today?"

"Fine," Helene answered before he could. She seemed dwarfed in her still-seated position. Carly was a tall woman, but he didn't think height was the only thing making Helene seem smaller in comparison. "At least, as well as it could, I suppose. There's a limit to what these old bones can do."

"That's not exactly the physical therapist's diagnosis," he interjected reprovingly. "He thinks you can make a full recovery if you apply yourself."

"Are you saying I'm not *trying*?" Helene demanded, her lips pursed. "It isn't as if I wanted to get hurt. As if I'm some hypochondriac who wanted to be disabled. I suffered a traumatic loss and my mobility in one fell swoop, and for you to suggest I might . . ." She trailed off, her short burst of anger fading to a more inward sorrow. She covered her face with shaking hands.

Feeling like a cad who might very well be taking out his own emotional frustrations on an injured, elderly woman, Daniel knelt by her chair. "I'm sorry. I wasn't implying that you don't want to get better. Chalk it up to a misguided attempt to . . . motivate you." She sniffed behind her fingers.

"Helene, I am sorry." All right, maybe she *wasn't* giving her physical recovery one hundred percent, but he couldn't imagine the emotional toll of the crash. He wouldn't be surprised to learn she was experiencing mild to moderate depression after losing her spouse. After all, he'd left Carly of his own accord more than a year ago, and look how much it continued to affect him.

He glanced up involuntarily, the mere thought of what it would have done to him if Carly had died prompting the need for visual reassurance that she was alive and well.

But she'd already disappeared inside, escaping the emotional undercurrents on the porch as easily as she'd kick off a stinky pair of running shoes. Sighing, he asked himself why he'd expected anything different.

Carly leaned into the scalding spray of the shower, so hot that the water actually stung her skin. A line from an old song played through her head. *Hurt so good.* Her lips quirked in a sardonic quarter smile. Maybe she liked running because it hurt so good. Certainly, allowing her mother to live with her during this undetermined interim indicated a masochistic streak.

What was I thinking? I am not equipped to deal with her. Even Saint Daniel was struggling to maintain his patience with Helene. That display on the front porch had disgusted Carly. She wanted to shake her mother, tell the woman to stop being such a goddamn victim. Which would affirm every suspicion Daniel had ever harbored that Carly's veins were filled with ice.

Cutting off the water with a flick of her wrist, Carly reminded herself that it was stupid to care what the man thought. He'd pledged to love her for the rest of her life, then abandoned her. He'd lost his right to an opinion.

Carly shrugged into a terry-cloth robe and quickly made her way through the empty hall to her room. She chose clothes haphazardly, ending up with khaki shorts and a scoop-necked top with wide sleeves. Skipping makeup entirely, she blew-dry her hair, then went downstairs. She hadn't given much consideration to her appetite, but the smell wafting through her house made her stomach rumble in anticipation. If Beth's peaches-and-cream pie was as good as this chicken-fried steak smelled, Carly would be the toast of campus.

Before Carly had reached the last step, Daniel appeared in the foyer. She paused, wary but refusing to go on the defensive, waiting to hear what he had to say.

"Your mom's already seated at the table," he said. "Beth says dinner will be ready in a few minutes."

She nodded, knowing that wasn't why he'd sought her out. "And?"

"I wanted to tell you how much I admire the way you're taking care of your mother."

What? "Sarcasm isn't like you, Daniel."

He exhaled audibly—half sigh, half chuckle. "No, I'm serious. I realized today that I was having a tough time maintaining compassion, and I only deal with her a few hours a week. She's here all the time. And you—"

"Aren't known for my compassionate nature?" she asked mildly.

"I was going to say, you like your space."

Not as much space as you gave me. The thought startled her. As did her response to his praise. She was more moved than she should have been. "Thank you."

He inclined his head. "There was one other thing I wanted to ask you about."

A favor, maybe? That could explain his softening her up with flattery first. She arched an eyebrow. There was a time when she would have said that open and honest Daniel was too straightforward for such a tactic, but how well had she really known him?

"The front porch," he said.

She blinked. "What about it?"

"The railing's a bit loose, some of the boards need to be replaced. It was something I meant to do before I . . . Anyway, the last thing I'd want is for anyone to get hurt. I'd like to ask your permission to at least shore up the railing. If Helene lost her footing, it would be disastrous to her recovery."

It was what Carly had found fascinating yet simultaneously dreaded about Daniel: his propensity for throwing her off balance. She'd been expecting some reprimand about how she hadn't shown an extended interest in her mother's medical appointments. Instead, he complimented her and sought her permission to do property repairs? If the divorce had been *her* idea, part of her would have wondered if this was an excuse to stick around. But he already had an excuse in Helene.

No, as far as Carly could tell, Daniel was making the offer out of the goodness of his heart. Or perhaps delayed guilt. Did he regret ending their marriage?

Did she? If she hadn't verbally shoved him away whenever he'd tried to discuss it afterward, would the outcome have been any different?

"I'd like to pay you for your time and labor," she heard herself say, sounding passably unruffled. "Or the supplies at the very least."

"I wouldn't hear of it," he said. "If we were still married, I would have done it for free months ago."

She met his gaze, that infinite blue. "But we're not."

"I know." He reached up, touching his index finger to the side of her mouth. The simple contact—was it a caress?—jolted her. Electricity sparked inside her, neurons firing throughout her body.

"Carly." His tone was an apology. For the desertion, for the overfamiliar gesture? But he hadn't moved his hand away.

She swallowed, her throat bone-dry. "They're probably waiting for us."

"Right." He stepped aside, letting her pass before asking, "The porch?"

"Knock yourself out." The strain in her voice kept her from achieving the desired casual effect.

As she preceded him into the dining room, it wasn't the deal she'd struck with Beth that forced Carly to take a seat. It was her refusal to flee Daniel's company just because his finger had brushed over her skin. Pride stiffened her spine, and she sat ramrod straight in her chair.

Thankfully, the tantalizing spread made it easier to think about something besides Daniel, who was seated at the other end of the table between Beth and Helene.

"Dinner looks amazing," Carly said, giving credit where it was due. "Beth, I'm going to have to start running even more, or I'll gain twenty pounds before you leave."

Helene made a soft, distressed sound that drew all eyes to her. "I hate the thought of your leaving."

"I'll visit you even after we've both gone home," Beth promised. Then she folded her hands, ready to say grace.

Carly obligingly ducked her head, but her attention wasn't on Beth's words of prayer but rather Daniel's words earlier on the porch. Was Helene not giving therapy her best effort because she was reluctant to go back to her house once she was well? Did she fear being alone? Carly would never understand her mother. After decades of living under Samuel Frazer's thumb, Helene should have been reveling in her newfound freedom. Apparently, the woman valued security—even in a warped, unequal form—over liberty.

Socially, Samuel had been glad for a beautiful wife who reflected back his own self-importance. His public treatment of her had been affectionate, if occasionally patronizing. At home, however, he'd had no patience for Helene, calling her worthless more times than Carly could remember. A dull anger throbbed low in Carly's belly. Why wasn't Helene doing everything she could to prove the dead man wrong. Didn't she *want* to stand on her own two feet?

It had been years since Carly had to share a residence with Samuel. Had he mellowed in his final years, tempered his outbursts with his wife? Now that Carly thought about it, by the time she had reached her teen years, Samuel's rages—his interest—had been consistently directed at *her*, not his soft-spoken wife. Occasionally, she thought she'd even glimpsed a kind of predatory amusement in his narrowed eyes, as if he was gratified to have a more worthy opponent. Or almost . . . almost as if he were . . .

Flirting. Carly's skin crawled. She had tolerated the instances her father struck her, figuring other kids got spankings and such. The instances of physical pain had never seemed as bad as the embarrassment she'd feel if anyone viewed her as weak, a victim to be pitied. But if he had ever laid a hand on her in sexual aggression, he wouldn't have needed to wait for a car crash to kill him.

"Amen," Beth concluded.

Carly's head shot up, her gaze shooting to her mother—a personified anchor tethering Carly to a past best left forgotten. "Have you thought about what you're going to do when you leave here?"

Helene's lips thinned into a parody of a kidding smile. "In a hurry to get rid of me?"

Yes. "Because you could live wherever you wanted," Carly continued, refusing to acknowledge her mother's joke, which really wasn't one. "You could sell the house."

The woman's fork clattered to her plate. "I lived most of my life in that home."

I know, I was there. And Carly was unaware of any fond halcyon memories that would inspire someone to stay.

Helene crumpled in her seat, tears evident in the warble of her voice though none were actually marring her eye makeup. "After everything I've already lost ..."

With the precision of overearnest stage actors in a badly written community theater production, Beth and Daniel both reached for her at the same moment, patting a shoulder and a hand. Carly's stomach turned, and she wondered if she'd be able to choke down any of the food in front of her.

People acted as if *she* were unnatural. Bloodless. Daniel had left because of it; even her career goals were in jeopardy because her superiors seemed to think there was something wrong with her. Why couldn't Beth and Daniel see what she saw? How could they remain so oblivious to letting themselves be manipulated?

She stabbed blindly at a piece of steak. The sooner she ate, the sooner she could legitimately excuse herself to work on her manuscript. She'd had unprecedented difficulty concentrating lately, and she'd fallen behind schedule.

Daniel, possibly in a diplomatic attempt to dispel the awkwardness, let out a near moan of ecstasy. "Beth, this food is beyond words."

The woman blushed with pleasure. Carly had already noticed how strongly her employee reacted to praise. Clearly, she wasn't used to receiving it.

"Cooking for someone who enjoys my food so much is its own reward," Beth said humbly.

"You know what's an even better reward?" Carly asked. "Cold, hard cash. You should think about catering."

Though Beth looked stunned by this suggestion, Daniel was already nodding. "Carly's right. My company's pretty small, but at least twice a year, I like to get everyone together for a meal to foster camaraderie. Usually I grill, but I'd love to hire you to help if you're available."

I am *right.* Carly straightened in her chair, the idea coming so swiftly she could actually feel the lightbulb illuminating over her head. After all, wasn't camaraderie just another definition for collegiality? "*Are* you available, Beth?"

The woman seemed confused. "To help Daniel? I suppose that depends on your schedule and Helene's."

"No. To help me. I'd pay you extra, of course. We're getting a new assistant dean at the college, Genevieve Baker. The person she reports to is out of the country right now, so I thought it might help Genevieve feel more welcome if I threw a small dinner party in her honor." Carly beamed, entertaining a vision of Saundra Arnold's expression when she learned that Carly was hosting an intimate gathering with delectable Southern home cooking that would put Saundra's apple pie to shame.

Daniel lifted his eyebrows. "I'm not sure I've ever seen you look this happy about spending time with your coworkers."

Since she couldn't truthfully counter that statement, Carly stared him down instead. "People change, don't they?"

"I'm not sure," he murmured, returning his attention to his plate.

"When you say a 'small' dinner party," Beth ventured, "what number were you thinking?"

"Maybe eight? No more than ten would be my guess. After all, the point is to make the woman feel welcome and help her get to know her colleagues. Difficult to do that by overwhelming her with dozens of new faces." That plausible explanation might help soothe the ruffled feelings of anyone not invited.

"Ten people," Beth mused, a faraway expression settling over her face. She looked younger, dreamier. "I think I could actually do that."

"What about me?" Helene wanted to know.

Beth cast a guilt-stricken glance at her charge. "Well, I'm sure Carly wouldn't set the party up for one of your therapy days. And I could do some early prep the night before once you're in bed. . . . It's workable."

Helene sniffed. "Good. I wouldn't want to be an imposition. Sounds as if you can work around me quite nicely. I'll just let the two of you decide on the schedule, and on the night of the party, Carly can stick me back in my room like some embarrassing great-aunt."

Carly ground her teeth. Why weren't Beth and Daniel rolling their eyes at the woman's subdued histrionics? But, no, they were looking at Helene with something akin to pity. *Hell, maybe I am unnatural and bloodless.* With her mother living under the same roof, Carly was losing perspective.

"To be honest, Mother, I assumed you'd be happy in the

relative quiet of your room, with a good book and a tray of Beth's fantastic culinary offerings. After all, you've made a point of letting me know how easily you tire these days."

Helene narrowed her eyes. "I can take a nap. I often do, although I don't expect you to take note of *my* daily activities. Not with your busy schedule. But don't forget, dear, I was on your father's arm for many faculty events. Being around people from higher ed for the evening . . . it will be just as if Samuel were alive again."

Carly almost shuddered.

"Are you sure you're up for the crowd?" Daniel asked. "Because I'd be happy to escort you for a night out. Take you to dinner at some favorite restaurant?"

Helene looked torn between recapturing some part of her marriage or having a handsome younger man squire her about town.

Filled with gratitude, Carly wanted to tell Daniel how generous the offer was. He was an affable, attractive man who'd never had trouble drawing people to him. He could keep his social calendar as full as he chose. Yet he was sacrificing time to hang out with his cold ex-wife, her increasingly petulant mother, and a porch in need of repair. She felt that familiar tug again: admiration for a person she couldn't easily peg, counterweighted by her confusion and dislike of being puzzled. *I don't understand him.* Knowledge was power, and when it came to Daniel Cross, she didn't have enough of either. He made her feel disturbingly defenseless.

She was too smart to go down that road, though. History scholars believed in studying the past to learn from previous mistakes. Having allowed Daniel to penetrate her armor years ago, she wouldn't make such a gross error of judgment again.

She cleared her throat. "So, Beth, did you learn to cook like this from your mother?"

"Not really." A flash of pain passed over Beth's face. "I have memories of her making extensive Thanksgiving dinners for people in my dad's parish, but my job was setting the table. She died before I ever took my first home-ec class. A car accident."

Helene sucked in her breath. "Just like my dear Samuel. Oh, you poor thing. I heard on some talk show that automobile accidents are the leading cause of death for adults in this country. I'm sure your mother would have been so proud of you."

Carly forked in a large bite of food to keep from commenting. Or snorting in disbelief. Interesting how Helene would make a rote statement about maternal pride when she'd always wanted her own daughter to be someone different. These days, Helene's disappointment manifested as sad-eyed chagrin that Carly had "let" Daniel "get away." As if he'd escaped some feminine trap. Growing up, Carly had endured complaints about what a burden she was to her father.

Why must you talk to him like that, Carlotta? You know it upsets him.

Your father's a very important man with a stressful job. You just have to be more patient and understanding.

Right. A seven-year-old was supposed to "understand" when her father leaned down to yell in her face because she'd spilled juice near one of his academic journals?

Carly withdrew from the conversation, a defense mechanism against the rage boiling up. What good did it do her to be furious with a dead man? She'd never be able to make him apologize from the grave. Distantly, she heard Beth recount cooking disasters from her adolescence, when she'd tried to make dinner for her father. Daniel and Helene laughed obligingly, but the joyful sounds made Carly feel more isolated than if she'd simply spent the evening alone in her office.

"... bundle of nerves the first time I cooked for Allen," Beth was saying. "I wanted everything to be perfect for him. I felt so lucky that he'd even noticed me, and dating him was—"

"No." Carly's head snapped up. Beth's nostalgia sounded too much like something Helene would say, too much like the beliefs Helene had tried to force on Carly. "A woman should be aware of her own self-worth, not depend on someone else to define it. You should never let someone else make you feel *lucky* for their attentions."

Her harsh tone was met with shocked silence. She and her soapbox had crashed the fun party.

"For the record," Daniel said softly, "when you asked me to be your date to that awards banquet, I was surprised."

So was I.

"And I felt like the luckiest man in the world," he added.

The heartfelt admission was too much, too invasive. It made Carly physically uncomfortable in the same way as someone who didn't understand the cultural principle of "personal space" and crowded others while talking.

She pushed her chair back. "I-I have to go. My book. But dinner was. . . ." Illuminating? Infuriating?

At a complete loss, and hating herself for it, she exited the room and took the stairs two at a time. She sought her laptop and its blinking cursor the way a nerve-jangled alcoholic craves that first soothing belt of liquor. Carly wanted to open her computer files and crawl inside.

She was much more interested in learning and writing about the lives of others than being forced to examine her own.

Ten

Expect Delays

A phone ringing in the middle of the night was never good. It wasn't as if the state called people at three a.m. to let them know they were lottery winners. Those were Beth's nonsensical thoughts late Saturday—no, she squinted at the clock, early Sunday—as she grappled for her cell phone.

"Hello?"

"Mom?" Not Joy, but Peter.

Beth's chest tightened so painfully she almost couldn't speak. "Joy? The baby?"

"They're okay. . . . I think. We're at the ER. Just a precaution," he added, sounding too alarmed himself to put Beth at ease. "She wasn't even sure we should bother you with it, but I thought you'd kill me if—"

"You thought right," she said crisply, already pulling a pair of weatpants on beneath her nightgown. "You're at Kennestone? I'm on my way."

⋘❀⋙

Tachycardia. Ten minutes ago, the word had meant no more to Beth than gibberish, but as she raced through yellow lights— offering up silent apologies for the ones that turned red and prayers of gratitude for those that were slower to change— *tachycardia* echoed in her mind like the ominous opening notes of Beethoven's Fifth. Essentially, the term meant that Joy had been experiencing an abnormally rapid pulse.

According to Peter, Joy's palpitations and dizzy spells had started Friday evening. She'd figured she would have to wait until Monday to speak with her doctor. But when she'd awakened from sleep an hour and a half ago with her heart racing, then nearly passed out when she stood up to go to the bathroom, she and Peter had decided not to take any chances. They'd loaded her up for the hospital, registered her to see a doctor, then called Beth and Allen. For all that Peter had made a concerted effort not to seem panicky, it sounded as if the doctors hadn't made any kind of diagnosis one way or the other.

Beth was only vaguely aware of parking her car and rushing through the automatic doors. She followed Peter's directions to the waiting room upstairs, for maternity cases, and spotted Allen slumped on a padded bench. She hadn't seen him since their awful fight, but she had little emotional reaction to seeing him now. No lingering anger over his cruel words, no wifely pride that he was trying to get his act together. Just an insistent need for news about her daughter.

"Any updates?" she asked as she drew to a halt in front of him.

"Beth." Relief saturated his voice, and he rose to hug her. "I'm so glad you're here."

She felt stifled in the embrace, but that was probably because fear had been making it difficult for her to breathe ever since she'd disconnected her phone call with Peter. Strangled with worry, she felt claustrophobic in Allen's arms. "Of course I'm here. Can we see her? Do you know anything new yet?"

He shook his head, looking tired and, for the first time, actually old enough to be someone's grandfather. "I probably got the same summary Peter gave you. But Dr. Nguyen promised to—"

"Mr. and Mrs. Overton?" A white-coated man with matching hair stepped forward, glancing from the folder in his hand back to them.

Beth managed not to launch herself at him and demand answers. "Y-yes, that's us."

His smile was slight, but calming nonetheless. Surely medical professionals about to deliver terrible news wore appropriately somber expressions. "Your son-in-law asked me to step out and talk to you about Joy's condition. She's fine, resting as comfortably as one can in a hospital bed, and we're monitoring both her and the baby. Arrhythmias in pregnant women are by no means uncommon but sometimes they're indicators of other conditions."

"Such as?" Beth asked, already dreading the potential answers. Allen reached down and took her left hand, either to lend comfort or because he himself needed the reassurance of physical contact.

"Rapid and erratic pulse such as your daughter has been experiencing could mean the existence of a heretofore undiscovered heart condition. Or a condition like hypertension or gestational diabetes."

Beth felt faint. "You think Joy has one of these conditions?"

He shook his head. "Most of the time, arrhythmia occurs just because pregnancy puts increased demand on the heart, and Joy's body has never been through this before. I wanted you to understand the less-likely possibilities that we're trying to rule out. Running a few tests is our way of protecting Joy and your grandbaby, but we're doing it as a precaution. Your daughter seems in excellent health."

Beth wondered if it was unseemly to hug a physician she'd met only a minute ago. "When can I talk to her?"

The man gave that small smile again. "Actually, she's asked for you already. I think three people squeezed into that little room at once would be a bit much, but maybe one of you could wait with the husband while the other visits, then switch?"

"You go first, Beth," Allen said.

She nodded her gratitude, hurrying toward the room Dr. Nguyen indicated. When Joy had been a sophomore in high school, she'd been in a fender bender when a friend of hers misjudged how much room she had to make a left turn. The other vehicle had plowed into Joy's passenger door. Beth had felt just like this when she got the call from the driver's mother. Even though she'd been promised that Joy was safe and relatively unscathed—the car that had ultimately hit them had made a valiant effort to stop first, so neither vehicle had been moving disastrously fast—Beth couldn't take anyone else's word for it. She had to see her daughter with her own two eyes, smooth her hand over her child's face. Hear Joy breathe, the way Beth had done when Joy was a baby in the crib.

And now her daughter was propped up against pillows, her hands cradling her stomach and her own baby. *God, where did the time go?*

"Sweetheart." The word came out choked with emotion. She swallowed hard and turned to Peter. "You did good calling her father and me as soon as you got here. Don't ever feel you have to 'protect' us."

Joy sighed. "But I hate to worry you, Mama. Especially with you and Daddy . . ."

"Your father and I will be fine." One way or the other. Together or separately. "And no matter what else happens, we both adore you. Peter, would you mind giving us girls a few minutes to chat?"

"Not at all, Mom." He squeezed her shoulder as he passed, and Beth thought, not for the first time, that her daughter had chosen well. Peter was a smart, decent man who loved and cared for Joy without ever being cloying or condescending. Devoted without being smothering, teasing without being snide. They were equals. He seemed to truly *appreciate* her.

In Beth's eyes, that made him darn near perfect.

"He seems like a good husband," she observed.

Joy's eyes were teary. "The best."

"Good," Beth said firmly. "That's what you deserve. Now tell me the truth. Are you okay?"

Her daughter lowered her head, her chin tucking toward her chest as if she wanted to curl up in a protective ball. "Scared," she admitted. "Constantly. It's like everyone wants to give you advice and it just makes me worry more. Too much red meat isn't healthy, too much fish might lead to a mercury problem. When should I worry if I haven't felt the baby move? It's *exhausting*."

Beth smiled tenderly, thinking that it never got any better. Not really. In some ways, it just got worse because you couldn't keep your child with you. Even though Joy was a grown woman now, Beth had been scared to death when she got Peter's call. Motherhood came with a lot of blessings and a lot of fear.

"I was nervous all during my pregnancy with you," Beth said, "so this is a do as I say, not as I do, but try to relax. The stress isn't good for either of you. Dr. Nguyen doesn't seem to think this is anything serious, just one of the many bizarre side effects of pregnancy. All kinds of crazy things happen to your body."

"I know." Joy leaned against a pillow, closing her eyes momentarily. "But I feel better hearing you say it."

Beth stood beside the bed and stroked her daughter's hair. Purple smudges of exhaustion beneath Joy's eyes marred her peaceful expression. "I should let you get some sleep."

"Don't go yet," Joy said drowsily. "I'm sorry Grandma Howard died before I got a chance to meet her, but I'm even sorrier that she wasn't there for you when you were pregnant. If there is ever a time when a woman needs her mom . . ."

During her own pregnancy, Beth had suffered conflicting emotions. She had desperately missed her mother, but on some level, she'd also been glad she didn't have to face her mother's disappointment in her. Confronting Reverend Howard with the news that she was expecting had been difficult enough. He'd never looked at her the same way again, even after she married the baby's father.

"Were you and Mee-maw close then?" Joy asked, referring to Allen's mother.

"Not really." Beth had always felt her in-laws viewed her as the harlot who'd disrupted their son's future. Which made later Thanksgiving and Christmas dinners *lots* of fun. "They . . . didn't quite warm up to me."

Joy opened her eyes. "Because of me?"

Beth bit her bottom lip.

"Peter and I were trying to have a baby, and everyone was thrilled for us. It wasn't like that for you, was it?"

Beth had expected to have this conversation someday, just not at four in the morning in a cramped, sterile hospital room. "There were differences," she admitted. "But I loved you just as much as you love your unborn baby. I couldn't wait to meet you."

"Is that how Daddy felt, too?"

Beth stared out the window at the still-dark world beyond. "You'd have to ask him that question. I think mostly he was young and scared, nervous about providing for both of us. But he adores you. You know that."

"I hope he showers you with adoration." Joy stifled a yawn, then echoed Beth's earlier sentiment. "That's what *you* deserve."

❧

Beth sat in the hospital corridor with Peter while Allen verified their daughter's well-being for himself. She found herself curious and a little apprehensive about what Joy and Allen might be discussing but decided that unless either of them volunteered the information, she wouldn't ask. With the initial surges of adrenaline fading, both Beth and Peter were crashing into fatigue. They sat together in supportive but tired silence until Allen returned.

Peter rose, hugged them both, then rocked back on his heels with a ghost of a smile. "Guess I'll go see whether that chair-ottoman combination in Joy's room is as uncomfortable for sleeping as it looks."

"Probably worse," Beth predicted with an answering smile. "Take care of—" She'd been about to say *her*, then thought better of it. "Each other. Promise?"

He nodded solemnly. "Promise."

Allen watched their son-in-law go, echoing Beth's earlier observations. "They're good together. I thought she was young to get married, but . . ."

Not so young. Beth turned to her husband, trying to sort through her present numbness and rediscover the strong feelings she'd had for him.

He met her eyes. "Don't know about you, but I could use some caffeine before I attempt the drive home. Can I buy you coffee and maybe an early breakfast in the hospital cafeteria? I doubt it's a four-star restaurant, but—"

"I'm sure it will be fine. No worse than dorm food, remember?"

He grimaced. "I think my palate's become more refined since college. Thank God greasy pizza and cheap beer were enough to keep me happy back then. You obviously didn't fall for me because of my sophistication."

She was taken aback by the joking comment. It was unlike Allen to be self-deprecating. "You'd be surprised. To a sheltered girl from a microscopic town in the North Georgia mountains, you embodied culture." The real question was why had *he* fallen for *her*? If not for Joy's conception, would they have ever stayed together this long? According to what he'd said the night Beth left home, no, but she wasn't sure how much credibility to give words spoken in such anger.

Which meant she wasn't sure where that left them. For now, the hospital cafeteria.

Allen picked up a couple of scuffed green trays and handed one to her. He eyed a pan of scrambled eggs that already looked cold and congealed even though the cafeteria had started their breakfast buffet only about ten minutes ago. Eventually he settled on some bacon and a bagel, while Beth stuck to a cup of fruit salad and coffee that smelled strong enough to be used as paint stripper.

"I miss your cooking," he said with a sigh.

Somehow, the compliment didn't excite her as much as Carly and Daniel's suggestions that she might be a good enough chef to take on some small catering jobs. It was one thing for Carly to look at her in a domestic capacity—Beth was her employee, after all—but she'd hate to think that, if asked what he missed about his estranged wife, Allen would mention food first.

She made a noncommittal sound that he was free to take as thanks and followed him to a table for two.

Once they sat, she automatically bowed her head for a moment of silent prayer, but Allen began speaking immediately. Almost nervously.

"So I went to my first meeting," he reminded her.

Her feelings toward him softened. Whatever became of their relationship once she moved back into the house—*if* she moved back into the house?—she was thrilled that he'd sought help for the gambling. He was a hard worker, resourceful and energetic, a devoted father, and he had always been a loyal husband. She would hate to see the man he could be eclipsed by the ugly addiction. "How was it?"

"Hard at first," he said. "But after I'd been there for about twenty minutes . . . liberating. It was freeing to be around people who were just like me. There's a line between social gambling and compulsive gambling. I've learned at work that I have to be careful how much I say or people like Ev go from thinking it's fun to play a hand of cards to treating me like some kind of criminal."

Or deadbeat. As she recalled, Allen owed Everett money. The other man was justified in his anger and concerns.

"Even with you," Allen said, "I was defensive because I knew you wouldn't understand. The first time I ever had a big loss, I *wanted* to tell you, Beth, but I couldn't figure out how.

And the thought of your reaction was paralyzing. Your views tend toward the judgmental."

She choked on a piece of melon.

"That came out wrong," he backpedaled, wide-eyed. "Maybe conservative would have been better. Or traditional."

But no matter how diplomatically he could have couched it, he had meant judgmental. Was that really how he saw her? It was true that she had strong moral values—they were ingrained in her—but after enduring her father's quiet condemnation on more than one occasion, she tried hard not to cast her own stones.

"After I hid that first loss from you, I won back the money and put it in our savings with no one the wiser. From there, it got easier to lie, and the whole thing snowballed." He said it almost reprovingly.

Beth bristled. She should be glad he was finally opening up to her, but it seemed that, even if it was only on an unconscious level, he saw her as enabling his habit. Why? Because it had been easy to lie to her? Because she hadn't made a habit of interrogating him?

Maybe sleep deprivation was causing her to overreact, but his tone was annoyingly reminiscent of her pregnancy when he'd adopted the unspoken position that it was *her* fault, even though he'd definitely been a contributing factor. While she was glad he'd embraced the truth of his gambling problem, she'd be truly ecstatic when he learned to stop blaming other people for it.

Allen rubbed a hand over his face. "I've offended you, haven't I?"

If she said yes, would he retreat, stop confiding in her? Would she be proving his assessment that she was judgmental? She sidestepped the issue. "I think that maybe I'm too tired to have this conversation right now. It deserves more care and thought than I'm capable of at the moment."

"You're right." He smiled. "What about next weekend?"

Her mind was too bleary to make the jump. "Next weekend?"

"I've been thinking about the suggestion you made, that I date my wife. I'd like to give that a try."

When he reached across the table to shyly take her hand, she was flattered. Was this what being wooed felt like? Granted, most men probably picked a more auspicious time and place than a hospital cafeteria in the predawn hours, but it was sweet that he was making the effort. Looking back, she realized there had never truly been courtship between them. There'd been infatuation—almost worshipful on the part of her dewy-eyed teen self—followed by marriage. Allen had never had to *work* for her.

She took a moment to think it over, even though she knew she'd say yes. (After all, as he'd pointed out, it had been her suggestion in the first place.) The good, dutiful Beth told her that making him wait, enjoying the idea of his squirming slightly, was petty and uncharitable.

The newer part of her had been heavily influenced by Joy's success in love and even by the less successful Dr. Frazer. Bolstered by her daughter's earlier words, Beth allowed herself to want something that she'd been taught as a child was misplaced ego. Maybe she *did* deserve a little adoration.

"Beth?" Confusion laced his voice. "This is what you wanted, right? Me to . . . work on my problem? Us to work on patching things up?"

"Yes, of course." But if he was paying attention, he would have noticed the lack of conviction in her voice. Strengthening their emotional bond was why she'd braved her fear of planes and flown to Houston; delivering the news that they were going to be grandparents had been more the catalyst than the goal.

So why, as she tentatively agreed to have dinner with him Friday night, didn't she feel happy and hopeful?

❦

Beth had dashed off a note explaining her absence in case she hadn't returned Sunday morning by the time Helene and Carly rose from bed. But the house was quiet and still in the first rays of daylight. Carly was normally an early riser, but Beth knew the woman had been up late writing, so maybe she'd sleep in this morning.

A spectacular idea, Beth thought, yawning so widely, her jaw popped. If she crawled into bed without bothering to change clothes again, she could get at least an hour of sleep before Helene awakened. But once there, she couldn't force her mind or body to relax. She rolled onto her left side, worried about her daughter and all the guarantees she couldn't give Joy on pregnancy or life in general; then she tossed to her right and thought about her goodbye to Allen. He'd hugged her again, as he had when she'd first entered the waiting room. This time, he'd ducked his head slightly as if he might kiss her, probably just a brief peck on her forehead or cheek, but she'd jerked away as if he'd tried to feel her up at a church picnic.

What is wrong with me? After Joy's wedding, caught up in a revived matrimonial spirit, Beth had daydreamed about ways her own marriage could be richer. Now, if she weren't careful, she could push her husband away permanently. Behind her closed eyes, she saw her father's face, the gentle reproach. He would advise her that she was supposed to forgive, to submit to her husband, that marriage was sacred. She believed that, didn't she?

A creak jolted her from her troubled musings, and she sat up, realizing that Carly was awake. If Carly had a different personality, Beth would offer to cook the two of them a hearty Southern breakfast and they could chat companionably over slices of crisp bacon and cheese grits. But she knew that Carly would probably start her Sunday with a run, then follow it with half a grapefruit or some kind of protein drink.

Restless, Beth kicked aside the coverlet. *I should try running.* A woman her age should pay more attention to her fitness. And that disquieting claustrophobic sensation still lingered. The thought of running with the wind in her face sounded oddly exhilarating. Weren't there emotional benefits, some kind of "runner's high" that enhanced a person's sense of well-being?

She pulled on a pair of battered canvas tennis shoes and opened the door to her room. Carly was just exiting the bathroom, securing her hair in a ponytail as she walked.

"I've decided to join you," Beth said, her tone unintentionally imperious. Funny how she sounded more decisive about something she'd resolved to do in the last two minutes than she did about seeing the man she'd vowed to spend her entire life with.

"Running?" Carly asked, unable to mask her surprise. She glanced at Beth's feet and raised an eyebrow.

Admittedly, Beth's shoes wouldn't get her through the annual Peachtree 10K, but they should suffice for her first jog around the neighborhood. She lifted her chin. "Yeah."

"All right. But don't expect me to slow down for you."

"Likewise."

The corners of Carly's mouth twitched, her eyes sparkling with suppressed laughter. In that second, she was a truly beautiful woman. Not just an elegant blonde with strong features and a great figure, but actually breathtaking. It was the first time Beth had ever looked at her and been able to imagine her employer married to Daniel.

"Let's get going then," Carly said, once more all business.

Carly hadn't been kidding about not altering her pace for Beth's sake. Within ten minutes, Beth had nearly lost sight of the professor. Which was just as well. Running left her sweaty and breathless. Having the tall blonde with her Swiss-precision movements out of sight enabled Beth to focus on herself instead of her embarrassment. She strove to find her own rhythm, even though, after two blocks salt stung her eyes and her knees were protesting.

What are you doing? her aching body seemed to ask. *You're not a runner.*

Why the heck not? Just because she'd never been athletic before, where was it written that she couldn't do something more than she had? Become more than she was? She was proud of her daughter, so nothing she'd done as a mother had been wasted, but when Beth looked back . . .

Her father had instilled in her strict teachings about being a good person, even while simultaneously preaching that it was human destiny to fall short. She'd entered her marriage guilty and apologetic, striving to be a good wife. Now, with an actual paying job, she wanted to be a good employee. Had her entire life consisted of trying to be good for other people?

After another block, she turned back toward the house but, spurred by a burgeoning, unfocused anger, she vowed to give it her all in the final stretch. She needed to *go*, needed to be . . . something.

Only Carly's presence on the front porch kept her from collapsing on the grass as soon as her feet hit the yard. Her lungs were on fire, and her muscles were screaming. If she sat down, they'd probably lock, making it impossible for her to get up again. She staggered toward the house, wincing inwardly at the prospect of taking the stairs. Another stupid outing like this one, and she'd need to borrow Helene's crutches.

I was right, her inner voice sniped. *You're* not *a runner.*

She'd thought that once she stopped, she'd feel better, but actually, stopping was worse in some ways. She barely managed to lurch toward the bushes before she threw up. This was not, Beth concluded, the much ballyhooed runner's high.

"It gets easier."

Beth turned her head to see Carly extending a bottle of water.

"You'll do better next time," Carly predicted. "If you alternate walking and running, you'll probably manage to keep down your breakfast."

There wasn't going to be a next time. If Beth weren't so winded, she'd say as much. She was going to accept her own limitations, maybe look into some other form of exercise because she was not cut out for this.

Yet, as she later unlaced her stinky shoes, she found herself wondering how much a pair of real running shoes cost.

⨞

Before class on Monday, Carly got Genevieve Baker's e-mail address from the secretary and sat down to write an invitation for dinner. The competitor in her wanted to do it now, before two or three other people on campus had the same idea. Unfortunately, the ulterior motive made her second-guess her straightforward, welcoming message of Southern hospitality.

Her first attempt was too brusque, a veritable summons. She edited it to read more like what she imagined Saundra Arnold would send. But then she couldn't reread it without wanting to gag.

That made her think of Beth, who had been a bit green beneath her red face this morning after her second attempt at running but had indeed kept down breakfast after admitting defeat much sooner and walking back to the house. Yesterday, she'd looked as if she had demons to slay, so Carly hadn't stood in her way. Beth was a grown woman; if she didn't have enough sense not to take off like an Olympic sprinter on her very first day, Carly wasn't going to interfere. Better that Beth indulged her momentary, self-destructive defiance through running than, say, a bottle of tequila. With that out of her system, maybe she could now find a real rhythm, start off at a slow jog and see where it took her.

Carly drummed her fingers on her desk. When she'd first met the older woman, she would have classified her as someone with shaky confidence, not entirely comfortable with herself. But she did well with others. Helene and Daniel had taken to Beth instantly.

Though *welcoming* didn't come naturally to Carly, it was probably right up Beth's alley. Before she'd consciously realized what she intended to do, Carly dialed her own home number.

"Frazer residence," Beth answered.

"It's Carly. About that dinner we discussed for my incoming colleague?"

"Yes?" Beth encouraged when the pause lengthened.

"Nothing. Never mind." What had she planned to do, ask the former housewife to draft an e-mail that might have a bearing on how Carly was viewed on campus and might, by extension, directly impact her career path? Carly determined her own successes and even failures, if it came to that. "I have a class to teach."

"Right. I guess we'll see you tonight."

Seemed a safe bet, since she owned the place. Carly hung up, exasperated that she was overthinking a damn e-mail. She typed a three-line message giving her title, saying that she'd like to host a casual dinner party for Genevieve to give the woman a chance to meet faculty, and would either of these dates work for her? Then she hit SEND and drew in a deep breath.

It was the unresolved tenure situation doing this to her. Carly didn't customarily doubt herself. She didn't flee dinners just because her ex-husband happened to be sitting at the table. She didn't ask random women with no professional experience for their help with her work. She didn't labor at her computer until three in the morning, filling pages with prose that with a growing frustration she feared was wooden and pedantic.

When Dean Murrin came back and made her official recommendation to the provost, Carly would either be granted the tenure she deserved, restoring her universe to rights or . . . Her mind blanked at the "or." What she wanted to tell herself was that she'd apply elsewhere—plenty of universities would be happy to have her, maybe even someplace where she fit in better with the campus culture. But she couldn't quite brook that possibility. Not getting tenure here at Ramson Neil would mean not reaching her goals.

Not beating her father.

Carly jerked to her feet, shuffling lecture notes she didn't really need. When she walked into the room, Kiss Ass smiled from his seat in the front and started to ask about her weekend but trailed off by the end of his sentence. She must look about as cheerful as she felt. Today she was speaking on Eleanor of Aquitaine, queen consort of not one but two major countries and, for a time, the regent of England.

Pacing at the front of the room, Carly started with Eleanor's background and marriage to Louis, working toward the fiasco of the Crusades and Eleanor and Louis' eventual annulment. Then came the woman's marriage to Henry, fraught with adulterous affairs and ending in Eleanor's political imprisonment. Carly paused, her lips quirking in a moment of dark humor. Despite the unwanted onslaught of conflicting emotions during Friday's dinner with Daniel, obviously there were worse conclusions to a marriage.

His image rose in her mind, his confession that he'd felt lucky that she would go out with him. Something treacherous and too much like longing snaked through her. Had he already started work on the porch? He'd mentioned that he might stop by today because of a light afternoon schedule. *I should have asked Beth while I had her on the phone.*

"Dr. Frazer?" Kiss Ass's usually smarmy tone was now one of befuddled concern.

Carly blinked. "You had a question?"

"N-no, ma'am." He exchanged apprehensive glances with a girl next to him. "We were just wondering . . . if there was anything else you wanted to add about Geoffrey de Rancon?"

Oh, my God. She'd trailed off in midsentence. In front of her class.

She cleared her throat. "I think we'll take our break a bit earlier than normal today, if no one objects."

No one did. She barely had a chance to move out of the way before they stampeded from the room to visit the vending machines and check text messages. Trailing behind her more exuberant classmates was Laurel, dressed once again in an utterly forgettable long-sleeved T-shirt and jeans, even though the temperature was supposed to hit ninety today.

The girl actually lifted her gaze from the floor long enough to glance in Carly's direction. Was that *pity* in the kid's shadowed eyes?

Great. *When a skittish teen dragging around her own invisible luggage cart of emotional baggage feels sorry for you, you know you're screwed.*

Eleven

❦

Contents May Shift During Flight

Damn, she was running late. She was *never* late, so why today of all days?

On a deeper level, she recognized that the lack of punctuality meant this wasn't real. But the Carly in the dream didn't seem to know that.

This was it: the oral defense in front of her dissertation committee. Carly planned to go into that room and kick academic ass, then celebrate by letting her new husband take her somewhere decadent for dinner and jumping his bones afterward.

Looking forward to all of that, she parked her car and opened the door. Wait, was she... *barefoot?* She couldn't go in there like that. Glancing in the backseat, she spied dozens of shoes jumbled together. Flats? *Those aren't mine.* Not that it mattered—she had to go. *Now.* Adrenaline flooded her system. She hadn't been this nervous since she brought home that report card in middle school, the only one from her junior high years that hadn't been all A's. Samuel had—

No. She couldn't think of him right now.

Thank goodness, she'd found a pair of matching shoes. She tossed them on the pavement and shoved her feet inside. Was she actually *shorter?* She made it to the learning auditorium in record time, not running into anyone along the way.

But the chairs were all empty, and the room was oddly shadowed. The dark seemed to magnify the sole sound—breathing. Where her committee members should be sitting, there was nothing but an upright coffin, slightly ajar.

"Well. Come closer, Carlotta, and let's get this over with," Samuel barked. "You've kept me waiting long enough." The form in the coffin was jostling around; she caught a glimpse of narrowed eyes set in decaying flesh.

She did not want to approach. She wanted to wake up. *It's a dream, you dummy. It's not real.* But her feet, crammed into ugly, too-tight flats, carried her forward. Was she going to trip? She'd done that once, when she was small. He'd rushed at her, his face dark with fury over some imagined slight, and she'd instinctively shied away, tripping over a damn topiary of her mother's. That had amused Samuel to no end. He'd laughed while she lay sprawled in mortification. He hadn't helped her up but grabbed her chin between his fingers as she'd tried to stand.

"I'm not going to whip you after all," he'd told her. "But I could if I wanted to."

Now he demanded in the exact same tone, "Aren't you going to begin the formal presentation? Christ, you're dumb.

And I had such high hopes for you—my wife's looks and my brains. Everything you are, you owe to us."

No, that couldn't be right. *Everything I am is in spite of you.*

"Oh, wait," he said silky. "I forgot. You're *nothing*."

She wanted to scream. But no sound emerged from her throat. *Shutupshutupshutup!*

"Couldn't get tenure, couldn't keep your husband, can't even—"

Carly did scream then. Not an angry rebuttal to his words, but an incoherent cry that bounced off the walls of her bedroom. Her heart pounded so hard it hurt her chest. Even as she turned to check the nightstand clock, she knew the time was irrelevant.

There was no way she was going back to sleep.

At first, Beth thought she was dreaming, but then the voice came again.

"Beth?" It was an odd whisper-shout. "Are you awake in there?"

"No," Beth mumbled. Though she'd yet to open her eyes, she sensed that the room was still dark. Surely it wasn't time to go running. If she could get her eyes open, she'd check. But apparently she wasn't curious enough to go to all that trouble.

A light rap sounded against the bedroom door. "Would it speed things along if I told you I come bearing gifts?" Carly called. "All right, technically, just one gift."

My birthday. Good Lord, she was forty-five. "Is this present worth getting out of bed for?" she asked around a yawn.

"Only one way to find out. I'll wait for you downstairs."

Five minutes later, Beth plodded to the kitchen. "Are you aware that it's barely six in the morning?"

Carly nodded. "I've been up since a quarter till five."

On purpose, because she'd wanted to work in the wee hours, or for other reasons? "Well, thank you for not waking me up then." Beth glanced around. "I don't see a box or gift bag."

"Here." Carly handed over a blue envelope.

The greeting card read HAPPY BIRTHDAY TO A GREAT EMPLOYEE . . . FROM AN EVEN GREATER BOSS.

Beth smirked. "You got me out of bed for th—?" But her question ended abruptly when she pulled out the gift card that had also been in the envelope. It was for a store that specialized in women's athletic gear and clothing. *One hundred thirty dollars?* "Carly. This is . . . You shouldn't have done this."

"Don't be silly. Those canvas shoes offer you no ankle support, and if you keep running in them, you'll probably wind up injured and unable to cater my dinner party."

Beth laughed. "Well, when you put it that way . . . Thank you." She was amazed that Carly had done this—aside from their two-minute conversation when Beth had requested the night off, Carly had never indicated that she even realized today was Beth's birthday.

Figuring that her cheap sneakers could get her through one last jog, Beth followed Carly onto the porch. Streaks of sun were starting to cut through the morning chill. By noon, it would probably be ninety degrees out here.

"So what are you doing tonight?" Carly asked as she jogged in place to warm up.

"Going to a late movie with friends. I had different plans but shifted them since Joy's on bed rest and can't go with us." Beth would have been perfectly content to take her daughter some food and just play cards or something, but Joy had insisted that her mother have a girls' night out. Even if it was just to the local cinema for a couple of hours. "This way, I can still be here to fix dinner for you and Helene and help her get through her nightly regimen of strengthening exercises." The woman still relied too much on a crutch; Dr. Rylan said she should have already started weaning herself from it for short, easy distances.

"Oh, but I do have plans for another night," Beth suddenly remembered. "Allen wants to take me to dinner."

Carly paused, as if she wanted to comment, but she all she said was, "Make him take you someplace nice."

As they started down the street, Carly surprised Beth by asking, "Do you miss him? Your husband, I mean."

Not always, but at odd moments, powerful nostalgia would grip her. "Sometimes. What about you? Do you miss Daniel?" She half expected a smart-ass response about how Carly would need him to be gone more in order to miss him.

But Carly looked as if she were giving the question sincere consideration. "It was an adjustment, after he left, but—"

"After *he* left?" Beth came to an involuntary stop in the middle of the sidewalk. She'd always assumed that Carly had been the one to walk away from their marriage. It didn't seem in keeping with Daniel's character . . . or with the way he still looked at his ex-wife.

"Anyway, as I said it was an adjustment. But I made the adjustment and moved on," Carly said dismissively. "And speaking of moving on?"

"I take it this is the part where you're done with your warm-up and will leave me in the dust?" Beth asked wryly, feeling her age.

Carly flashed a smile over her shoulder. "You can think of it as fairy dust, full of sparkly birthday wishes, if that helps."

Strangely enough, Beth thought with a laugh, it did.

❧

"Dr. Frazer," came the department secretary's voice through the speakerphone, "I'm putting through a call on line one from Genevieve Baker."

Carly picked up the extension, glad for an excuse to quit reading an absolutely abysmal essay. "Hello?"

"Is this Carly?" asked a warm, throaty voice dripping Southern. She sounded like Scarlett O'Hara and Kathleen Turner's love child. "Gen Baker."

"Yes, this is Carly Frazer. I take it you got the e-mail I sent yesterday?"

"I did! And a week from Sunday would be just perfect. Thank you so much for the thoughtful invitation. I can already tell I'm going to love Ramson Neil. Everyone seems impressively competent and friendly to boot." A note of wicked humor stole into her voice. "You wouldn't believe some of the political rivalries I've dealt with on other campuses."

"Oh, I might."

"Is there anything I can pick up to bring to the dinner? A bottle of wine? Dessert? Nicely aged single-malt scotch?"

"Bring whatever your beverage of choice is, and that way even if the company sucks, you know you'll have a decent drink to get you through."

The other woman laughed. "Good rule of thumb. Some of the meetings I've been to would have been more productive, or at least more entertaining, if everyone had been allowed a flask."

Well, it was too soon to tell what Carly would think of Gen Baker in person, but it was refreshing to know the other woman wasn't obsessed with being politically correct. *If she doesn't bake pies, she's my new best friend.* After they got off the phone, Carly decided to get to class a few minutes early rather than return to grading papers. She went down the hall to the faculty lounge for a mug of coffee.

Out of the corner of her eye, she saw a couple up against a wall, the guy leaning close toward the girl, whose back was pressed to the glass of a display case. At first, Carly rolled her eyes, wondering if the young, sex-crazed imbeciles weren't aware that there were more appropriate—and certainly more comfortable—places to make out. But something in the tableau made her do a double-take. The body language was all wrong. Intimidating, not playful.

The young man was tense, radiating anger and dominance. The girl, in a cantaloupe-colored shirt and dark jeans, was shrinking away but had nowhere to go. They were both speaking softly, but there was a menacing undertone to his voice and a higher squeak to hers. *Laurel.*

Carly assumed it was the girl's boyfriend who had her cornered. He was obviously a domineering jerk, and Carly was tempted to smack him on principle. She was equally tempted to smack Laurel. Even a passerby could see the guy was bad news, and Laurel had a real brain in there somewhere. *Ditch the SOB. It's not as if you're a defenseless child trapped in the guardianship of—*

"Laurel!" Carly's voice reverberated through the corridor. "Hope you did the reading. There's going to be a quiz later."

The guy—tall enough to intensify Carly's dislike—sneered over his shoulder. "Do you mind? Class hasn't started, and we were having a private conversation."

She stopped, crossing her arms over her chest and piercing his gaze with hers. "Actually, this is considered a public hallway, junior."

What she said was irrelevant, but her expression and tone got through to him. Like most bullies, he was a coward who didn't like to waste his time with anyone who bothered standing up to him.

"Whatever." He straightened, shooting Laurel a derisive look. "I'm out of here."

As soon as he turned away, the girl shuddered. It wasn't clear from her expression whether she was relieved or chagrined that he was going. Carly wanted to shake her until her teeth rattled.

It wasn't true that Carly had scheduled a quiz for the day,

but just because no written questions were planned didn't mean she couldn't call on her students for class participation.

She decided to kick off her lecture with some verbal review. "Laurel," she said with bright cheeriness, "would you like to tell us what you think made Eleanor of Aquitaine such a unique woman in history?"

The girl jumped in her seat. "M-me?"

"You are the only Laurel in this particular class," Carly pointed out pleasantly. "So, Eleanor of Aquitaine. What made her so notable?"

"Her property holdings," Laurel mumbled, already looking away again.

Carly snorted. "Oh, come on. This isn't a middle school history class. You can go deeper than that."

Red-faced, the girl shifted in her seat. Carly maintained eye contact, patently ignoring Kiss Ass, whose hand had shot up in the air.

"She led troops into battle," Laurel said.

"True. But so did a handful of other women, as far back as biblical times. Women in China and India, later women such as Joan of Arc."

For a moment, anger shone bright in Laurel's eyes. It was a good thing Dean Murrin was out of the country, Carly thought in resignation. It could come back to bite her on the well-toned butt that she was being "hard" on a female student. Right now, she didn't care. So she continued to stare down Laurel, patiently waiting for an answer worth the words it took to articulate.

"Courtly love," Laurel bit out. "Women were often treated

like chattel, and the cultural shift Eleanor popularized encouraged men to put females on a pedestal instead. Even to swear obedience. She wielded power not by subverting her femininity, as one might argue historical figures like Joan of Arc did, but by embracing it. She led men into battle, but she also gave birth to ten children and set court fashion."

"Interesting points," Carly praised. "Thank you."

The look she got in return was far from a *You're welcome.* Laurel seemed pissed at being singled out. *Good.* Carly hoped the girl nurtured that anger. It could be amazingly motivational.

Better to be a pissed-off and bitter success than a willing victim and loser.

As a teenager focused on becoming valedictorian, Carly hadn't been as boy crazy as a lot of her peers. Even as an adult, she'd never subscribed to the theory that she needed a man. Still, coming home to a sweaty, shirtless male made Carly's heart beat unexpectedly fast and she suddenly felt more sympathetic on the subject of lust-addled impulses.

Parking the car in the driveway that ran alongside the house, she found it difficult to tear her gaze away from the sight of her ex-husband's muscular torso. He'd always kept in good shape; he worked outdoors and was a recreational athlete like herself, but he looked even better now than she remembered. Not that she allowed herself to remember often.

Even in the early days of their marriage, she'd suspected that she couldn't be quite as close as Daniel wanted. She simply wasn't wired that way, but she'd let him convince her that he loved her as she was. Although his love had turned out to be short-lived and ultimately conditional, it had been more than anyone before him had ever managed. If, in their time together, she hadn't reached that level of intimacy that inspired sonnets and Oscar-winning movies, she'd still experienced a cataclysmic physical joining that had both lured and repelled her at the same time. When she and Daniel had sex—

Oh, hell. Was he coming over here?

She got out of the car and met him where the grass stopped and the cement began. His eyes connected with hers, and she was startled by the longing that pierced her. For the past two years, any sexual desire she'd felt had been more like an itch between her shoulder blades—existent, but in a mildly inconvenient and easily ignored way. What mortified her the most about her reaction now wasn't how difficult it was to dismiss but the possibility that he might guess at her feelings.

She made a point of looking past him. "How's the porch coming?"

He dragged his forearm across his damp forehead, glancing over his shoulder. "Not bad. What about you? How's life in the higher ed?"

"I had an interesting moment with a student," Carly said. "I don't understand her. She has real potential but seems determined to sabotage herself. I'd rather not let her."

Daniel grinned. "Then she doesn't stand a chance. What's the plan, force her to discover her own fabulousness whether she wants to or not?"

"Refuse to let her hide, anyway."

Carly's mind snagged on Laurel's eventual response, what she'd said about a woman being powerful not because she tried to shirk being female but by manipulating society to value females more highly. Carly felt an inexplicable scrape of anxiety in her gut. *I don't shirk my femininity.* She wore heels and skirts nearly every day and looked damn good doing so.

"You seem deep in thought." Daniel's smile had softened into something dangerously tender. "This student's really gotten to you, hasn't she?"

"Don't buy into the idea that I'm a kinder, gentler Carly," she warned. "It's just that the kid ticked me off." There was something about Laurel's overall air of kicked-puppy resignation that made Carly angry.

"Even if it's true that you're only interceding for selfish reasons," Daniel said, sounding as if he refused to believe that, "this girl is lucky she met you. Once you've decided on a course of action, you don't let anything stand in your way."

"Right. I'm too focused and single-minded," she said wryly. In the last months of their marriage, it had been a major source of contention, that she'd been unable to put aside her driving goals and escalating workload to invest more time in their relationship and home.

"Focus isn't always a bad thing," Daniel said.

"Funny, that's not the impression you gave me when you took off."

"Carly." He reached out, one large hand cupping her cheek.

Don't say you're sorry. She'd managed, for the most part, to interrupt or shrug off his apologies because it was easier not to acknowledge how sorry she was, too. Marriage had made her feel like a square peg in a round hole, and Carly wasn't accustomed to being bad at something. Whenever Daniel had tried to express legitimate disappoint, she'd heard Samuel's voice in her head, mocking her as a fraud and a failure. As a result, she'd grown increasingly snippy and aloof, punishing Daniel for injuries he hadn't inflicted. For the first time since she'd met Beth, she half hoped the woman worked things out with her lying, gambling husband. Women like her were *meant* to be wives, skilled at it even.

Women like Carly? Not so much.

She jerked away from the heat of Daniel's touch. If circumstances were radically different—if Beth and Helene weren't both inside, for instance—Carly might invite her ex-husband in the house and allow him to screw her temporarily senseless. She'd been restless and on edge all month and would welcome the physical release. But even if it weren't for the presence of accidental chaperones, Daniel's many talents didn't run toward no-strings-attached sex. He'd want to talk afterward, to "connect."

Which wasn't one of *her* talents.

"I should let you get back to work," she said.

His eyes dimmed with disappointment but he nodded, accepting the strategic retreat. "You know me. Once I start a project, I get antsy about seeing it through."

So a couple of wooden slabs merited conscientious follow-through, while their *marriage*— She'd already said more than she'd intended to on that subject this afternoon. Carly stalked toward the house, taking only a few steps before it occurred to her that she would have to overcome her pride enough to ask for a favor.

Eyes closed, she stopped in her tracks. "By the way, I heard back from Genevieve Baker, the woman for whom I wanted to host a small gathering. She's agreed to two Sundays from now. I realize it's an imposition, but would you be willing to take my mother out somewhere that night? Maybe dinner? I'd foot the bill, of course."

"I don't want your money," Daniel growled. "And it's not that big an imposition. You adjust your schedule, make a few sacrifices for people who are like family."

"So you'll do it?"

He fell quiet, contemplating the request. "I don't know, Carly. She seemed so animated at the thought of staying for the party. It might do her some good to—"

"You're the one who made the offer in the first place!" All she was doing was asking that he check his schedule and consider following through. Why the hell did the man have a reputation for being such a great guy when he was constantly reneging? "I was just trying to take you up on it, but if you didn't mean it, then don't worry. I'll make other arrangements."

This time when she strode off, she had no intention of stopping again. She made it as far as the bottom step of the porch before he called out to her.

"Carly! Damn it, Carly, wait."

She took the stairs two at a time. She was reaching for the front door when Daniel grabbed her arm.

Whirling around, she jerked away. "Don't touch me."

"I'm not sure I ever have," he said, his expression strained with an ugly mix of anger and pain. It was all the uglier because she knew she'd put it there.

If she were a more generous woman, she never would have hated him for leaving her. He deserved someone open and loving who would gaze at him adoringly and bear him chubby babies. Someone who dotted her i's with hearts, Carly thought viciously.

"What does it take to touch you, Car?" The anger was rapidly draining from his face, leaving only a dignified anguish.

She wanted to cry and despised them both for that. "Well, if I have to explain it you . . . ," she drawled coldly.

"I hurt you," Daniel said. "And I regret that. But you were wounded when we met. Long before that, probably. What happened? How can I help?"

I don't want your help. But it was a lie, and the horrifying bubble of emotion in her throat wouldn't permit the words anyway.

He was too close, breathing in her space, his hand smoothing her hair. "You can talk to me."

Who did he think he was kidding? If she'd been able to talk to him, in that ridiculously soul-baring way he meant, they'd still be married now.

But his hopeless optimism knew no bounds. "Just let go," he whispered.

Against everything she thought she was, she *wanted* to take that advice. Disjointed sound bites and fragmented images flashed through her mind, most of them from the past month. The site of fresh earth on her father's coffin, the disdain of

Saundra Arnold and the not quite pity of Dean Murrin, the moments when Carly's gaze had met Daniel's and she'd lost her breath, the grating sound of her mother's voice, the inescapability of her father screaming at her in her nightmares, the ballooning terror that he'd been accurate in his assessment of her.

Daniel was right: She was in dire need of letting go. But the only outlets she'd ever mastered were physical.

Instead of rejecting his touch this time, she angled into it, letting his labor-roughened palm rub against her cheek. She brought up her own hands, threading her fingers through his hair. Since they were so similar in height, she didn't have to stand on her toes to capture his mouth in a searing exorcism of a kiss. Keen arousal, sharp enough to be painful, shot like lightning across her abraded nerves. She nipped at his lower lip, feasting on the remembered taste of him. She drove her tongue into his mouth as if the lewd action could drive out her demons. For one glorious moment, he gave back everything he got.

He gripped her shoulders, their kiss so carnal they might as well be having sex on the railing for the neighbors to see. But then Daniel lifted his head. Carly made a mewling sound of protest she might never forgive him for.

"Carly, we—"

"If you utter any variation of the phrase 'We should talk about this,'" she said between ragged breaths, "I will castrate you."

He clenched his jaw but kept his voice level. "You have an astronomical IQ. So you're smart enough to know that lashing out like that is just a form of running away."

"You're my *ex*-husband, remember?" She opened the front door without looking back at him. "I don't have to run away. You took care of that for me."

⁂

Beth arrived downstairs eager to break in her new shoes, sports bra (worn under a modesty-preserving synthetic T-shirt), and special socks meant to minimize moisture and blisters. To tell the truth, she was also looking forward to the morning companionship. It was odd—considering Carly was a woman who kept time by the start and finish of academic semesters and publishing deadlines while Beth measured the years by her daughter's birthdays, not to mention that Carly could run marathons while Beth barely made it to the end of the street without shin splints—but she'd discovered in these a.m. excursions a kinship she'd never expected.

Were they becoming friends?

And if they were, would the budding friendship entice Carly to confide in her? Something was clearly wrong. The other woman had come home from work yesterday, the front door slamming shut behind her, and gone straight to her room. Neither Helene nor Beth had seen her again all evening. Beth might have concluded that Carly was troubled by something at work except that, ten minutes after her uncharacteristically dramatic entrance, Daniel had packed up his tools and left in stony silence.

As Beth had dressed this morning, she'd tried to determine a tactful way to ask about a situation that was none of her business. She might not have the guts to do so in the normal course of a day, but she'd noted that in the minutes when Carly was warming up, she was more relaxed and more susceptible to personal interaction.

Unfortunately, it looked as if this morning wasn't going to afford that opportunity. Beth drew up short in the doorway of the kitchen, surprised to find her employer not in running clothes but wearing a rumpled pajama set of cantaloupe-colored pants and matching tank top as she poured cornflakes into a bowl on the counter.

Disappointment filled Beth—a vaguely surreal feeling. If someone told her a month ago that she'd be voluntarily crawling out of bed at dawn to go exercise, would in fact consider it one of the high points of her day, she would have laughed until she couldn't breathe.

"Morning," she said, her tone cautious. For Carly to miss her daily run, whatever was bothering her had to be worse than Beth had imagined. "I take it I'm on my own today?"

"I was up most of the night," Carly said. "Writing."

"Okay." Beth cast a furtive glance toward the downstairs suite. "You'll probably be getting ready for work by the time I get back. Can I talk to you about something before I go?"

Carly hitched an eyebrow in question.

"It's about your mother," Beth began. "I'm worried about her."

"Of course you are. She's such a delicate flower," Carly muttered, turning to put the milk back in the refrigerator.

Tread carefully. "Even you have to admit she's been through quite a—"

" 'Even' me?" Carly asked, her voice deceptively light. "The heartless queen bitch of the universe?"

Beth winced. "I would never say that."

"Not if you wanted to keep your job," Carly agreed with a thin smile.

As awry as this conversation was going, it had at least answered one question. They had not become friends. Beth felt squarely categorized as "the Help."

Still, it was Helene whom she was being paid to help, so she pressed forward, determined to do her job even if no one in the house was making it particularly easy for her. "I'm sure the pain and difficulty are very real obstacles for her, but she just isn't making the progress that Dr. Rylan expected to see. Daniel and I have—"

The way Carly stiffened at the mention of Daniel's name momentarily disrupted Beth's flow of thought. She'd known divorced couples who wouldn't even be in the same building with each other, but Carly and Daniel's separation had always seemed amicable in comparison. *What happened?*

Stifling her curiosity, she returned to her initial concern. "Anyway, we weren't able to figure out the best way to get through to Helene and thought you might be able to point me in the right direction."

"You want my advice?" Carly plopped her bowl of cereal onto the table. "Stop catering to her emotions. And to her emotional manipulation. Don't offer her choices. Just tell her what to do, and Helene will spinelessly acquiesce. She always does."

Beth gaped. In a single breath, Carly had called her mother spineless and manipulative. Did she truly hate her?

"You came to me with this," Carly reminded her matter-of-factly. "Did you want me to give you some motivational piece of fluff, or did you want advice that's going to work? I know my mother."

All evidence to the contrary. The two women barely spoke to each other and the more time Beth spent with each of them, the more visible the cracks beneath their superficial civility became.

"I doubt that." But as a mother with her own grown daughter, Beth had to admit, "It's a two-way street, though. I'm not sure Helene understands you any better than you understand her. For instance, when it comes to your divorce, she—"

"If I'm ever overcome with the sudden desire for a therapist," Carly snapped, "I'll find one who knows what the hell she's talking about. You're my injured mother's paid companion, not a psychologist."

Leaving her untouched breakfast at the table, Carly stood and exited the room. Beth was torn between wanting to smack her for her rudeness and wanting to hug her. Carly's need for that therapist was becoming more apparent every day.

But having problems didn't justify treating other people like dirt. Beth was tempted to follow her boss and insist that she would not be talked to that way, but she hesitated. She'd rather not start her morning by getting fired before breakfast. As screwed up as things might be under Carly's roof, Beth wasn't ready to go back to her own home.

❦

Running really did help. As Beth jogged, her thoughts ebbed and flowed, a gentle but constant tide. She'd called Joy every day since the ER incident but decided to see today if her daughter was up for a visit; Helene could either tag along, which would be good for her, or stay home with no assistance for a few hours, forcing her to depend on her own mobility. *Maybe I'll make some of Joy's favorite cookies to take with me.* She also spent some time thinking about the menu for Carly's upcoming dinner party . . . and entertained tentative plans to spit in Carly's food.

No, that would be juvenile.

"*Two* people acting badly is not an improvement," she admonished herself.

It wasn't until a man wielding a hose in his yard turned in her direction that she realized she was talking out loud to herself. Beth could feel her cheeks warm. Luckily, she was probably red-faced from exertion and he wouldn't be able to see her blush.

"Good morning," she called to him.

"Not really," he replied. But his rueful smile kept her from thinking the entire world had woken up on the wrong side of the bed. "I think I've killed more darn plants. You know anything about gardening?"

"Just enough to be dangerous." She slowed, following his gaze to wilted flowers that had been planted alongside the short sidewalk running between the driveway and front door.

He'd dropped the hose and fisted his hands on his hips.

"First the tree I planted in the backyard didn't take, *then* the daylilies, which I was told were near indestructible—"

"What happened to the daylilies?" she asked. At her own house, she had several varieties that she loved.

"Thrips." The man spat the word like a curse—which most gardeners would consider fitting. The tiny bugs were a common spring menace and had been worse this year than most. "Now this."

"Planting near the sidewalk can be tricky," she commiserated. "You have to take into account the extra heat reflected from the pavement. And you have to make sure you give the plants enough room to thrive. I learned that the hard way with some hostas."

He chuckled. "So far the only plant thriving around here is that stupid thing." He jerked his thumb toward a climbing rosebush planted in the front flower bed, much too close to the door. "I kept cutting it back just so I could get outside and realized I was encouraging it to grow more. In my defense, it was here when I moved in and not one of my own gardening mistakes. I think I'm going to yank it entirely."

"Might be your best bet." She wasn't a fan of climbers, having once had a traumatic experience with rambling rector. Beth was convinced that it was a second cousin to kudzu and that the two plants were conspiring to take over the world.

"I'm Bart, by the way. Bart McKenna. Retired here last year. You live in the neighborhood?"

"Retired?" she echoed, surprised. His close-cropped dark hair had gone gray, but his handsome face was mostly unlined, with a square jaw that showed no sign of softening. She suspected that this man was in good enough shape to run with Carly without getting winded.

"Semiretired after twenty years in the Marine Corps," he clarified. "I'm part owner of a sports bar with a couple other guys and have way too much time on my hands. I can't remember what the hell sounded so good about *relaxing*. I thought I'd travel, garden, take up golf. My swing's worse than my gardening."

She laughed. "And the travel?"

A shadow passed over his face. "My wife's idea. We spent so many years moving around based on where the military assigned us, she thought it would be a kick to go places just because we felt like it. But she died two years ago. Now traveling just seems like a lot of trouble."

Beth's conscience twinged. It seemed wrong that she wasn't making more of an effort to save her marriage when other people lost their spouses in untimely tragedies. "I'm Beth," she said. "I live two streets over, but only temporarily. I work for a woman there. It's a short-term assignment." Considering this morning's exchange, perhaps *very* short.

Bart wiped his dirt-streaked hands unself-consciously on the front of his faded jeans, then offered one to her. "Glad I met you while you were still here then."

"Me too." She shook his hand. "But I should probably head back. My employer wasn't in the best of moods this morning, and I—"

"I wouldn't want to keep you. But maybe sometime when you aren't on the clock, I could buy you a drink and pick your brain on perennials?"

Beth's mind went blank. Had a good-looking man just asked her out? Or was she reading too much into the face-to-face equivalent of posting a few questions on an online gardening forum?

"I-I'm married," she stammered. "I mean, I'd be happy to talk with you sometime, but I . . . You weren't asking me on a date, though. Were you?"

After a split second of looking as flustered as she was, he smiled. "I was, no offense intended. You aren't wearing a ring."

"None taken." She looked reflexively at her bare left hand, at the absence of the very ring set she used to fiddle with whenever she was apprehensive and in need of security. "We're separated, my husband and I."

He paused, as if unsure what the correct response was, finally offering an uncertain, "That must be difficult for you?"

"Some days more than others," she said truthfully. "Nice meeting you, Bart."

"Take care."

Well, that was awkward. But as she made her way back up the sidewalk, a girlish grin tugged at her lips. A good-looking ex-Marine had deemed her worthy of pursuing. Even though there'd doubtlessly been a smoother way for her to handle his interest, the overall effect was still a giant ego boost.

While she'd had reason in the last month to question whether she'd spend her remaining years with Allen, even when she'd thought they were headed for divorce, she'd never pondered the possibility of dating. She hadn't considered other men a possibility since her freshman year of college.

Everyone—Allen's parents, Allen himself, even her father to some extent—had acted as if she'd limited *Allen's* possibilities with her pregnancy. He'd been barely a man and suddenly his life had been predetermined. But the fact was, her options had been stripped away, too. At least, it had felt that way at the time.

But everything was different now. She had . . . choices.

A heady, dangerous word.

❦

It was difficult to avoid your own gaze in the mirror. Carly had left off the bathroom light when she staggered into the room. Still, the combination of silvery moonlight and artificial rays from a streetlight provided enough illumination to make it clear she looked like hell.

She splashed water on her face, then bent with her hands braced against the marblelike vanity, letting the silence wash over her. *God, I'm tired.* Ironic, since she'd caved to exhaustion and gone to bed "early" instead of revising chapter ten.

Minutes ago, she'd jerked out of bad dreams that she couldn't remember, thank the Lord for small mercies. She was grimly reminded of Coleridge's line from "The Rime of the Ancient Mariner" about water being everywhere, but not a drop to drink. Never in her life had Carly so badly wanted to rest. But sleep held no solace for her, only jumbled memories and fantastical fears.

She suddenly shivered, feeling eerily alone in the dark.

If you're alone, it's your own damn fault. Her rage had been unfairly directed at Daniel yesterday evening. After all, she'd kissed him. Any resulting negativity fell on her shoulders, not his. And Beth? Carly was not by nature an apologetic person—and God knew Beth had been overstepping professional bounds—but she lamented the cold anger with which she'd attacked. *Would serve you right if she up and quits.*

Heaven forbid. Not only would Carly be responsible for making new, last-minute catering arrangements for Genevieve Baker's dinner, but she'd also be left to deal with her mother.

Well, Carly had already planned to write Beth a sizable check for the groceries and extra labor required for the dinner party; she'd just up the amount significantly. The extra money would be far more useful atonement than a few clumsy words trying to make up for something that couldn't be taken back.

And what about Laurel Rogers? Carly asked herself as she padded back to her room. *You can't pay her off.*

The girl, who had attended every class since the summer semester kicked off, had been conspicuously absent today. Coincidence or the result of Carly's sharp-tongued prodding yesterday? Or, more unsettling, had the boyfriend Carly annoyed taken his irritation out on his hapless girlfriend? Why had Carly even intervened? The students she taught were legally adults, entitled to screw up their lives if they so chose. *Without* Carly's assistance mucking it up further.

Lecture, quiz, grade. Don't get involved.

Somehow, she doubted that quaint motto would go far in convincing Dean Murrin that Carly deserved to be a tenured member of Ramson Neil's faculty.

In the privacy of her own thoughts, Carly herself questioned whether she deserved it.

⁂

"I still don't understand why Daniel couldn't come with us," Helene complained on Friday, as Beth helped her out of the car.

Because he has his own business and his own life. That seemed like a pretty basic concept to grasp, but Beth suppressed the uncharacteristic sarcasm.

"You know he has to work hard to keep his business afloat. His employees depend on him." Before Helene could assert that *she* depended on him, too, Beth added cheerfully, "Besides, you're stronger now than you were a couple of weeks ago. You and I are perfectly capable of being on our own without a big strapping man to come to our rescue."

"You can tell me the truth," Helene said. "Carlotta's run him off again, hasn't she? He barely even pauses to say hi when he comes to work on the porch now and he makes sure he's gone before she gets home. Why does she have to be so difficult?"

Overlooking Carly's prickliness, Beth asked, "Do you assume all the problems between them are her fault?" While Helene had known the couple far longer than Beth had, perhaps having a history with them had robbed the older woman of her objectivity.

"Daniel is a teddy bear. Heart of gold, that boy. And Carly . . . is Carly. She's always been terrible with men."

"You mean things ended badly with all the men she dated before him?"

"All the men?" Helene huffed out a breath of disbelief. "She almost never dated."

Beth opened the door for the other woman. "So when you said she was 'terrible with men,' you weren't basing that on specific instances, just her lack of a track record?"

Helene scowled. "I don't want to talk about this. I need to concentrate on my session."

"You got it," Beth promised. But even after the discussion was aborted, she had trouble shaking her preoccupation.

It was something she never would have expected to have in common with Carly: a lack of formative romantic experience. Reverend Howard had discouraged dating, but even if he hadn't, Beth's innate shyness with the opposite sex had kept boys from chasing her. Allen had shown just enough interest to give her the confidence to respond. She wondered now: If some other boy had smiled at her like that, would she have thought herself madly in love with *him*? Had she given her heart—and body—to Allen Overton as much from gratitude as affection? A disquieting thought, and one that made her cringe at how needy she'd been in those days, away from home for the first time and desperate for a little tenderness.

Carly, on the other hand, was not someone who inspired tenderness. Had she scared off interested young men? She was a leggy blonde with a beautiful face and far more confidence than Beth had ever possessed. So why on earth had she never dated? The more Beth learned about Carly Frazer, the less she understood her.

She wasn't even sure on any given day whether she liked the woman. She was frequently rude and self-important. So why, earlier this week, had Beth genuinely found herself hoping they might be friends? The encounter in the kitchen, which had put that hope to rest, had been the last time they'd exchanged more than a sentence. Even though Carly had resumed her morning and evening runs, she spared Beth little more than a nod before leaving her behind. Yet Beth felt inexplicably compelled to defend her employer whenever Helene spoke critically of her.

For now, however, Beth had her hands full with Helene; her issues with Helene's daughter would have to wait.

When Dr. Rylan pressed to know whether Helene was doing all her exercises as prescribed at home, Beth had to intercede.

"It's imperative that you're honest with me," the man was saying. "If our initial diagnosis was wrong, then we may need to consider surgical alternatives."

"I've done everything asked of me," Helene said mulishly, her gaze fixed on her lap.

Beth cleared her throat from the guest chair.

"Ms. Overton?" The doctor peered over the top of his wire-rim glasses. "Is there something pertinent you can add?"

"Helene does try," she said, mostly to be diplomatic, "but she manages only the bare minimum of what you and Benny ask her to do. And I worry that I'm enabling her. It's my job to get things for her and make sure she's not putting undue strain on her leg, but the lack of mobility—"

"Can cause stiffness and worsen the problem," he said, swinging back to Helene. "Mrs. Frazer, we've discussed this."

Helene sniffed. "I can't believe you're ganging up on me this way. *I'm* the one who was in the accident. *I'm* the one who lost my beloved husband."

"Oh, Helene. I—" Beth was out of her chair and had taken two steps when the woman looked up, freezing her in place with a glacial glare.

Then Helene cut her gaze away and addressed the doctor as if Beth weren't even in the room. "I believe I'd like to go to the gym and see Benny now."

While Dr. Rylan was the physician in charge of her case and examined her regularly, it was a specialized therapist who worked with her during her one-hour sessions.

"All right," Dr. Rylan agreed.

Helene swallowed, lifting her chin in a picture of courage. "I'll do my best, I swear. It's just so . . ."

When she broke off, Dr. Rylan patted her soothingly on the shoulder. "I know. We all understand what you're going through. We're only trying to help."

Nodding, Helene appeared to forgive the man. Forgiveness for Beth, as evidenced sixty minutes later, would be more difficult to come by.

"Benny said you had a wonderful session," Beth bubbled as she helped Helene to the car. "Your best yet. Great work! I knew you could do it. Is there anything special you want to do to cel—"

"You set that up," Helene accused as she lowered herself into the passenger seat. "You ambushed me."

"That's not true." Beth stood her ground. "Like Dr. Rylan said, we're all trying to help."

Not for the first time, Beth experienced a frisson of wrongness. They were all trying to help *Helene*. Who was comforting Carly, who'd lost a father? Granted, she didn't seem like a person who would accept comfort graciously, but shouldn't her own mother be trying?

"Help?" Helene scoffed. "By ganging up on me? Kicking me when I'm down? I never took you for a cruel woman, Elisabeth. I swear you're getting more like my daughter every day."

At a loss for the best way to respond, Beth shut the car door, buying herself a moment's respite from her querulous charge. More like Carly? She'd lost all perspective on whether that might be good or bad.

Twelve

❧

Layovers

"Mama?" Joy's concern came through the cell phone as clearly as if she sat there on the bed next to her mother. "Are you sure you're okay?"

Beth chuckled. "You asked me that already."

"I know." Some of Joy's worry faded into wry amusement. "But your answer wasn't very convincing. If you're worried about me, don't be. The OB says I'm fine."

"I know, honey. It doesn't stop me from worrying entirely, but I promise, I really am okay." She'd just been seized with the urge to call her daughter, to hear Joy's voice as a touchstone after surviving a week with two women who didn't talk to each other enough to fight but clearly couldn't stand each other.

"Are you nervous about your date with Daddy?" Joy asked almost shyly.

More conflicted than nervous, but she chose not to share

that with her daughter. "Maybe a little." She thought of Bart McKenna—not so much the actual man, since she'd spent only a few isolated minutes with him, but the idea of him. A single man, without any vested interest, attracted to her as a woman.

If there was anything harder to imagine than her dating other men, it was discussing other men with Joy.

"I think he's nervous, too," Joy confided. "But in a good way. Excited, you know? I should let you go so you can get ready."

Ready? Beth glanced down, wondering if she should have put more effort into her appearance. She was wearing a skirt and a short-sleeved cranberry sweater, a color she thought was flattering on her. Her hair was brushed, she'd done a light application of cosmetics, and she wore her mother's pearl earrings. But it wasn't as if she'd spent any extra time deliberating or primping.

Hoping that Joy didn't pick up on her lack of enthusiasm, Beth said goodbye, jumping a little when she realized she wasn't alone.

"How long have you been standing there?" she demanded of Carly, who was leaning in the doorway.

"Only a moment. I didn't want to interrupt your call. Is your daughter okay? No more problems with the baby?"

Beth had told Helene and Carly about Joy's trip to the hospital and explained that if anything came up with the pregnancy, she would have to leave the house with little notice. "She's doing well, thanks."

"Good." Carly straightened. "It seems the same cannot be said for my mother."

"Did something happen? I've only been upstairs a few minutes," Beth said warily.

"I was referring to earlier today. You must have really ticked her off." A hint of a smile played about her mouth. "As soon as I walked through the door, she made it known I should fire your ass. Of course, she's far too well-mannered to ever say that. I gather you took my advice on how to handle her handicap?"

"Only to a point." Beth stood. "I didn't bully her. I just encouraged her, with Dr. Rylan's backing, to try harder."

Carly rolled her eyes. "She's right. You're definitely evil incarnate. I should toss you into the street."

"Glad to see you're taking the situation so seriously." Beth sighed.

The younger woman looked startled. "Why would I do that? I know what a good job you're doing. I'm not going to lend credence to her woe-is-me slant. Did you think I would?"

No, but somehow it aggravated Beth even further to see Carly make light of the situation. She'd had enough for one day of Carly and Helene's enmity for each other. "Maybe we can talk about this some other time. I should be leaving soon. I asked for the evening off, remember?"

"Of course." Carly backed into the hall. "Have a nice time. But Beth . . . ?"

"Yeah?"

"I meant what I said about you . . . doing a good job," she clarified softly. She jabbed a hand through her blond hair. "Thank you."

Beth's jaw dropped. "You're welcome."

But Carly had already vacated the space where she'd been standing.

⋘⋙

Allen had made reservations for two at Ray's on the River, a premier seafood restaurant overlooking the Chattahoochee. As Beth handed her keys to the valet, she found herself hoping that Allen had been able to restore his—*their* finances. This wasn't exactly a two-for-one burger joint. In fact, now that she was here, Beth wondered briefly if her skirt and pearls were dressy enough.

Standing just inside, Allen wore a blue suit with no tie and an anxious expression. He beamed when he saw her, the smile so boyishly handsome that it gave her vertigo—the past and the present superimposing themselves over each other in a dizzying overlap.

"Beth, you look beautiful."

"Thank you. You look very handsome yourself."

"Any trouble finding the place?" he asked. He'd been here a couple of times over the years on business; she never had.

"No." It had been a longer drive than she'd expected, but the time in her own company had been a blessed relief after dealing with other people all week.

The hostess showed them to a table and mentioned the award-winning wine list. Once they were alone, Beth asked if Allen had any interest in sharing a bottle of white with her.

"You go ahead," he encouraged with a shake of his head. "I'm abstaining from alcohol, at least for the time being. One of the issues discussed at the meetings is that a lot of us gambled in social settings where we were also drinking. That doing one can act as an unconscious trigger for the other. I've been to three meetings now," he said proudly.

"Three, already? So it's more than once a week?"

He shrugged. "Different locations have different schedules and rules. I've been experimenting to figure out what suits me best. Besides, with you gone, I've got way too much leisure time, too much sitting around in my own solitude."

Was that his way of saying that he missed her or that her absence made him worry he was more likely to entertain himself with gambling? Pragmatically speaking, probably both.

The waiter came and introduced himself, leaving them with information about the night's specials while he got their drinks. Beth selected the shrimp and grits while Allen splurged on the swordfish steak. After double-checking out of courtesy that he didn't mind *her* having some wine—and being utterly relieved by his answer—she also ordered a glass of chardonnay. She couldn't shake the feeling that she needed it.

For a man who hadn't wanted to admit he had a gambling problem, Allen was surprisingly loquacious on the topic now. He spoke about some of the people he'd met at meetings, what he'd learned about them and himself even in a short time, how he was looking for new hobbies to replace the thrill of gambling and might take up fishing, and how he was striving to repair his friendship with Everett. Beth was sincerely happy for him. Was it petty of her, then, to notice that by the time the food arrived, the only question Allen had asked her about herself all night was whether she'd had difficulty finding the restaurant?

Given that observation, it jarred her when he suddenly raised his water glass instead of cutting into his fillet. "To you."

"M-me?"

"My beautiful wife, who's taken care of me all these years, who's taken care of our equally beautiful daughter, and who gave me the swift kick in the butt I needed to take better care of myself. Thank you."

It was the second time in as many hours someone had thanked her and she felt just as disconcerted now as then.

Beth clinked her glass against his. "You're welcome."

After that, they fell into a discussion about their daughter, sharing mutual parental pride over a delectable meal, two wine refills, and a sinful dessert.

"Beth." Allen slid his credit card into the bill folio and reached for her hand. "Unless you've changed drastically in the last couple of weeks, you've had more to drink than your usual limit. Why don't you let me drive your car? I can leave mine in the area and have someone bring me back for it tomorrow."

A sound plan. The world wasn't exactly spinning, but Beth felt cocooned in a warm, sleepy haze that meant she probably shouldn't get behind the wheel. "All right."

He rubbed his thumb across the inside of her wrist; her pulse fluttered beneath the touch. "Would you like me to drop you off at Dr. Frazer's . . . or do you want to come home for the night?"

Home. A word with so many poignant meanings and associations, the very connotation designed to fill a person with longing. Did she want to go home again? There was a guest room, of course, but they both knew that wasn't what he was suggesting.

"I took the night off," she heard herself say. "I don't have to be back until morning."

Pulling into the driveway, watching their house come into focus through the windshield, was for Beth at once dreamily unreal and completely mundane. How many hundreds, *thousands*, of times had she sat in the passenger seat while Allen punched the electric garage-door opener?

He squeezed her thigh. "I'm so glad you came with me."

She lifted his hand and pressed a quick kiss to his skin. He smelled good. He still used the soap she liked, which she supposed was hardly a surprise. He'd used the same brand for years.

Inside the garage, she swung her feet out of the car and had an embarrassed moment when she realized Allen had been on his way to open the door for her.

"Sorry," she said.

"Don't be." He was shamefaced. "If I remembered to get your door on a more regular basis, you would have known to expect it. I guess I just wanted to be on my best behavior tonight."

And what about when tonight was over? In light of all his gallantry, it would be hypercritical to ask. But the question gnawed at the back of her mind.

He flipped on the light in the kitchen. "Can I get you anything to drink? There isn't any wine, but maybe water or coffee?"

"Trust me, I don't need any more wine. Ice water is fine." Watching him grab a glass from inside the cabinet, she realized with shock that she felt more like a guest here than she did in Carly's kitchen, which she'd subtly taken over as her own domain. Silly, since this kitchen had been hers for years, but she felt oddly detached.

She crossed the room to the stained-glass windows she'd always loved so much, but their brilliance was best viewed during daylight hours. Almost experimentally, she pressed her fingertips against a pane.

"Beth? Everything all right?"

"Yes." Her path might not be as straight as she'd girlishly assumed it would be when she said her vows, and she might not be entirely sure of her destination, but she had faith that she'd end up where she was meant to be . . . just as soon as she figured that out.

His leather shoes slapped at the tile as he approached. Instead of handing her the water, he set the glass on the table. Then he came up behind her, wrapping his arms around her and bending to kiss the side of her neck. It had always been one of her major erogenous zones, exquisitely sensitive but not a place on her body that made her self-conscious. The first few times Allen had kissed her breasts in college, she'd been too ill at ease to relax and enjoy it.

Now she leaned against him, the predictable sensations

rising within her. She kept her hands at her sides, simply letting herself be wanted.

His palms spanned her waist. "Have you lost weight?"

Could he actually tell that in just two weeks, or was he merely trying to flatter her? "I've taken up running."

"You?" Chuckling, he nuzzled her hair. "Doesn't sound like the Elisabeth I know."

Somewhat awkwardly, she turned in his embrace, facing him. "I'm not sure I can be that Beth anymore."

He cupped her face. "That's all right. We'll change together. Improve with age." Then he kissed her, not with a lot of technique but with an unrestrained passion she couldn't help responding to.

The woman who'd waited in vain all night for her husband to come to bed seemed like a long-ago stranger now. *This* woman was wanted by her husband, was more physically aware of her muscles and her rights to pleasure and her own reactions. If he moved his hand—or hers—where she wasn't ready for it to be yet, she simply slid it away. If he touched her in a way that sharpened her desire, she didn't hold back her response but let him know she wanted more.

She refused to let either of them rush, and he obliged. After the first few eagerly thrusting kisses, he slowed down, delighting in her and letting her touch him however she wanted. They moved in unhurried stages from the kitchen to the living room, where they half sat and half reclined on the couch, and finally to their bedroom. He peeled back the striped comforter and reverently laid her against the dark sheets.

It wasn't as awkward as she might have feared, having sex with her estranged husband. The wine helped, but instinct had kicked in, too. Allen was the only man who'd ever made love to her, and her body was primed for his touch. The only clothes left between them were his briefs, which he left on while he stroked down her body, finding her clitoris and dutifully bringing her to orgasm before shucking his underwear and sliding into her still-pulsing dampness.

Riding out her own separate aftershocks, she tried and failed to meet his rhythm. He didn't seem to mind. Murmuring her name, he tightened his hold on her, picking up speed as he neared his own climax. He threw his head back in a wordless shout. Then the room was still.

"Beth." His voice was sleepily content. "That was . . .."

Informative. She wiggled out from beneath him, her thighs sore and sticky.

He was slow to move his arm off her. "Where're you goin'?"

I don't know. But she wasn't coming back here. "Bathroom."

Once there, she moistened a washcloth with water from the bathtub faucet and sat on the side of the tub, contemplating how to handle the rest of the night. And the rest of her life. It had been good sex—a satisfying swansong to a long marriage—but there was a difference between decent afterglow and love. After she'd found her release, dispelling the mist of wine and arousal and affectionate nostalgia, she'd been left remarkably clearheaded. By the end, watching him pump into her, she'd felt more like an observer than a participant.

There'd been no deep, spiritual reconnection. Oh, she'd always love Allen. She'd spent over half her life with him, and he'd given her Joy. But Beth was no longer in mourning for what they could have been together.

Was it selfish that she was more intrigued by what she could yet be?

She wrapped a charcoal gray towel around her body and returned to their bedroom for her clothes. And the inevitable conversation. Allen wasn't quite snoring, but his breathing was deep and even. He was on the cusp of peaceful slumber, piquing her guilt. What were the chances she could break her news gently, then slip out, leaving him to sleep?

"There you are," he mumbled, reaching out a hand but not opening his eyes. "I was beginning to worry."

"Allen, thank you for tonight." She stood in the light spilling from the bathroom and drank in the sight of his face, her memory imprinting this as goodbye. "It was wonderful. All of it. But it also helped clarify some things for me."

He squinted at her. "Like what?"

"This isn't going to work out." She gave him a bittersweet smile, thinking of all he'd meant to her once and wondering why she couldn't recapture those emotions now, when he might truly appreciate her. "I won't regret the life we shared, but—"

"What?" Fully awake, he maneuvered up on his elbows. "Of course we're going to work through this."

No, because to do that, both partners had to *want* to work through their problems. She hadn't missed him nearly as much as she should have in the past few weeks. Even as taxing as the Frazer women could be, Beth had enjoyed having a job and a new routine—one that hadn't included her husband. She'd liked experimenting with new recipes instead of cooking the dishes she knew were his favorites, taking up a new hobby, knowing that she was still vital enough that men might flirt with her.

She was hesitant to verbalize any of that, though. The last thing she wanted to be was deliberately cruel.

Bolt upright now, Allen took both her hands in his. "Is this because of the gambling? You know I'm getting help for that. I can't promise so soon that I'll never place another bet, but if you give me more time . . ."

She'd given him so much time, her entire adult life. How could she explain that she wanted to reclaim it? "It's not just the gambling. Before Houston, I didn't even know about the gambling. And I went there for a reason."

"To tell me about the baby?"

"Joy's news was the impetus for the trip, it gave me a pretext for doing something rash, but getting on that plane was the act of a desperate woman. I wanted you to see me. I wanted us to . . . It doesn't matter now."

"Don't say that. Your feelings matter. I do see you," he said earnestly. "We can have everything you wanted."

She smiled sadly. "What I wanted has changed. I'm sorry, Allen."

He hung his head, looking defeated as he tunneled his hands through his hair. "I should have been a better husband. Living here on my own has made me realize how much you do, how much I took for granted. And that's only the laundry and the dishes and homeowners' association crap. You had even more on your plate when Joy lived here."

Without realizing it, he'd reinforced Beth's point. If he loved her as much as he thought he did, would he really be noticing the trivial tasks like laundry? Should he not have instead been discovering how much he missed her smile or how much he hated sleeping alone?

"You weren't a terrible husband," she said. "You provided for us. You cared for us. You were a faithful spouse and loving father. I think we played the best game we could with the hands we were dealt."

He winced. "Please, no card metaphors."

"Sorry."

Neither of them spoke for a moment. All of the words seemed small and insignificant, too trite to sever ties with the father of her child and the only man she'd ever loved. The enormity of the moment washed over her, and tears pricked her eyes. *This is really it.*

"Are you okay?" he asked quietly.

No. "I will be. We both will," she said, squeezing his hand. "I should . . . I should go. Do you want me to come back in the morning so we can get your car?"

He shook his head. "I can call Gary. He's that guy I told you about, kind of my sponsor? Or Everett."

"Okay." She swallowed. "Should we . . . How do we tell Joy?"

"I think she'll have an easier time hearing it from you."

Whether he believed that or was seizing the excuse to

duck the thorny conversation, Beth accepted the responsibil-
ity with a nod. This was her call, and she owed her daughter
an explanation.

Allen's voice was thick with the same emotion she was
fighting. "Elisabeth, are you sure I can't change your mind?"

Far from it. It would be so much easier to stay in the secure, if deficient, confines of a twenty-six-year marriage than
to break up a family and strike out on her own—completely
alien territory.

"You could," she admitted. "Probably without even trying
very hard. So I'm asking you, please, not to try."

⚜

Feeling a bit like a cat burglar, Beth removed her shoes on the
front porch of Carly's house and strove to be silent while she
unlocked and opened the front door—closest to where Helene slept. In her bare feet, she glided along the foyer, trying
to avoid the places where the floor creaked.

A dim light shone from the kitchen. Had someone left it on
for her? As she approached, however, she realized that Carly
stood at the counter, her back to Beth. She appeared to be
eating pecan pie straight out of the ceramic dish. Beth didn't
know what whisper of noise gave away her presence, but Carly
suddenly whirled, her fork gripped in her fingers like an im-
promptu weapon.

"Elisabeth! Christ, you took ten years off my life."

Beth would have said they were even for earlier, when she
hadn't realized Carly stood outside her room, but given that it
was the dead of night, she suspected Carly's shock was worse.

"I didn't mean to scare you. I saw the light on and thought I'd turn it off before I went up to bed."

"Oh." Carly slid a sheepish glance toward the pie dish. "I don't usually eat junk food in the middle of the night. Deadlines seem to bring out the compulsive eater in me. You've heard of the freshman fifteen so many college kids gain? A lot of people attribute it to dorm food or keg parties, but I think it's students nervously chowing their way through all-nighters and trying to finish term papers."

She's babbling. Beth must have really scared her. "My freshman fifteen was due to pregnancy," she said matter-of-factly. "Is there any more of that pie left?"

Carly dished up two plates and carried them to the table, stopping at the fridge to retrieve a canister of spray whipped cream. It was nowhere near as good as the real stuff, but it was perfect for one o'clock in the morning bingeing. "How was your date?"

"Great restaurant, pleasant company. I ended my marriage." Despite the gravity of the situation, she found a certain dark amusement in Carly's wide-eyed speechlessness.

"Well." Carly swallowed. "Maybe this calls for something stronger than pie. I probably have a bottle of vodka in the cabinet."

"I'm good with the pie, thanks."

"And the ending-the-marriage thing? Are you good with that?"

"I think so. It will take time." Her stint here would probably be finished in a couple more weeks, sooner if an exasperated Helene convinced Carly to get rid of her. Where would she go next? Allen had said before she left that he'd give her the house, but she had no desire to live in the home they'd built. They could sell it and split the money, which they'd need for separate residences. "I know it's only summer now, but fall's coming."

Carly raised her eyebrows. "You lost me. Are you being metaphorical?"

"No." Beth laughed. "I meant fall is actually coming. It's supposed to represent the end of the year, but I guess after all the years of putting Joy on the school bus, the beginning of September always felt like New Year's to me."

"Me too," Carly said. "We have semesters all year-round, but there's nothing quite like that fall back-to-school rush."

So this year, instead of September being a new start for Joy, it would be a new start for Beth. Heck, maybe *she'd* go to school—she never had gotten her degree. Or she could brainstorm ways to use her cooking skills to provide some income. Whatever direction her life was going to take, she didn't have to figure it out before dawn. She yawned, the sugar-laden pie acting as a sedative.

"Can I ask you a personal question?" Carly said.

Hadn't she been doing that already? "Do I get to ask you one in return?"

"No."

Beth couldn't help laughing. *At least she's honest.* "Go ahead."

"Did you get married because you were pregnant?"

"Yes." Beth could claim that, of course, she'd loved Allen

and had believed, hoped, that he also loved her, but the truth was, he wouldn't have proposed if it hadn't been for Joy.

"So you spent all these years together before finally calling it quits, but you don't resent Joy?" Carly's voice was almost childlike in her simple wonderment, devoid of its usual acid.

"Of course not. I love her. She's my—" But being someone's daughter wasn't always a guarantee of unconditional love, was it? "That's not why *your* parents married, is it?"

Carly snorted in laughter. "Because Helene was knocked up? Hell, no. I'm sure she came to her wedding night as pure as the driven snow." The acid was back.

Sighing, Beth carried her plate to the sink. "If you ever want to talk about this thing with your mother . . . or Daniel."

"There is no 'thing' with Daniel."

"Do you wish there were?"

Carly was quiet for a long time before she finally stood. "I have to get back to work."

I'll take that as a yes.

Knowing that this was liable to be one of the most difficult things she'd ever done, Beth raised her fist and knocked on the door. Peter opened it almost immediately.

He hugged her, the friendly touch almost bringing tears to Beth's eyes. She was glad that, when she left, Joy would have his sturdy shoulders to lean on.

Blinking back the urge to cry, she thrust a plastic container at him. "I made more cookies. White chocolate macadamia nut for Joy, peanut butter chocolate chip for you."

"You're gonna spoil us." But his wide smile made it clear he didn't mind. He ushered her into the small but charmingly decorated house.

Joy was sitting in an upholstered rocking chair, reading.

"Don't get up," Beth said. "I'll come to you."

They hugged, Beth reluctant to let go.

"Do I smell cookies?" Joy asked impishly.

"I'll pour three glasses of milk," her husband offered.

Pecan pie right before bed the other night, followed by a day of compulsive baking and stealing bites of cookie batter. Beth would need to expand her running regimen if she kept this up. As soon as Peter left the room, Joy rubbed her hands together.

"So? I didn't want to call yesterday because it seemed too pushy and I realize you may not want to share all the details of your love life with your kid, but—"

"Oh, honey, let's wait just a second for Peter, okay?"

Joy hesitated. "Okay."

He came back with a tray Beth recognized as one of their wedding gifts. Three coffee mugs, presumably full of milk, flanked the open cookie container. Beth stood, taking the tray from him and placing it on the coffee table. Peter studied her face and moved closer to his wife, leaning against the arm of her rocking chair.

"I wanted to talk to both of you," she said, "about Joy's dad and me. He and I had a really good conversation the other night. I think we're both in better places for it, but we're not . . .

We're going to . . ." This had been so much easier in Carly's kitchen. Finding the words to tell her own daughter was excruciating.

"Mama?" Joy's lower lip trembled.

"It will be all right," Beth promised. "We both love you as much as we always have, and that's never going to change. We even love each other, but not—"

"Oh, Mom, no. You can't. You just . . . you just have to be patient with him."

Beth swallowed an inappropriate laugh, hearing her own words thrown back at her. Hadn't she counseled Joy when she got married that it was a wife's job to put up with her husband's sometimes considerable shortcomings? Looking back, Beth had too often encouraged Joy to keep her expectations low, telling her that she didn't have to take as many advanced classes if the workload was daunting, that the rigors of medical school might not be for her, that balancing motherhood and a career might be too difficult.

I should have been a better role model. I should have told her to be true to her heart and not let fear—hers or mine—stop her.

"It's not about him," Beth said. "Not completely. Your father is trying very hard to make positive changes in his life, and you should be proud of him. I am."

"Then is this . . . is—" She swiped impatiently at tears and a runny nose, hormones taking her from zero to actual sobs in seconds. "My fault?"

"What?" Beth had heard that children of divorce tended to blame themselves, even unconsciously, but it was the last thing she had expected from her grown daughter.

Joy rolled teary eyes as Peter crossed the room for a box of tissues. "I can count. And when I was in the hospital, you all but confirmed it."

"That was decades ago, darling. This isn't about you or your father. It's about *me*." It sounded so shockingly egocentric out loud that Beth faltered, waiting to be struck by lightning or at least reprimanded for self-absorption.

But instead, her wonderful, beautiful daughter—*Allen and I clearly did something right*—sniffed twice and nodded slowly. "All right."

"All right?"

Joy, looking a bit lost, cast an anxious glance at her husband and visibly calmed. "I'm not h-happy about it, of course. But you've always been there for me. After everything you've d-done, I can't . . . I have to support you in this. If you're sure it's what you want?" she asked with transparent hope.

"I am." It was becoming more true with each passing second.

Peter turned his concerned gaze from his wife to Beth. "You know that if you need a place to stay for a little while, you're always welcome here." He waited a minute, then offered a tentative smile. "Especially if you bring cookies."

❧

"Carly!" Saundra Arnold approached with a wide smile pasted on her face, an immediate red flag. "And how was your weekend?"

"Fine, thanks." Carly continued measuring out ground coffee. There should be stiff fines for people who poured the last of it and didn't brew more. Maybe the death penalty for people who committed the offense on Monday mornings.

"I hear you're holding a little party at your place?"

"Very little, just a cursory representation of several of our departments." Shapiro, from humanities. Wilson Eckett, from chemistry, and his wife, Shayla King, from interdisciplinary studies. The provost and his wife. Natalie Reaser, head of human resources, and her fiancé. And, of course, the guest of honor. "In fact, even with the few invitations I limited myself to, I still went over the number I gave my caterer." She hadn't expected everyone she'd invited to be able to attend on such short notice.

"Dr. Frazer?"

The voice was timid, but audible, and both women turned toward the entrance of the faculty lounge. Laurel Rogers stood there, wearing a man's lemon yellow button-down shirt over a pair of baggy khaki pants. She looked washed-out and dwarfed by her own clothes. Carly was seized by the wholly insane urge to yell, "Where the hell have you been?"

The girl cleared her throat. "I know your official office hours don't start for another few—"

"I can join you in my office now." Carly punched the POWER button on the coffeemaker, her good deed for the day, and nodded a quick farewell to Dr. Arnold. She fell in step with Laurel, and they reached her office a moment later.

"Come in. We've missed you in class," Carly said.

"That's what I wanted to talk to you about. Class." Laurel paused, then glanced up from the chair she'd taken, meeting Carly's gaze. "I want to drop Western civ. But I'm past the deadline for dropping a course without either the professor signing off on the decision or taking an academic penalty."

"You want to drop the course? You're one of the best students in there! And trust me, I don't give that praise casually."

"I'm aware."

Sarcasm? Maybe there was hope for the kid yet.

"Generally if a student wants a prof to okay this decision, the student offers a reason for the change of heart. Class too tough for you?" Carly challenged. "Just can't cut it?"

Laurel glared for a moment before lowering her eyes. "Personal problems. The specifics aren't anybody's business but my own. Suffice to say, I don't think I can give your course the attention you keep telling us it deserves."

Carly leaned back in her chair. Was this her fault? She'd bullied the girl, and Laurel, true to character, was retreating. "No."

The girl's eyes flashed. "You can't stop me from dropping—"

"I wasn't finished," Carly said softly. "You said you were having 'personal problems.' I can only assume that if they're major enough to disrupt your work, they're also potentially upsetting, which means maybe this isn't the best time for you to make the decision."

"That isn't any of your business either," Laurel countered, but her tone had lost some of its vehemence.

She has a point. Laurel was technically an adult with the right to make her own decisions, even really crappy ones. So what had happened to "lecture, quiz, grade, and don't get involved"?

Carly sighed. "Wait until the end of the week," she advised. "If you really want to drop, I'll sign the forms, no questions asked. But in the meantime, swing by class if you can. I think you might get something out of the lectures and . . . the rest of us might get something out of your participation."

Laurel's eyes widened. "I-I'll think about it," she said finally. "But I'm not promising anything."

"Not asking you to."

The girl stood. "I'll be back on Friday."

Watching her go, Carly thought that perhaps refilling the coffeepot hadn't been her only notable good deed today after all.

❧

Carly thrashed in her sleep, her subconscious dredging up old memories that she could ignore during waking hours. But not now.

Seventeen, freshman year. Home for winter break—nowhere else to go. Her dorm had closed for two weeks.

She was in her old room, which looked more like a suite at a bed-and-breakfast than a place where a teenager had ever lived. A few Colonial pieces, an antique porcelain doll on the bookshelf, nothing so tacky as posters of rock groups. She'd spent the last two hours reading in her pajamas, gratified to have the house to herself.

Samuel and Helene had attended a faculty party with an open bar that night. Once they arrived home, Mrs. Frazer went straight to bed. But Samuel poured a bourbon, then came upstairs to tell Carly good night. He stood in the doorway of her room, throwing his shadow across her. For all that Samuel Frazer was a cold, unpleasant man, there had been a few rare occasions when he'd been almost silkily proud of her. Those moments were the worst.

"Women's studies? Doesn't even sound like a real program. Although I guess I know plenty of men who would sign up to *study* women." He brayed with laughter over his own wit, his smile too leering to be companionable. "Guess there was no point in challenging your old man's chemistry prowess, was there, girl?"

Refusing to be baited, she stayed silent, wishing desperately that he'd go away.

He stepped inside her room, and she experienced a moment of almost superstitious outrage, as if she couldn't believe the vampire had crossed the threshold uninvited. Samuel smirked. Far from being oblivious to his daughter's discomfort, he savored it with the same relish as his bourbon.

"Still, you hold your own, GPA-wise." He continued the one-sided conversation jovially. "Bet you're grateful you got my brains."

By her teenage years, she hadn't wanted *anything* of his; it was on the tip of her tongue to say so. She told herself she was no longer a child to be browbeaten by his harsh words and mercurial tirades. This wasn't like the time when she was thirteen and he'd backhanded her—she'd tasted her own blood and Helene had kept her home the next day so that no one could ask about the swollen lip. At seventeen, though, she was no longer a kid. If he laid a hand on her, she'd call the cops. It's what any self-respecting woman would do.

As if trying to make out someone's face across a dim, smoky bar, he squinted. "You're turning into quite a woman, Carlotta. Damned if you aren't."

Her stomach churned. Somehow the calculated commendation creeped her out far more than the times he'd insulted and berated her. She'd noticed through her high school years the speculative way he'd begun to look at her. The gleam in his eye made her flesh crawl. She'd assured herself, when she could even bear to ponder it, that it was in no way a *physical* interest. In all likelihood, he was drawn to her because the more she excelled in school, the more he saw himself in her. Samuel exalted in his own image.

The reality of that night was that he'd finished his bourbon, flashed one more nasty smile, knowing that deep down his strong daughter had wanted to hide under her covers, and he'd trailed his clammy fingers over her cheek before lumbering down the hall to join Helene. Carly had shut the bedroom door and locked it.

This was not, however, reality. This was her nightmare.

Wanting to recoil in any way possible, she squeezed her eyes shut, willing the nightmare phantom away. But she felt her father lean in closer, felt his warm, bourbon-scented breath on her face.

"Yes, quite a woman," he cooed. "Not like that woman I married. She's a shell who doesn't have an original thought in her head. Not even legal to drink, you can probably hold your liquor better than her. Helene will be passed out for *hours*."

He reached out one meaty hand, still smiling that awful grin.

No!

Carly's mind finally rebelled, jerking her out of the ghastly reimagining. She came fully awake, barely managing to leap from the bed before she gagged. Making it down the hall to the bathroom was out of the question. She dove for the wastebasket on the other side of her nightstand. Why couldn't she purge the lingering fear and disgust and hatred as easily as she could purge the contents of her stomach?

Tears welled in her eyes, unfamiliar sensations squeezing together, crowding her lungs and choking her from the inside.

She grappled for the bedside lamp, needing to see, to reassure herself that nothing lurked in the dark corners of her room. With shaking hands, she knocked the cordless phone off the nightstand. She picked it up, intending to put it back on the charger, but clutched it to her chest instead. Only one person had ever made her feel truly safe, his innate goodness temporarily blotting out much of the ugliness she'd grown up with. The ugliness that had taken root deep inside her.

Like a sleepwalker, she dialed his number, aware of what she was doing but not acting on her own volition. The chirpy sound of his phone ringing snapped her out of her trance, though. *What am I doing?* A beat of quiet, then another ring. Calling her ex-husband at two in the morning? To say what, that she was scared there was a monster under her bed? Another ri— She mashed the END button with her thumb before Daniel could answer.

Not even a full sixty seconds later, her phone rang.

She'd just discovered something else to admire about historical times. No caller ID or star 69. No grabbing the phone and foolishly calling an ex in a moment of temporary insanity. Carly imagined that back in the days when people's chief modes of communication were ink-dipped quills or the Pony Express, there were fewer impulsive mistakes.

She eyed the receiver. If she ignored the call, it might wake up Beth and Helene. Plus Carly would feel like an even bigger idiot than she already did. "Hello?"

"Hey, what is it? Your mother didn't fall or anything, did she?"

"No. It's not her. It's— Never mind. I'm sorry I woke you." Lord, she *hoped* she'd awakened him, that he was alone. The middle of the night had always been Daniel's favorite time to surprise her, rolling over and making love to her long after the hurry of the day had subsided, when she'd fallen into a deep enough sleep that she wasn't writing lecture notes in her head.

He'd tried to give that to her, those moments when she could finally let go, but she'd resisted. Even though she'd grown up in a house where she felt like she had to be on her guard every moment, it wasn't until she fell in love with Daniel that she experienced how truly vulnerable she could be. She hadn't liked it.

"Never mind waking me up," he said. "Call whenever you need me. Just tell me what's wrong."

Whenever you need me. The words lacerated her. She didn't *want* to need anyone, yet here she was huddled in a ball in the floor of her room, blindly dialing him. "I'm sorry," she repeated. "I'm sorry I'm such a mess. I'm sorry I was such a—"

"Carly, stay put. I can be there in five minutes."

Not without breaking several major traffic laws, but she didn't object. It wasn't until after she hung up the phone that she realized she was crying, which explained the alarm in his voice.

Even if he ignored the speed limit, she had some time. Moving with bone-deep weariness, feeling she'd aged a hundred years since she'd lain her head on the pillow that night, she started cleaning up both herself and the room. Fifteen minutes later, she'd restored some semblance of normalcy in her appearance and set the rinsed-out garbage can on the back porch. She wanted to call him on his cell phone and say it had been a false alarm, but she knew he'd ignore her. Push past her comfort zone and try to be by her side—again.

Didn't he ever learn?

Having replaced her camisole top with a flannel shirt over drawstring pajama bottoms, she dragged her comforter down the steps, like a kid with a security blanket, and decided to wait for Daniel on the front porch. By the time his truck's headlights hit the porch railing, she'd situated herself in the padded wicker love seat. Even at this hour it was warm and muggy outside, but the worst of the Georgia humidity had eased. Now the air was soft, a dewy caress against her skin.

He bounded from the pickup, hair on end, gray T-shirt inside out. "Carly?"

The wealth of tender concern in his voice was intolerable, like some well-meaning idiot hugging you when you were already trying not to cry and sending you over the edge. That was a phenomenon Carly had witnessed in other women. She herself rarely cried. And she never hugged.

Apparently Daniel had missed that memo. Instead of taking the available chair positioned across from her, he invaded the love seat, scooping her into his arms and squeezing her to him. "Whatever it is, I'm here."

"No kidding. I can't breathe."

He pulled back, his expression contrite.

When he didn't say anything, she realized he was waiting for her to start. Where? *Why?* Would her picking at old scabs really achieve anything besides ugly scars? But she owed him something. Not even Carlotta Frazer was such a raging bitch that she'd wake a man in the middle of the night, make him drive across town, then tell him to get lost without at least a bare-bones explanation.

"I had a bad dream," she said lamely. She probably sounded like an eight-year-old.

"What about?"

He'd asked her that several times during their marriage, and she'd mostly prevaricated that the nightmares were difficult to remember once she was awake. Lying went against her abrasively forthright nature, and she didn't do it well. "My father."

"The crash?" he guessed.

She shook her head.

"Do you miss him?"

Unable to stop herself, the nightmare too fresh in her mind, she shuddered in revulsion. "Hell, no. I'm—" What, relieved he was gone? What kind of human being took morbid joy in the demise of a parent? She barely even qualified as an abused child. It wasn't as if anyone had locked her in closets for days on end. She wasn't a victim.

Aren't you? How long did she think she could pretend that she was flourishing professionally? Even if she *did* manage to procure tenure, how much did it really matter? In marriage, in her personal life, she was every bit as worthless as he'd always—

"Hey. Hey!" Daniel jostled her left shoulder. "I lost you for a minute there. Where'd you go?"

"No place good." She scrubbed her hands over her face. "I'm so tired, Danny. So goddamn tired."

He didn't even wait for her to finish the sentence before he'd started repositioning himself on the seat, tucking her against his broad shoulders. She was horrified by how desperately she wanted to let herself lean on him. Just this once. Just for now.

"Rest," he said, stroking her hair, offering comfort so seductive she could barely keep her eyes open.

"I can't." Her stiff muscles wouldn't cooperate. "I know I pushed you away. I know if I had a lick of sense I'd just relax and let . . . I *can't*." Frustration battered her, ruthlessly finding all the fissures in an aged and weakened dam. Hot tears stung her eyes and rolled down her cheeks.

"It's okay," he lied, more chivalrous than helpful.

She laughed. "What definition of 'okay' are you using, Daniel? Take a good look. I am one fucked-up piece of work. I always have been. I just . . . I was able to hide it better. It should be better now that the SOB's dead, but it's not. I keep—"

"Your dad." Daniel was rigid with tension. "What the hell did he do to you?"

She almost laughed again, more hysteria than humor. Had there ever been a person who less embodied a *dad* than Samuel Frazer? "Nothing much. It's not like you think, not how I'm probably making it sound."

When had she stood up? She dropped the blanket from around her and started pacing. "He was impossible to please. He wanted me to be the best, but not if it meant outshining him. He wanted Helene to keep her mouth shut unless it was to proclaim his brilliance or parrot back his own opinions, but then he belittled her for not being able to think for herself. He ordered our house in his own self-image, wanting us to reflect back the things he loved best about himself. He was cruel, a quick-tempered tyrant.

"When I was a girl, I lived in a constant, nonspecific terror of him. Now that he's gone, I should feel safe. But I'm terrified that . . . that—"

"Go on," Daniel urged.

Go *on?* She was bleeding to death emotionally, her insides pouring out, and she wanted nothing more than to stanch the flow. Pressing her arms to her stomach, she doubled over. "I'm scared to death that he got what he wanted after all, that I've become just like him."

There. That was the worst of it. Worse even than the sometimes-unholy glint in Samuel's eye. Far worse than the nightmares and the deep-seated fear that she would never get tenure, that she would fail. What if she'd actually become the thing she loathed the most?

"Carly." Her name was no more than a breath as Daniel

rose. He didn't reach for her this time, didn't crowd her or grab her. Instead, he simply braced his feet and spread his arms, opening himself to almost certain rejection.

She was rooted to the spot. Only a few feet separated them, but it might as well have been the length of Napoleon's doomed march through Russia for the dread she felt and distance she perceived. *Run away,* she wanted to tell Daniel. *Save yourself.* He had, once. Exhibiting well-honed but short-lived survival instincts, he'd tried to wash his hands of her.

"Why do you keep coming back?" she croaked.

"Because you're here."

His courage flowed between them like an electrical current, a psychic jump start, lending her just enough to propel her into motion.

She was already arching up to meet his mouth when he bent down to kiss her. The scent and taste and feel of him were dizzying. Carly had never realized how erotic solace could be. His hands stroked a rhythmic pattern over her spine and she angled her hips, pressing closer to his body. Her blood beat hot in her veins, and her nipples were already hard points. She wanted him to touch her there; she wanted him to touch her everywhere.

She sucked at his lower lip, releasing him long enough to say, "More."

He let her press him back onto the padded bench and she straddled his thighs, her hands braced on the coarse wicker behind him. As they exchanged long, drugging, openmouthed kisses, she rocked against him, grinning at his moaned response. When his hands skimmed up under her shirt, she tried, for the neighbors' sake, to stifle a cry of her own. She hadn't bothered putting on a bra, and the slide of his skin against hers was so perfect, she could have wept.

She felt his smile against the hollow of her throat as he asked, "More?"

"God, yes."

He clasped her hips, temporarily immobilizing her. "Here?"

Pretending to misunderstand the question, she took his hand in hers and slid it down her abdomen to the juncture of her thighs. "I was thinking, *here*."

His chuckle was as rich a caress as his touch. "We can stay on the porch if that's what you want. But I didn't exactly come prepared for this."

Condoms. It had been so long since she'd had sex, she'd forgotten. With a groan, she bumped her forehead to his. "I have some upstairs." Which suddenly seemed like a very long way away.

"Race you to the top," he whispered.

Trying to stifle laughs and creaks and Carly's curse when she stubbed a toe, they found their way through the dark to the bottom of the steps.

"If this is a race," Carly managed between kisses, "you're cheating."

His thumb brushed her nipple beneath the soft flannel shirt. "Complaining?"

"*Yes.*" But only because the condoms were still too far away.

It wasn't until they sneaked past Beth's closed door and

finally entered the bedroom that Daniel's expression became solemn. "I know you were upset tonight, Car, and—"

"Take advantage of me," she instructed, already rifling through the nightstand. "I insist."

He flashed her an endearing grin. "Well, if you're sure."

What she *was* was so turned on that stringing together coherent words was becoming an effort. She wanted Daniel with her, inside her, all around her. He lunged for her, and they hit the bed in a roll, kissing as they debated without words who would be on top. She won.

When they were both naked and he was stretched out before her like some decadent pagan feast for her enjoyment, she lowered herself in aching fractions of movement. Daniel growled at her slow progress, and she almost laughed, feeling giddy, *powerful*—and she definitely hadn't shirked being female. She'd never been so grateful to be a woman. Closing her eyes, she leaned back and found her own celebratory rhythm.

Just as her inner muscles clenched and tremors began, Daniel rolled her over, rearing back and burying himself in her, heightening her orgasm so much that she almost shouted his name. Her pulse pounded in her ears, and little dots appeared in front of her eyes. The perfect state of being, as far as she was concerned, sated and not quite conscious but not asleep. Resting, without dreaming.

Without opening her eyes, she felt for his hand amid the sheets and raised it to her mouth, kissing his fingers. *Thank you.*

He gathered her against his chest, the lullaby of his heart beneath her head.

She yawned. "You shouldn't stay. Helene, Beth . . ."

"I'll go soon."

"Soon." Carly snuggled deeper into his hold.

And slept.

Thirteen

Returning to the Correct and Uptight Position

Carly woke in gradual golden stages. She'd been out cold. Was this what a bear felt like, coming out of winter hibernation? She'd lost all sense of time, merely floated in a black sea of blessed oblivion.

But her perfect contentment lasted only until she realized there was a leg tangled with hers beneath the covers. A hairy, muscular leg.

"Daniel!" Her eyes flew open. Sunlight streamed into the bedroom, and her ex-husband was sprawled naked partially atop her. "Daniel, wake up."

"Go in a minute," he mumbled. "Just need a sec to recover."

"That was hours ago," she said, a dart of amusement piercing her exasperation.

Hell. What was the point in rushing him? Since Beth had taken to getting up early and running, she'd probably seen his truck in the driveway by now anyway. *Maybe I can convince her we were up here discussing blueprints for the porch.*

She laughed aloud, prompting Daniel to open one eye curiously.

"Laughing at my morning hair?" he demanded.

"No, but now that you mention it . . ."

He reached around her to swat her bare backside. But some of the playfulness left his tone when he asked, "How'd you sleep?"

"Like a rock," she admitted. "A well-laid, deeply satisfied rock."

The corner of his mouth twitched. "I do aim to please."

She thought of their honeymoon. "I remember."

"So." He sat upright. "This is the part where you kick me out?"

"I have to get ready for work. And so do you," she added, not wanting to spoil a nice moment by reminding him of all those times he thought she'd been more into her work than her marriage.

"Very true," he agreed. "I don't want to get off schedule and upset any of my customers. Some of them can be a little . . . high maintenance. Like this one professor? I'm restoring her front porch, and she— *Oof.* Technical foul," he complained, grabbing her arms. "You can't hit a guy with a pillow before he's had coffee."

"Coffee? Don't tell me you were going to venture into the kitchen. I was hoping you'd toss on your clothes and climb unobtrusively out the bedroom window."

He searched her face. "You are kidding?"

"Mostly." She would prefer hustling him out of the house with as little interaction with anyone else as possible.

"Ashamed of me?" he asked lightly.

Ashamed of myself. The sex had been amazing. She hadn't slept that well in . . . ever. And she was awed by Daniel's generous spirit. But in the clear light of day, the memory of how clingy and weepy she'd become was tough to swallow.

"I see."

Carly blinked, feeling as if she'd missed a crucial part of the conversation. "What?"

"I know that look. You're regretting last night," he surmised.

"Not all of it." She squeezed his upper arm. "Come on. You know that was . . . intense for me. I loved being with you. I-I hope we can do it again. The sex part, anyway." The part with her sobbing on the front porch sucked.

His mouth twisted. "Booty calls? Is that how you see us?"

"I don't know! I just woke up. We're divorced, for crying out loud. I wasn't prepared for a morning-after postmortem."

His back to her, he stood and pulled on his jeans. When he turned around, his expression had softened minimally.

"You don't have to answer this now, Carly, but I will need one eventually: What *are* you prepared for? I've regretted a thousand times walking out on you, and I wouldn't blame you if you refused to give me a second chance. Although," he said drily, "that particular horse may be out of the barn already.

"The thing is," he continued, "if you do decide to give me—give us—that chance, it has to be different than it was before. I won't repeat the daily friction of loving a woman who kept me at arm's length."

"I am sorry for that. You deserve love." The real kind, not the limited version that might be all she was capable of.

He brushed his knuckles below her cheekbone. "So do you, Carly. So do you."

❧

Since they'd ruled out the shimmy-down-the-drainpipe exit, Carly agreed that she'd go downstairs and fix some coffee for both of them while he showered. She also agreed to run out to his truck and grab his generic change of clothes. In his line of work, Daniel explained, he always made a point of keeping a clean set handy.

Carly wondered if Beth might already be out running, but no, the woman was icing a round pan of freshly baked cinnamon rolls, the smell of which made Carly groan in ecstasy.

Looking over her shoulder, Beth smirked. "Good morning, sunshine. Sleep well?"

Narrowing her eyes, Carly threatened, "Not one word when he comes downstairs."

"Or what?" Beth challenged with a barely disguised giggle.

Carly had once been considered the terror of all incoming freshmen; now she couldn't even unnerve her makeshift cook. "I could fire you, you know."

"Three days before your dinner party?" Beth snorted. "I don't think so. Good luck finding anyone else to put up with you at my salary."

Knowing she couldn't argue either of those valid points, Carly shook her head and turned away before Beth saw her grin. Carly never could have guessed a month ago how much she'd come to like Beth. And, hard though it was to believe, she didn't think Beth minded putting up with her.

By the time Daniel was dressed and ready to go, Helene had also gotten out of bed. The four of them shared a simple meal so absurd that Carly felt like Franz Kafka and Lewis Carroll might approve. If breakfast lacked the exterior drama of waking up as a cockroach or falling down a rabbit hole, the internal currents were definitely surreal. She was sitting across the table from the man who had divorced her, while her employee, a conservative preacher's daughter, seemed thrilled that Carly had hit the sheets last night. Beth could barely pass sugar for the coffee without making it a double entendre. At the opposite end of the spectrum was a glowering Helene— the woman who'd insisted countless times that Carly shouldn't be alone. Instead of being overjoyed that her once beloved son-in-law might be wooing Carly again, the woman was so sour that Carly's face puckered every time she glanced in her mother's direction.

Even given Helene's obvious displeasure, Carly was shocked at the way her mother whirled on her once Daniel drove away. "This is tacky even for you, Carlotta."

"Excuse me?" Carly was more nonplussed than indignant. Since when did Helene lash out so aggressively?

She'd always been quietly critical, a counterpoint to her husband's malicious bluster. Carly had spent much of her adolescence wishing her mother would grow a spine, wishing she would just once snap and tell Samuel to shove it when he was belittling her. With him gone, it seemed like an opportunity for Helene to come out from his shadow, to discover herself, the way Beth was in the wake of her separation.

Helene was changing all right, but steadily for the worse. It was as if, with Samuel dead, his widow was having to play both parts of the dysfunctional duet—victim *and* bully. *Or in my mother's case, Jekyll* and *Hyde.*

"You wait until everyone's gone to bed and summon your ex as if he's some . . . some boy toy! Then flaunt him in front of us this morning. Did you spare even a moment's consideration for how you might embarrass Beth?"

Beth looked startled that Helene, who'd been sharp-tempered with her all week, was suddenly worried about her delicate sensibilities. "I'm fine. Besides, it's *Carly's* house. You and I are just visitors."

Yet another one of this morning's surprises. Carly searched her memory banks. When was the last time anyone had gone to bat for her, defended her even though she was eminently capable of doing so herself? It was unexpectedly touching.

Warmed by Beth's allegiance and mellowed by last night, Carly simply sighed. This certainly wasn't worth the agitation of a screaming match. "I don't understand, Mother. Didn't you want me to patch things up with Daniel?"

"I wanted you to be worthy of him in the first place! But you weren't, were you?"

Carly heard Beth's sharp intake of breath but responded before her empl—before her *friend* could. "I'm not sure that I was." And she wondered, in light of what Daniel had said this morning, if she could be. If she could live up to all that he needed and rightfully deserved. "But it's none of your business. Instead of fretting about me, you should invest your energy in getting well."

And then get the hell out of my home.

"Dr. Frazer?"

Carly diverted her attention from the computer notice that the textbooks she'd requested for the fall were no longer available to the young woman standing in the doorway. It took her a split second to place Laurel Rogers. Though her clothes were as baggy as ever, she'd skimmed her hair back in a ponytail, revealing an attractive oval face and a purposeful gaze that Carly hardly recognized.

"Laurel. Come in."

The girl hesitated, then tightened her hold on the backpack she had slung over one shoulder. "I don't want to keep you. I just wanted to say . . . I know I've missed a couple of classes, but if it's still all right with you, I want to stay in Western civ."

"Glad to hear it." Carly smiled. "Just for my own personal reference, in case a situation like this ever arises again, was it something brilliant I said that changed your mind?"

Instead of laughing, Laurel seemed to take the question seriously. "Actually, no. It was my own decision. That personal matter I mentioned?"

Carly nodded.

"I broke up with my boyfriend." It came out a whisper. Laurel was still a long way from belting out "I Am Woman" feminist anthems, but every song needed a few introductory notes.

"The guy from the hall?" Carly clarified. "Good call. You're better off without him."

"I know that. And it's what got me to thinking. I dumped him so that I could be . . . well, so that some things could be different. And quitting your class didn't seem different—it seemed like old habits. So anyway, I'm staying." She jutted her chin out defiantly, then ruined the effect by adding, "If that's okay?"

"We would be glad to have you," Carly said, mentally pumping a triumphant fist in the air. She'd asked Daniel not long ago if he thought people could change; remarkably, it seemed they could. "Don't forget. There's a quiz on Monday."

"Got it." As she was leaving, Laurel blurted over her shoulder, "Thanks for not letting me give up."

Aw, you didn't need me, kid. Laurel had found her own power to stand up for herself.

It was a thought that nagged at the back of Carly's mind the entire way home, like a lingering melody you can't remember the name of. But when she stepped inside the house and saw her mother in the front living room, it all coalesced. For years Carly had mistakenly assumed that her simmering rage was directed at her father, while her mother was more to be pitied. She'd never realized how angry she was at Helene, too.

Lifting the remote control, Carly snapped off the television set. In the background she heard kitchen noises, presumably Beth making initial preparations for this weekend's dinner.

"I have something to get off my chest, Mother." Talking to Daniel about her father last night had been like lancing an infected wound. Eventually, Carly hoped she'd heal. But the immediate aftermath wasn't pretty or clean. There was a disgusting, puslike fury that needed to be wiped away. And she'd been overlooking the major source of that fury for years.

Helene shrunk back against the sofa cushions. "Has Elisabeth said something hateful to poison you against me? You know I tried to be her friend, but—"

"A student of mine came to see me in my office today—a timid teenager who's been dating a jerk. It turns out she had the backbone to stand up for herself and leave him."

Looking bored, Helene eyed the remote. "Good for her. I fail to see what this has to do with me, though. After all, you've never bothered sharing your work anecdotes with me before."

"Really, Mother? You really don't see what this has to do with you? Then maybe you're actually as stupid as he always said you were." While it was disturbing to use Samuel's words, she needed her mother to know how it felt. *All those years.*

"Carlotta!"

But Carly couldn't be swayed by her mother's outrage; she was too busy choking on her own, thick as bile. "I alienated my own husband, so maybe I'm not fit to judge your decisions as a wife. But if you couldn't find the balls to stand up to your husband when he belittled you, couldn't you have at least stood up for your child?"

"I'm sure I don't know what you mean." Helene's tone was arctic.

"He was a monster! You *know* that. You heard how he talked to me—how could you not? He was usually screaming! Even if you pretended not to notice how he started looking at me once—"

"You shut your ungrateful mouth," Helene ordered, her voice quavering. "Your father was—"

"Do. Not. Say he was a great man. Not ever again in my hearing."

That myth had been rammed down Carly's throat from all sides—from her mother, from people in higher ed who knew him by reputation. The legend of Samuel Frazer, Great Man, could die along with him. She was happy to put the nails in that particular coffin.

"He was intelligent," Carly conceded, even that small, flattering truth difficult to get out. "And he was somewhat gifted in chemistry. But those don't exempt him—or you—from basic human decency!"

"He . . . I put up with a lot, accepted it as my role," Helene whined. "Some of his ideas, if they'd come to fruition, could have changed the world. And I would have been standing right at his side."

His ideas had often proven to be cost-prohibitive or otherwise impractical in application; in the end, they'd been little more than academic pipe dreams. But Carly couldn't care less about his legacy in chemistry. She was distraught over what legacy she'd inherited—from both her narcissistic, damaging parents. "I was a *child*. Did you let him come after me because it took the pressure off you?"

"You horrible, horrible wretch," Helene hissed, looking ugly and old. Years of barely masked bitterness were beginning to etch grooves on the former debutante's face.

Trying to restore the tattered shreds of her calm, Carly left the room. She'd said what she needed to, but she refused to stand there as a target under her own roof while the woman who should have loved and shielded her hurled more insults.

Helene lobbed one last attack, her screech distorting the Southern drawl she normally used for company. "I weep for the other babies I lost. I didn't deserve *you*."

I quite agree.

⁂

"Please tell me she's ready to go." Carly spoke through gritted teeth. "Daniel will be here any minute—and our guests will start arriving soon after that!"

"Not yet. I'm still working on her, but it will be okay. We have time," Beth lied. If the situation weren't so tense, she might have found Carly's frazzled demeanor endearing. Beth found herself wanting to impress everyone tonight on Carly's behalf.

They were cutting the schedule a little too tight, though. Daniel had wanted to pick up Helene earlier but had ended up working a landscaping job that afternoon—a project that was behind because of rain delays. And Beth couldn't drive

Helene to his place because she needed to finish food preparations. No one even broached the possibility of Carly taking her mother.

The two Frazer women alone in the car? Lord, no.

Frankly, Beth was surprised at how well they'd managed in the same house. When she'd overheard most of Carly and Helene's conversation, including Helene's hateful insinuation that she wished her daughter had never been born, Beth had braced herself for the ill will to escalate. But it had grown deceptively calm.

The night of their argument Carly had taken dinner in her room and Helene, with a new Personal Enemy Number One, had reverted to being sweetness and light with Beth. Her manner was saccharine and unbelievable now that Beth had taken a clearer look at what lay beneath, but at least Helene wasn't making her days directly unpleasant.

With the exception of being flustered about this dinner—and about Daniel, who'd continued to work on the porch so that it would be finished by tonight—Carly seemed more centered than Beth had ever seen her. When they'd first met, she'd admired Carly's poise but it had been an aloof self-possession that made her unapproachable. She wasn't distant now, merely ... serene.

Well, not right at this *moment*. But in general.

Beth rinsed her hands at the kitchen sink. "I'll go check on your mother again." Helene had raised passive resistance to a new level. She was getting dressed for her dinner with Daniel, but had "slipped" after her shower. And changed her mind twice about what to wear.

"Thank you. I can't deal with her," Carly admitted. She had fallen back on the same strategy she'd employed when Beth first came here, doing her best to ignore her mother's presence. At the time, Beth had viewed Carly as cold. Now she thought Helene should consider herself damn lucky that her daughter even let her stay.

"Should I tell her that, ready or not, she's leaving this house in fifteen minutes, even if I have to drag her bodily in her slip?"

Carly's face broke into a bright, sunny smile. "Yes, please."

The doorbell rang, and Beth paused. "Want me to get that first?"

"It won't be the guests yet," Carly said. "Just Daniel."

Just? The slight blush climbing Carly's cheeks belied her nonchalance.

Beth chuckled. "I'll leave him to you, then."

There had been no more mornings when she woke up to find Daniel's truck parked outside, but he'd not only come by to complete the porch repairs—he'd started calling Carly when he got home. She'd disappear into her room to wait for his calls, shutting her door and reminding Beth of when Joy was a teenager in the throes of major crushes. Before, the only noises that had come from down the hall from Carly's room were the machine-gun staccato of typing and the occasional alarmed cries at night. Now, more often than not, there was the husky murmur of Carly's voice as she talked to her ex-husband, their conversations punctuated by the occasional wicked giggle.

Beth had never been more pleased to see two people re-connecting. Staying in the marriage hadn't been right for her and Allen, but that didn't mean second chances were wrong for everyone.

She knocked on Helene's door, a cursory formality before she pushed it open. "Daniel's here." *So get your butt in gear.* But as gratifying as the direct approach might be, Helene was too mulish for that. She'd only dig in her heels and find some way to go even slower. The trick with Helene was to cater to her own delusional view of the world, the one in which she was persecuted and everything was conspiring against her.

"I know it's difficult for you to get ready by yourself," Beth said, "so I came to see if I could help you."

Helene, sitting at her vanity, turned with narrowed eyes. "You mean that daughter of mine sent you to chase me out."

"Carly didn't send me. I volunteered," Beth said truthfully. "You haven't had an evening on the town in such a long time, and I knew it would be important for you to look your best. Need any help?"

The woman's thin shoulders slumped beneath the royal blue top she'd finally chosen. "Well, my hand's not as steady with makeup as it once was."

"Okay." Beth did a mental rundown of kitchen duties. The slow-cooked roast was simmering in chopped onions and red wine, scheduled to be ready an hour and a half from now. Beth would first bring out appetizers, which were ready to go, followed by the cucumber-and-tomato salad for the first course. She still needed to get dessert in the oven, once she'd taken out the corn bread biscuits, three-potato casserole, and vinegared green beans, which were currently cooking; the pie would have plenty of time to bake during dinner.

For now she could spare a few minutes here.

"Do you think this outfit looks all right?" Helene asked innocently, as if she hadn't already made a couple of wardrobe changes. "Maybe it's too dressy. Daniel might only be taking me for barbecue."

"Now you know that's not true." Exasperation leaked back into Beth's tone. "He asked *you* to pick the restaurant before he made the reservation. And you look beautiful."

On the outside, at least.

What kind of mother was so completely careless with her child's happiness and well-being? Though Beth didn't have all the details, and knew better than to ask for them, she had pieced together that Carly had been emotionally abused by her parents. Overtly by her father, who sounded like a nut job with anger-management issues, but perhaps more insidiously by her mother. In standing idly by, had Helene impressed on her daughter that she wasn't entitled to—didn't *deserve*—any better than what her father inflicted on her? That she wasn't worthy of love or even common courtesy? Had Carly grown up in a home where no one showed her kindness?

"Ow!" Helene jerked back, cupping her hand over one eye and glaring with the other. "You stabbed me with the mascara wand."

"Oops. Sorry." With effort, Beth kept her thoughts to herself and finished the older woman's makeup in record speed. "There. Perfect! You guys should probably get going now. They're predicting that a thunderstorm will blow through later, so this is your best chance to get to the restaurant without driving in bad weather." Spring storms in Atlanta could be powerful forces, but often ended quickly, fading with flickers of distant lightning and marked more by high winds and hail damage than actual rain accumulation.

"Is this really dramatic enough for an evening look?" Appearing not to have heard anything Beth had just said, Helene gave her reflection a critical once over.

"Let's be honest, Helene. Smoky eye might be lovely on a twentysomething girl going to the theater, but on women of a certain age?" Beth allowed herself a slight smile. "You don't want to look like some sad ex-diva trying too hard to recapture her youth by troweling on the makeup."

Helene stiffened. "Are you—?"

Divine intervention came in the form of the doorbell. "Oh, it sounds as if the guests are arriving. I have to help the hostess, but I'll let Daniel know you're *all ready to go*." She power-walked out of the room before Helene could find reason to delay any longer.

Beth reached the foyer just in time to overhear a female voice chirping that she was sorry to be early but that, having never been to Carly's home, she'd allowed more time than she needed.

"No problem at all," Carly said. Only someone who knew her well would see the panicked look in her eyes beneath the composure.

Daniel, who knew her well, surreptitiously gave her elbow a supportive squeeze.

The brunette in the dotted Swiss dress held up a bottle of Bacardi with a ribbon tied just below the cap. "Where can I put this?"

Carly caught Beth's eye, obviously seeking some reassurance that Helene was ready for departure. Beth inclined her head slightly.

"Elisabeth, come meet Dr. Shayla King, one of Ramson's wonderful professors. Shayla, this is Beth, the genius behind the delicious smells wafting through my house. Why don't you follow her to the kitchen?"

"Right this way," Beth said with a smile. "Would you like me to go ahead and mix you a drink? Or maybe I can get you an hors d'oeuvres?" With any luck, Carly and Daniel could march Helene outside and have her gone before anyone else arrived.

Unfortunately, "marching" seemed to be out of the question. When the next guests appeared, their outerwear beaded with silvery rain drops, Helene was leaning on her cane, doing her damnedest to seem too frail for the simple journey to the front door. The guests—an older married couple both wearing black—turned out to be the provost and his wife.

The man immediately crossed the room to Helene. "Mrs. Frazer, I haven't had a chance to personally convey my condolences. I didn't know Samuel well, but his reputation preceded him."

Helene darted her daughter a venomous look. "Yes, he was a *great* man."

Simultaneously, the provost's wife had been greeting Daniel warmly. "Daniel! How lovely to see you. I didn't realize you and Carly had gotten back together."

"Er . . ." Daniel swallowed, glancing questioningly at his ex-wife for direction. Not that she noticed because she was too busy contemplating matricide.

Outside, the wind howled ominously.

"So," Beth chirped, "who wants a drink?"

—⇽✦⇾—

After greeting another wave of guests—only one person was missing now—Carly excused herself to the kitchen to get a platter of hors d' oeuvres.

"I was going to bring those out for you." Beth glanced up from the dough strips she was layering over top an apple pie. "I just needed one more minute to finish this."

"Don't worry. I wanted a second back here to breathe," Carly said, her blood pressure still soaring from the aborted scene with her mother. Daniel, God bless him, had announced that he wouldn't want Helene to miss reservations at her favorite restaurant and propelled her out the door. *I owe him big-time.* He could have whatever form of thanks he wanted. Smiling over that thought, she said, "Now all we need to make this Get to Know Genevieve dinner perfect is—"

"Genevieve?" Beth asked. "That's who called while you were greeting Dr. Shapiro. She's on her way but got a bit tied up at her new house, where she apparently had to wait for a repairman all day. She said she would be here soon."

Carly lifted the tray of marinated mushrooms and mini quiches. "Excellent. Then I'll just take these to circulate through the room. People are already enjoying the red pepper hummus you set out. And the fried pickles," she admitted with a shake of her head.

Laughing, Beth chided, "I told you. It's a Southern delicacy."

"Yeah, well, just between you and me, we Southerners are weird." Grinning and feeling as if this dinner might turn out to be one of the best ideas she'd had in years, she pivoted toward the doorway.

Only to drop the silver tray when a thunderclap rattled the house.

"Oh, *crap!*" Carly's exclamation came as much from being startled as from watching the appetizers slide onto the floor.

"Five-second rule?" Beth asked wryly.

"Five-second what?"

"Right, you don't have kids. Never mind. I was kidding anyway."

"Beth, I am so sorry." Looking down at the food they could no longer use, Carly was reminded anew of how much work the other woman had put into this evening. "You'll come have a glass of wine with us later, right?"

Beth blinked. "You sure?"

"Absolutely! You'll need to come take credit for all the food, assuming I don't ruin any more of it."

"Accidents happen. Refresh your guests' drinks, and I'll get the salads plated as soon as I've got this in the—" She broke off as lightning flashed an eerie silver-blue just outside the window, followed by another booming burst of thunder. "Wow, they weren't kidding about a storm tonight. I hope Genevieve's driving extra carefully."

Carly winced. The entire point of tonight had been a welcoming gesture; it seemed inhospitable that she had the newest member of Ramson Neil's faculty driving to an unfamiliar neighborhood in this kind of weather. She'd no sooner had that thought than her mind flashed to Daniel. *Please let him drive safely.* He'd only just reappeared in her life, and she wanted to keep him unscathed and free from harm. She hoped that if Helene was distracting him as he drove, he'd overcome his noble streak long enough to politely ask her to shut up.

"Carly? Your guests need their hostess," Beth said gently.

"Right!" She rejoined everyone in the front parlor but barely had time to hand the provost's wife a glass of wine before the phone rang again. Irrationally, the sound made her jump as she envisioned Daniel once again. *I wish he was here.* She would never forgive herself if he hydroplaned or didn't see a car in his blind spot because of compromised visibility; he was only out on the road right now because Carly couldn't tolerate being around her mother.

Beth appeared in the room's entryway. "Carly?"

"If you'll excuse me just a second," Carly told the provost.

As she turned, Dr. Shapiro filled the space she'd vacated, chatting easily with the couple. Because Carly was used to dealing with her colleagues in mixed and often frustrating settings—charged meetings where people from different departments didn't always have the same agendas; committee work that always seemed to include that one person whose sole purpose seemed to be annoying everyone else—she sometimes forgot how much she genuinely enjoyed being around some of them. Dr. Shapiro had traveled all over the world and always had fascinating anecdotes to share. And the provost—if Carly could temporarily forget that he would have a major impact on whether she received tenure and if she overlooked his misplaced respect for her father—was a benevolent patriarch, encouraging his faculty members to think of one another as one big family.

She swallowed as she reached Beth, hoping more than ever that her future was at Ramson Neil. "Everything okay?"

"More or less. That was Genevieve calling from her cell again. She said that navigating traffic is getting a little more complex because a lot of the streetlights have lost—"

Lightning struck outside so close that Carly could feel the sizzle in the air; a collective gasp filled the room the same split second that it was plunged into darkness.

"Power," Beth finished.

"Well, Carly." The provost beamed over the top of his wife's head as he helped her into her coat. "This has been one evening we won't soon forget."

"Couldn't you try?" Carly joked. "As a favor to me."

Natalie Reaser from HR laughed. She was standing by the front door, waiting for her fiancé. He and Beth were helping Dr. Shapiro look for the car keys he'd set down. The search probably would have been brief if it weren't being conducted by flashlight. "I want your aplomb. At Todd's and my engagement party, I felt like my head would explode if the smallest thing went wrong."

Carly pressed a hand to her chest, feigning dismay. "Oh, no, you don't think something went wrong with *my* party, do you? Just because the entrée didn't get done and I dropped most of our finger foods and the guest of honor never actually came . . . *Pfft*, minor hiccups."

"That's the kind of bring-it-on, can-do attitude we like to see at Ramson Neil," the provost said approvingly. "Seriously, you were grace under pressure, something I'll be sure to mention when I have my meeting with Beverley on Thursday."

The woman was due back in the country on Tuesday, which Carly had temporarily forgotten in the midst of everything else going on in her life.

"Oh, and one other thing." The provost opened the front door for his wife but glanced back just as they'd stepped onto the porch. "Tell Mrs. Overton that I'll also be mentioning her to our housing partners."

Carly beamed. "Will do, sir." Stumbling across a lead for what might well be a new job for Beth could be the best thing that came out of tonight.

"Found them!" called a male voice. Seconds later, Dr. Shapiro and Natalie's fiancé appeared to make their goodbyes.

When everyone had gone, Carly sagged against the front door and exchanged glances with Beth. "What say I fix us some drinks?"

"Strong ones," Beth agreed, her features looking even younger by candlelight. Their earlier search had turned up a motley assortment of tea lights, aromatherapy jar candles, and a few birthday candles, although Carly couldn't imagine how long they'd been sitting at the back of a kitchen drawer.

In preparation for this evening, Carly had set up a mini-bar of sorts. But, although a few had accepted a glass of wine, almost everyone had eschewed cocktails once dinner plans had changed. Beth had scheduled the food to be fresh and piping hot more than an hour into the evening, giving people plenty of time to arrive, socialize, and have before-dinner drinks. The power outage meant that most of the items on their menu hadn't had enough time to finish cooking. Carly thought people also drank less than usual because everyone wanted sharp reflexes for the drive home. The rain had slowed to a trickle, but electricity was still out and there were bound to be tree branches and other debris blown onto the road. She was relieved that Daniel had thought to call her from the restaurant to let her know they'd made it just fine and would wait out the worst of the storm there.

Carly pursed her lips. "Your poison of choice is rum and diet cola, as I recall?"

"Good memory." Beth sounded impressed.

"Wasn't that long ago," Carly said. But if felt like a lifetime ago. It felt like . . . a parallel existence. Someone who was her, but not. An alternate Carly whose life had been simpler in many ways.

Lonelier, too. She couldn't quite imagine what the past few weeks would have been like without Beth's and Daniel's support.

"You know what?" Beth said. "I think I'm in the mood for a new drink."

"Such as?"

"Surprise me," Beth suggested.

"Okay." Carly splashed a bit of Southern Comfort into some cranberry juice and topped it off with some lime. "By the way, you were brilliant tonight. Completely saved my ass." There was a time when Carly would have had trouble admitting such a thing or even feeling grateful for someone else's help. Tonight, she couldn't help being impressed by Beth's ingenuity.

Since they'd had to scrap their dinner plans and since the ice cream Beth had bought in anticipation of pie à la mode would eventually start to melt, she'd scrounged through Carly's kitchen and found enough supplies for a good old-fashioned ice-cream social. There'd been fruit, hastily crumbled cookies, whipped topping, two flavors of ice cream and some frozen yogurt, which had thrilled Natalie Reaser (who was obsessed with fitting into her wedding dress next month).

"We used to have ice-cream socials all the time at my dad's church," Beth said. "It was easy enough to do once I thought of it."

"People had fun." Carly handed over the drink. "I just feel bad that no one got to eat your food. I hope you don't feel the evening was a waste."

"Are you kidding?" Beth settled onto the sofa as Carly fixed herself a martini. "With the way you were chatting me up to the provost, it was the best career networking I've ever done! Of course, I'm pretty sure it's the *only* career networking I've ever done. Does he have any say in that dorm-mother job?"

"Hard to tell. It's not an official on-campus dorm, just a small independent housing facility that's in partnership with us. It only takes female tenants, and there has to be a responsible adult living on the premises. You might have heard the provost mention, the last lady who had the job was young, not terribly older than the students residing there. She loved it, but she's getting married, so they want someone new in place before fall."

"And you think I should apply?" Beth asked, looking sincerely interested in her opinion.

Carly bit her lip. "That's up to you, but there is something I need to talk to you about. *This* position—"

"You're kicking out your mother," Beth surmised.

"It's that obvious?" Carly plopped down on an ottoman, wondered if Beth would think her a terrible person.

"I don't think the provost noticed you wanted to throw Helene under a bus, if that's what you mean."

"It's not like I plan to put her in a box on a street corner," Carly defended herself. "I'll pay for her to have someone come to her house on a part-time basis, or we can look into finding her a retirement complex where she'd be around other people her age, maybe someplace with an on-site physical therapy staff, but—"

"She can't stay here. I agree."

"You do?" Carly stopped, discomfited by just how *relieved* she felt at Beth's empathetic tone. *Am I turning into one of those people desperate for the approval of others?*

"You moved her in because she needed assistance during her recovery, but one of the things I realized with Allen is that you can only help people when they *want* to be helped. I'm not convinced that her staying here is going to do anything further to improve her condition, and her presence certainly isn't doing you any favors."

"I doubt Helene will be gone as early as tomorrow," Carly said, trying not to sound hopeful, "but it needs to be done soon."

"For what it's worth, speaking as a mother, whatever happened during your childhood?" Beth leaned forward. "It wasn't your fault."

Carly was so startled by the left-field comment that vodka splashed over the rim of her glass onto her hand. "I-I know that." Logically. Intellectually. "But thank you."

"Now, whatever mistakes you make from here on out? Those are entirely your fault," Beth said impishly. "Please tell me that Daniel will move in here soon after your mother vacates the premise and I'm out of a job?"

"If you needed to stay for another week or so to figure out your next move . . ."

"I appreciate it, but I may spend a few days with my own daughter, help her get the nursery ready. That kind of stuff. And don't think I didn't notice how you sidestepped the issue of Daniel."

Carly belted back a hefty dose of vodka. "I'm not sure. I definitely don't think he should move in soon. I need some time to . . . readjust. And if we're going to start—" What, dating? It sounded silly. She'd been *married* to the man, was already been more intimate with him than any other person she'd ever known. It wasn't like he would ask if he could call her and take her out to a movie.

Or, hell, maybe it was. The idea was sweetly appealing.

With an impatient shake of her head, Carly tried to remember which track her train of thought had been heading down. "If we're going to get involved again, he has some stipulations."

"Are they unreasonable?"

He wanted her to see a therapist, either as a couple or separately, for herself. The prospect bothered her. Take time from her writing and teaching to *pay* someone so that she could feel like something was wrong with her? And the idea of sitting there for an hour "opening up" to someone? It was uncomfortable, if not out-and-out creepy.

Granted, even as painful as her conversation had been with Daniel on the porch, she'd felt wonderful afterward. But since she and her therapist probably wouldn't be concluding their sessions with cathartic sex, she deemed that irrelevant.

"His requests aren't unreasonable," Carly admitted. "They're just . . . difficult."

Beth smiled. "Most things worth having are."

❧

Déjà vu. It was five in the morning, and once again Carly lay sleepless in her bed, staring at the dark ceiling. Ironic, since the only reason she'd reluctantly booted down her computer at four thirty—she'd been in "the zone"—was because she hadn't been able to keep her eyes open. Her mind was racing.

Part of it, she knew, was the dread of today's confrontation with Helene. Her mother would not react well to being told to leave and such scenes were draining. Odd, that her mother would rather be miserable in the house of the daughter she hated than live in her own home, but Carly had accepted that she'd never understand the way the woman's mind worked. Balancing the dread nicely was knowing that Helene would be gone soon.

No, her insomnia wasn't so much trepidation as anticipation. She had much to think about, having rediscovered her stride on the manuscript, with Beverley returning this week, Daniel . . . *It's official. I'm not gonna get any sleep at this point.*

Moving more by sense memory than conscious decision, she dressed in shorts and a T-shirt. She laced up her running shoes, even considered waking Beth but then decided that it was still too early for that. It wasn't until Carly was literally reaching for the doorknob that she turned to grab her car keys.

She got in the car and sat there as the sun got brighter and morning birds grew louder. Was she really going to do this? Did she really want to? As she made the twenty-minute trip, she told herself numerous times that she could turn around without anyone ever thinking her a coward. No one would even know.

You would. So quit being a wuss and drive. Deep down, she knew she needed to see him.

Filled with grim pride in herself, she parked the car outside the gates of the cemetery and started up the paved path. It was insanely pretty here, blades of dew-kissed grass sparkling in the sun, bright flowers everywhere. The cemetery was atop a hill that created a picturesque vista, although she imagined it was a damn pain to lay out burial plots. No one wanted his coffin shoved into the ground on a slant.

There were a few flowers at the grave of Samuel Frazer

and she felt a passing curiosity about who had left them. Colleagues? Faculty wives? Other people who'd bought into his fairy tale of brilliance and scientific altruism? Had he really hoped, once upon a time, to make the world a better place . . . or had he simply wanted the credit for doing so?

She shoved her hands into her pockets, wondering why she'd bothered to come. It wasn't as if he could give her any answers. She supposed she could make some ceremonial sign of forgiveness—someone with a big heart like Beth's would probably see it as healthy, the right thing to do. But Carly was not one of those people.

"I'll never forgive what you did," she said quietly. "You were a bastard. You took sadistic glee in making me doubt myself, making a kid think she could never be good enough, and I don't know *why*. I don't know what the hell was wrong with you. I don't care. What I care about is that it ends with you."

She took a deep, cleansing breath. Maybe she didn't need to make peace with him after all, but with herself. She couldn't change the past. But she could vow to be more than a selfish, career-focused, emotional bully. She wasn't doomed to repeat her father's life or even her own mistakes.

If she wanted to try again with Daniel, if she wanted to change . . . well, hadn't she always found a way to achieve her goals? Confidence and newfound optimism burned so hot inside her that she imagined herself to be glowing on the hill—incandescent. She must have looked otherworldly to anyone driving by, easily mistaken for a ghost. But the season for ghosts had ended.

"I don't want to see you in my dreams or hear your voice in my head," she said firmly. "This is goodbye." Walking back to her car, she buzzed with fierce victory. It was time for her father to stay dead.

And time for Dr. Carly Frazer to start living.

Fourteen

❧

Preparing for Takeoff

"You don't have to do this, you know." It tore at Beth's insides to watch the way her daughter valiantly fought tears.

Joy sat in the living room of the home she'd grown up in, surrounded by boxes. "Mama, you're underestimating me. I *want* to help. I know I can't do any of the heavy lifting, but let me do this." She was wrapping fragile items in paper while Peter, Allen and Allen's friend Gary loaded heavier pieces into the truck outside.

Beth started to remind her daughter that even more help was on the way—Carly said she'd be over as soon as she'd dropped the polished manuscript in the mail. But maybe Joy truly did need to be here rather than pushed aside. It was still Beth's biggest regret in ending her marriage—that her daughter had been hurt by the decision—but it would be best for all of them. Joy was a mature woman from a loving family with lots of support; she would heal.

Truthfully, Beth had to admit the packing process was emotional even for her. The real estate agent she and Allen had met with had said that getting out all the nonessential clutter, leaving only a few key pieces of furniture and color accents, would help their home stand out in the crowded housing market. But when you'd shared twenty-six years with someone, you accumulated a lot of clutter.

She'd heard the unfunny jokes about an ended marriage coming down to divvying up CD collections, but you couldn't tear memories in half. In some ways, she and Allen would be forever fused together by what they'd shared. Walking away from those collective experiences was bittersweet, but she looked forward to new experiences. Both Joy and Carly assured her she was going to be a "natural" at her new dorm mother position. On paper, the bulk of her responsibilities was administrative, but she'd been warned that she might want to keep her door open in case one of the young women needed advice or a shoulder to cry on.

"If you're sure you're okay here," Beth told her daughter, "I'll go get some more stuff from the bedroom."

Joy nodded.

Beth had waded into the walk-in closet and was considering whether some of her old clothes were even worth packing and unpacking, or if they should be donated to a nearby women's shelter, when she heard footsteps behind her.

"In here," she called. "In case someone was looking for me."

Allen poked his head in the closet. "Hey."

"Hey." She hesitated, not sure what to say after that. There hadn't been a lot of acrimony between them since she'd made her decision, but the awkwardness was enough to fill a moving van all on its own.

"Didn't mean to bother you. Just came to get some suitcases," he said. "I figured I might as well use those for packing some stuff instead of just using cardboard. Unless you wanted the luggage?" he asked as an afterthought. "Or we could each take some pieces."

"And break up the set?" She shook her head. "Keep them. You travel far more than I do."

Maybe once she got settled into her new place and her new job, she'd think about traveling between semesters. She hated planes, but another cruise might be nice someday. She'd buy a big, brightly colored case, maybe with paisley swirls or playful polka dots.

The kind of suitcase she'd recognize as hers the instant it hit the baggage carousel.

⋘◈⋙

"Why are there suitcases?" Carly froze on the driveway, looking through the back windows of her car.

Daniel sighed. "Because you don't have enough trunk space. The surprise would have worked much better if you had."

"I agreed to a one-hour therapy session," she reminded him warily. "If you're kidnapping me for some weeklong couples therapy retreat in the mountains, I'm going to kill you in your sleep."

He laughed, opening her door. "Our first appointment with Dr. Sloan is actually *next* Friday. No retreat in the mountains,

I promise. But how would you feel about a long weekend at a beachfront resort?"

My hero. Would there ever be a time when she wasn't caught off guard by his romantic gestures and unbelievable thoughtfulness? It still felt strange, but no longer unpleasant, to let herself be loved by someone—kind of tingly, like when one of her feet fell asleep.

Tingling now in much more intimate parts of her body, she threaded her fingers through Daniel's hair and kissed him deeply.

"Mmm." He pulled his head back but kept his arm around her. "Careful. Much more of that and we'll miss our plane."

Once they reached the airline ticket counter, where he could no longer keep their destination a complete surprise, Carly asked, "Are we going to the same place we went on our honeymoon?" That would be just like the sentimental fool.

"No. Everything's been so great between us, I didn't want to scare you off with unintentional wedding overtones."

She thought that over. "I appreciate the consideration, but I think you'll find I don't scare as easily anymore."

"Good to know." He pulled her against him. "Just don't get too used to these spontaneous weekend getaways. Next Friday, we really *are* going to see the therapist. But I thought we should celebrate your tenure first."

She had so much to celebrate now—Daniel being at the top of her list. She'd be sure to tell him so tonight, perhaps after she'd had a tropical drink and gotten him naked.

"What are you smiling at?" he asked.

"I'll tell you later," she promised.

They didn't encounter any hassles going through security and spent the time at the gate reminiscing about their honeymoon. And debating whether they were still young and limber enough to reenact certain parts of it. They also talked about some of the autumn projects his company had signed on and her badgering Laurel Rogers into testing out of a prereq to enroll in one of Carly's upcoming classes. In seemingly no time at all, their flight had been boarded and Daniel was using the flimsy excuse of looking for the other end of his seat belt to touch her ass.

Through the speakers overhead, the pilot welcomed everyone and cheerfully advised them to "relax and enjoy the flight."

Carly planned to do exactly that.

Tanya Michna is a summa cum laude graduate of the University of Houston–Victoria. Her first writing-related job was there in college, and she's been writing professionally ever since. She lives with her husband and two children outside Atlanta, Georgia.

Baggage Claim

❧

TANYA MICHNA

This Conversation Guide is intended to enrich the
individual reading experience, as well as encourage us
to explore these topics together—because books,
and life, are meant for sharing.

A CONVERSATION WITH TANYA MICHNA

Q. What inspired this story?

A. I usually start with the characters. As a wife and mom myself, I was intrigued by Beth, who has tried to do everything right as a wife and mother yet is forced to admit in the opening chapters that her marriage has gone wrong.

For the story itself, I was inspired by the idea that sometimes the right person passes through your life at just the right time, even if you only recognize that in retrospect. Someone who gives you advice you don't even know you'll need, someone who turns out to be the business contact that helps you get your next job. In Beth's case, the "right" person is Dr. Carly Frazer, even though the two women are unalike in temperament and life experience. Beth dropped out of college as a pregnant freshman; Carly is a college professor. I worked briefly at a university and am well-acquainted with faculty members and administrative staff at several institutions, so that familiarity was an inherent part of my inspiration for Carly.

Q. Of the two main characters, Carly is more abrasive and less sympathetic. Did you worry about readers not being able to relate to her?

A. It's true that Carly is very guarded and driven. She's far from perfect, but aren't we all? There are dozens of examples of fictional characters who are compelling even if they're not always likable. I also have faith in readers—one of the joys of reading a book is getting inside a character's head, getting to know what makes that person tick, and watching as he or she evolves. As we better understand Carly and see her reach out to others, whether grudgingly or gracefully, she becomes someone we can really root for.

Q. This is your second novel for NAL Accent. Was your writing process the same for both Baggage Claim *and* Necessary Arrangements?

A. As I mentioned, my approach is to start with characters, so that part was very similar. *Necessary Arrangements* is about two sisters, one of whom is fighting cancer. Since I have a sister I'm close to, and have lost loved ones to cancer, writing that story was very difficult for me. In the early stages of *Baggage Claim,* I expected that this novel would be easier. What I've learned is that it's *never* easy—which is probably a good thing. Just as my characters struggle and learn and change during the novel, I also face challenges and struggles as I write that make me a better writer in the long run. From that creative turmoil comes a novel that offers a richer reading experience.

Q. *The inciting incident for this book occurs when Carly and Beth take the wrong suitcases off the airport carousel and must meet later to switch them back. Has this ever happened to you?*

A. Actually, yes, but not at the airport. When my husband (then fiancé) and I were in college, we took a long bus trip from south Texas to New York so that he could meet my father. As you can probably imagine, we were nearly dead on our feet by the time we arrived two days later. We ended up with another person's duffel bag, while ours continued up the road. Thankfully, we were able to exchange luggage the next day.

More recently, my five-year-old daughter came home with a white-and-pink lunch box that we didn't realize wasn't hers until I opened it that afternoon to clean it out. It interested me what you could tell about a person from the inside of her lunch box. In my daughter's lunch box were a spoon with cars and trucks on the handle and a worn thermal container covered with action heroes for her soup; an observant person could deduce that she has an older brother and often gets hand-me-downs. In the lunch box that didn't belong to us was a note reminding the child of an important appointment after school—none of my business, obviously, but I couldn't help wondering what kind of appointment and creating various scenarios for the unknown family. When you're a writer, it doesn't take much to kick-start your imagination!

Q. Would you say that your books have a common theme?

A. No, my stories are thematically varied. However, I do think all of my writing showcases my fascination with relationships—how people help one another, hurt one another (intentionally or not), and ultimately connect. In *Necessary Arrangements*, the focus was on the relationship between two sisters and on beginning romances, from a first date for one couple to an engagement for the other. In *Baggage Claim*, I examine the relationship between two strangers who grow to be friends, relationships inside marriage, and the different ways parents can impact the lives of their children.

Q. Instead of letting herself get depressed about the upheaval in her life, Beth tries to embrace change. She becomes excited about the opportunity for a fresh start. Many people, however, avoid and fear change. Are you someone who finds a fresh start invigorating or alarming?

A. I have to admit, I'm getting more cautious and settled than I used to be. We moved around a lot while I was a child. In college, I changed my major multiple times and routinely redecorated my apartment. When my husband and I first got married, I found it thrilling to change jobs or houses. But we've been together for twelve years now, have two children, and are active in our community. I have a sense of belonging that I didn't truly experience for the first twenty years of my life. I'm probably more resistant to change because I have more to lose.

In that respect, I find Beth to be incredibly brave. Even small changes can be monumental if you're going against twenty-six years of ingrained habit. Inertia and fear keep lots of people in unhappy relationships because they're either scared to rock the boat and make the situation worse, or because changing something that's become so much a part of their lives simply doesn't occur to them.

Balance is probably key. Making capricious changes simply for the sake of change isn't healthy, but neither is stagnating. I keep an open mind when it comes to trying new foods, visiting new places, meeting new people. Every time I start work on a new book, I am both invigorated *and* alarmed. Plus, did I mention my two beautiful children? Still youngsters, they're changing practically every day, so my husband and I always have new joys and new challenges to keep us on our toes.

Q. As you've promoted your novels, what has been the most memorable response you've received from readers?

A. I have been amazed and humbled by what readers have shared with me. One woman e-mailed me that reading *Necessary Arrangements* made her feel closer to her sister than she'd felt since her sister's death; she thanked me for giving her that gift. Another woman I met while speaking to her book club applauded my character's strength in the face of adversity and shared her own true story of battling a childhood illness that the doctors said she had no chance of surviving. Now, more than ten years later, she has happily proven them wrong. When I was first published, I couldn't have imagined the ways in which my books have touched other people or how their responses have moved me. I look forward to hearing from people who enjoy *Baggage Claim* and to meeting new readers!

Q. Do you ever get a chance to read for fun? What's on your "to be read" pile?

A. I absolutely make time to read, and I encourage others to do the same. For most of us, life is hectic, but I truly believe that books enrich us—we glimpse different perspectives, gain compassion for characters unlike ourselves, rediscover the power of imagination, and travel by proxy to new locations. . . .

Recently, at a hair salon, I was gratified to hear the woman in the chair next to me discussing with her stylist how much they both loved to read. I couldn't help myself! I apologetically said that while I hadn't meant to eavesdrop, I was thrilled to hear others say they find books as important as I do. Before long, we were chatting like old friends, swapping author recommendations and inviting each other to book club meetings. (Speaking of book clubs, I have a page on my Web site where I periodically recommend both books and recipes for club meetings. And I love talking to book clubs either in person or through speakerphone or Internet chats.)

There are always a dozen or more books on my "to be read" list—I add them faster than I cross them off! Here are a few of the titles I'm looking forward to reading: *The Girl Who Chased the Moon* by Sarah Addison Allen, *A Dance with Dragons* by George R. R. Martin, *The Treasure Keeper* by Shana Abe, and *What I Did for Love* by Susan Elizabeth Phillips.

Q. What's next in your writing life?

A. More books! Although I don't yet have specifics, there are always new characters percolating in my subconscious. I look forward to "meeting" them and sharing them with readers.

QUESTIONS FOR DISCUSSION

1. Both Carly and Beth have been shaped by their pasts, specifically by their parents. Were you surprised by their responses to their upbringing, their ways of coping? Might they have responded differently?

2. In *Baggage Claim*, there are two sets of estranged spouses—Beth/Allen and Carly/Daniel. Why do you think these romantic relationships are ultimately resolved the way they are? Would you have resolved them differently?

3. Loneliness is a powerful emotion in the novel. Beth feels lonely in her marriage. Carly seems to have spent most of her life on her own, yet is determined to fight off feelings of loneliness. Allen's loneliness prompts him to want to reconcile with Beth. How powerful is loneliness in your own life and in the lives of the people you know?

4. Beth, Daniel, and Bart McKenna, the ex-Marine who lives in Carly's neighborhood, attempt to garden with varying degrees of amateur and professional success. Considering how much time, money, and effort a garden can demand, why do you think it's such a popular hobby for so many?

5. When Carly tries to throw a dinner party for some of her colleagues from the college, the evening doesn't proceed as planned. Have you ever supervised or planned a business or social event that went awry? How did you make the best of the challenges that arose?

6. At the end of the book, do you think Carly makes the right decision about her mother, or should she handle the situation differently?

7. What character do you think changes the most during the course of the story, and why?

8. Carly and Beth are obviously two very different women who've chosen dissimilar lifestyles—yet they're able to forge a bond that empowers both of them. What traits do you think the two women have in common? Will they remain in touch after events of the novel end?

9. What significance does running have in the story? How does its meaning differ for each woman—or does it?

10. Carly and Beth meet at the beginning of the novel as a consequence of inconveniently switching luggage. By the end, their mistake can be viewed as an unexpected blessing. What moments of serendipity have occurred in your life? Have you met people or had experiences that you couldn't truly appreciate until much later?